TATTOOED ANGELS TRILOGY

Judgment

TATTOOED ANGELS TRILOGY

Tattooed Angels Trilogy

JUDGMENT

VALERIE WILLIS

4 Horsemen
Publications, Inc.

4 Horsemen Publications, Inc.
1497 Main St. Suite 169
Dunedin, FL 34698
4horsemenpublications.com
info@4horsemenpublications.com

Cover by Valerie Willis
Typesetting by Autumn Skye
Edited by Heather Teele

Library of Congress Control Number: 2022948987

Paperback ISBN-13: 978-1-64450-072-9
Hardcover ISBN-13: 978-1-64450-586-1
Audiobook ISBN-13: 978-1-64450-585-4
Ebook ISBN-13: 978-1-64450-071-2

DEDICATION

I want to thank all my friends and family who encouraged me to finish this trilogy! (And that goes out to my Ruths, Chris, Diana, and my Shadow Legion Gang too!)

Most importantly, a special thank you to my loving husband Justin for putting up with those nights I refused to come to bed.

Thank you to Shannon for being my constant cheerleader and fellow artist at heart, plus reading right behind me as I finished edits! God bless you for that!

To all of you out there still making your path, never give up.

ACKNOWLEDGMENTS

Thank you to my amazing support team, both local and afar! From Alpha and Beta readers to my small collection of volunteer editors to the Writer's Atelier gang and Racquel Henry to Writers of Central Florida and Thereabouts.

I cannot forget family and friends who cheered me on!

You are all so amazing!

A special thanks to Joel, Kim, Karen, Ryan, Trudy, Carlee, Troy, Richard, Margaret, and the many other eyes who helped edit and polish this piece!

TABLE OF CONTENTS

TRIGGER WARNING

This story contains themes of genocide, suicide, verbal and physical abuse, bullying, violence, and murder, which may cause a reader distress. Read with caution, and please understand this is a fictionalized world, but some of the events are very realistic in nature. This is a trilogy about overcoming the tribulations of the past, present, and future as you uncover who you are and who you wish to be. This book features some very scary, real historical disasters, fictionally retold to capture the despair and fear that may have transpired.

I

DIE TRYING

Present Day

I fear I have failed my brother.

The start of my inability to protect him was a slow fall from grace before I plummeted into the endless pit of despair.

The day they fell under his reincarnation spell, I should have known something was not right with Hotan. He carried a distant look in his deep, green eyes; he kept secrets from me. Ignoring it was a dire mistake that would endanger all of us, even the innocent people of the world. I was their watcher, protector. I don't know exactly what created this chaos which surrounds us now. So much has been destroyed for our sins; it makes me sick with guilt.

Decades ago, I decided I could no longer allow myself to watch without intervening. My dreams are forever haunted by the faces of my fellow Levites, seeing them reborn only to die again. My memories are filled with centuries of disasters and horrific wars. Many of these I have seen and experienced firsthand in my efforts to track the others as promised. It took centuries for me to realize that idly watching their lives was not enough. This was my mistake.

I am troubled by my brother's hidden sins. It is time I set things right. I must atone for my own failures by doing what my brother could not. Life was complicated in the beginning. I trusted Hotan, but at some point along the way, he lost trust in himself. Am I not remembering some important clues from so long ago? There are so many gaps in my mind where memories should be… Have I lived too long? Is this the cost of remaining awake, unlike the others, as time went by?

With a gasp, Talib snapped out of his darkening thoughts. A wave of power echoed through his soul with an icy sensation, stinging and pulling at him. He had associated this power with his brother in the past, but with the old Hotan dead, it meant this was another entity—one which sought out his brother and now, the new Hotan. The power tugged at him to look north toward the unseen beacon. Silence fell over him from where he stood sheltered within the cathedral. A cold sweat slithered across his temple and his jaw tightened; this power easily matched his own. *No, it is stronger.*

Swallowing back the choking sensation of fear, he whispered, "The power that haunted my brother has returned."

"What has returned? What are you talking about?" Lucius turned away from the candles by the holy water fountain to the paling gentlemen behind him. "Talib, what on earth is going on?"

"There is no time to explain." He ran down the aisle between the rows of pews, pulling off his white suit jacket in hopes of freeing himself of any physical restrictions. "It is coming for Hotan!"

With amazing agility, he slid across the black hood of an Audi A8, his silver hair flashing in the sunlight. He rolled himself upright and jerked the driver door open. There was no time to worry about the consequences for what he was about to do. The tires screamed as he floored the gas pedal. He needed to reach the source of the terrible power before it found its target. Gripping the steering wheel tighter, his palms were clammy, and his jaw ached from clenching his teeth. Every muscle in his body grew taught under the pressure of the approaching, unavoidable battle.

The power being released shared a presence similar to Rebirth but took on a more negative tone. Instead of an exertion of power and life, this one consumed it—a black hole void of compassion. He could safely concur this was the element of Death. A coldness struck deep into his core, the grip of it making breathing painful and rattling his nerves. There was no other explanation; this was an immortal who became the embodiment of a terrible element, the one element none of them truly possessed. Whether Death realized Hotan was not the same entity it had chased in the past was unknown.

The Audi raced down busy roadways, disregarding street signs, traffic lights, and even the pedestrians crossing its path. Talib let his power free, allowing it to stretch ahead like a tidal wave. This was something he had not done in hundreds of years, and unlike the others, it did not exhaust him to unleash his element to this magnitude. People were baffled as they stopped their cars at green lights, pulled their vehicles off to the side, or found themselves sitting down on the sidewalk for no apparent reason. Being able to control the element of Judgment had its advantages as his power cleared the route.

Hotan's apartment building drew closer, and he felt the presence of other Levites. Hotan, Jacob, and several others were under the cold presence which loomed above them. The demon sat on the rooftop like a vulture, waiting patiently for the perfect moment to swoop down to its meal. The weight of the immortal's presence sent chills across his skin as he caught a glimpse of the shadowy figure.

Fae, the element of Intelligence, had concluded that something had been chasing his brother all these centuries. The clues left behind in books and records left a pathway of mass destruction which devoured an unfathomable number of lives. Entire cities, nations, and cultures had been wiped out in its wake. He hadn't revealed his knowledge of the destruction, but for her to recognize it within the history books was horrifying. She pinpointed events, huge and small, with similar characteristics, but the entity responsible for all of it was still a mystery. Disappearing colonies, unexplained wars, and natural disasters all happening within isolated areas were linked to this phenomenon. It started shortly after they left the island of paradise that they had called home, and sadly, escalated at an alarming rate.

What did my brother do to create something so evil? Why did I fail to notice this was a separate entity? I was there to help him; all he needed to do was ask. Was he too ashamed of what he had done to even tell me? And now, this child who bears Hotan's legacy must face the sins of my brother before he can master his powers. Lord, this cannot be the way you want this to end. A child against a monster is never a fair fight.

He slammed on the brakes. The tires squealed in response but weren't stopping fast enough. He yanked the emergency brake lever up and sent the car sliding. It turned ninety degrees before skidding to a complete stop. The air filled with the pungent smell of burnt rubber as he flew out of the car; the streets were too congested here to move all of them out of the way. Even with the aid of his powers, the bumper-to-bumper traffic left no room to move all the cars without causing injury.

Bursting into a full run, he left the car far behind. Stepping up and over car after car was proving too slow. Sprinting off to the right, he took an inhuman leap to the top of the nearest building; centuries of physical conditioning and the advantage of immortality allowed him to do the impossible. He ran with urgency toward the power source, leaping effortlessly from roof to roof, drawing closer with amazing speed. Reaching his destination, he skidded to a stop, spraying pea gravel across the rooftop. Panting, he quickly caught his breath, quelling the stinging in his lungs.

He looked wearily toward the back of a black trench coat flapping in the wind. The man's black hair gave way to the wind while he remained as motionless as a statue, unbothered that he was no longer alone. They stood there with nothing more than the slapping of the coat filling their ears. His chest ached from the frightening sensation urging him to flee. His mind flashed a lifetime's worth of glimpses reflecting those same broad shoulders.

Why do I feel like I know him? I have seen this man many times at different times and centuries, but...

The full scale of those memories and where they came from were beyond him, far out of reach. The nostalgic chaos of emotions inside his soul told him he had found the source of his brother's sins, but it was a threat he had lost memory of somewhere during his lifetime. This was the man in black which plagued the deepest reaches of his own mind and the nightmares Hotan suffered.

"Stop!" The determination in his voice was startling even to him; standing tall, he was prepared to do anything necessary to stop the element of Death. "He is not who you think he is!"

"Who are you?" Standing motionless, the deep, calm voice mused, "No one has ever found me, let alone been brave enough to speak to me in that tone."

"I am Talib. I was the brother of Hotan." As his lips hit the last word, there was a change in the man's power.

He is targeting him.

"Brother of Hotan?" The man shifted to peer over his shoulder, revealing the dark pools of black which glowered back at Talib. "My, my, you definitely must be. No one carries the genetic coding for silver hair in today's time. I guess I can call you uncle."

"Uncle?" It all made perfect sense. *I have been so blind.*

My brother attempted to bring her back, but that is not what came to him. There is no time to be shocked or question what was revealed in this instant. I can only take the information and run with it...

"I am so sorry. My brother, your father, is gone. I cannot undo what crimes have been committed against you, but please understand, this boy is not who you think he is. The person within this building is someone who looks like him and holds his powers, but Hotan's soul is gone. The boy knows nothing of my brother's wrongdoings. If you wish, we could finish that business here between the two of us."

"Then a look-alike will suffice." Sneering, he turned around to face him, his wild smile sending chills through Talib's entire being. "And will you attempt to stop me?"

"Yes." His body tensed. He planned to use the small revolver tucked in his back holster, and the handle of the gun urged him to shoot. "You have no right to take innocent lives. So many have been killed by your hand and had nothing to do with your endeavors to kill my brother. It must end; I will not allow this slaughter to continue further."

"Sorry, I guess I have a nasty habit of losing my temper." The nonchalant shrug was followed by a step forward. "Do you even realize who or what you are facing, Uncle?"

He is trying to play mind games with me; it won't work.

"I do not care what or who you are." He pulled the gun, and the man responded, black flames leaping off his skin, crawling outward like snakes. "You will be stopped here. I am his protector, and I owe that child my life for what my own brother has done to him."

"So be it, Uncle. Know that Iapetos, harbinger of Death itself, was the one who ended your life. Reborn from the cold womb of the dead and rejected by his own father." The black irises became glassy as he continued his growling speech. Another step closer sent Talib's heart racing. "I will not be satisfied until I have sucked the life from the soul that once was my father's. I will devour it; it will be mine."

"It pains me to know such evil was created by my own flesh and blood." As his fear mounted, he took an involuntary step backward. The man's power resonated through him like bony fingers of ice scratching at his soul.

You cannot take Hotan away from me!

An eerie calm washed over him.

BANG!

He squeezed the trigger.

The kickback from the revolver shook his arm and left his ears ringing, but his aim was impeccable. Gunpowder stung his nostrils as he sighed. He had landed the shot front and center—a single hole in Iapetos' forehead. His head fell back, still wearing the maddening grin. The relief was short lived, however, and Talib's blood ran cold as Iapetos started laughing. Tilting his head forward again, Iapetos stared him in the eyes. Talib emptied the revolver into the demon before him. There were no more chances for negotiations, or patience to entertain mind games. He hit the heart and neck, anywhere deemed vital to assure a kill shot, praying it would do damage or at least slow him. To his horror, Iapetos' laughter grew hysterical, and the small black holes lacked any sign of blood.

How does one kill Death itself?

He threw the empty gun to the ground in frustration, but his resolution to stop Iapetos stood firm. Swallowing down his fear, he ran toward his opponent. Pulling a hidden dagger from his shirt sleeve, he plunged the silver blade deep into the neck of the soul-eating beast. It was then that he felt something demonic in nature. He had only succeeded in entertaining the harbinger of Death. Before he could withdraw from his dire mistake, a firm hand had grasped his neck. Coldness like nothing he had ever felt snaked its way into his body and soul. His power had no sway here, and he felt his life seeping into Iapetos' fingers.

I have failed again.

Is this the coldness everyone feels when they begin to die? What a terrible, comfortless sensation. I have felt sorrow so many times but never the heartlessness of cold such as this.

How horrible to die with no chance of aiding others, unable to send even a simple warning, as his power pulls my soul so far from me. Even my powers have been yanked from me. Dear God, the others do not stand a chance against this immortal named Iapetos.

He could do nothing. He was flung away from his killer like a wet rag. As he hit the ground, the last thing he saw was the rooftop door opening, revealing Hotan's shocked face. His eyes rolled back as the darkness of death pulled him from the present, muffling the shouts and numbing the grip of those rushing to his body.

Why must he be so much like my brother in appearance? Run away, child. A demon is here to devour your soul. Can you not see he has killed me?

Ah, I hear music now.

Yes, the song Hotan sang at the club before Shellie's own death. Jacob said it was "Die Trying" by Art of Dying. What an appropriate song for me to hear as I fade away into the next life.

Oh, my dear Saphellia! I finally got you back, and here I go, leaving you behind. I am so sorry, my dove. Please understand my intentions. You always understood me so much better than I understood myself.

I wonder if it is true that one's life flashes before them as they arrive at Heaven's Gate…

2

GOD GAVE US LAND

938 BC

"Talib, wake up!" Small hands pushed their weight into his ribs, and he groaned in response. "We have so much to do today!"

"Not now." His muscles still ached from assisting the farmers with their harvest the day before; wincing, he rolled away. "Hotan, give me a moment to wake up."

"Fine." The ten-year-old boy's green eyes were bright. Letting go of his side, he headed for the door. "But I'm ready to go."

These were happier days. The air smelled clean. Skyscrapers, roads, and other signs of modern civilization did not exist in this peaceful time. These were the days of my mortal life—something I have rarely recalled—when I had no idea of the never-ending struggle that would be thrust upon me. Looking into those green eyes, I do not think he even knew the terrifying things he would set into motion through his misguided decisions.

Smiling wide, Hotan ran out of the tent, and Talib couldn't help but smirk as he watched him go. His back was sore, but it would have to wait with so much work still needed in the fields. As the chief's eldest son, he was the one everyone looked to for answers and, more importantly, to set an example. Grabbing the stiff golden chunk of bread, he gnawed on it as he poured water into a basin. Finishing his meager breakfast, he splashed the sleep from his face, ready to return to the harvesting.

Pausing, he looked down at his rippling reflection and his bright, silver eyes. *I am losing the boyish features of my youth.* Crow's feet had started to form at the corners of his eyes. It wouldn't be long before he would take on all the responsibilities waiting for him as an important advisor and leader within his village.

"Talib?" Her voice reminded him of a songbird, and it made his heart flutter when she said his name. "May I come in?"

"Please, Saphellia, you are always welcome." Turning to the entryway, he grinned at the tall, brown-haired girl who blushed under his stare. "What can I do for you, my dove?"

My God, if I had known how much more beautiful she would become after this... Even as I lay dying, my heart races at the memory of the morning before we became husband and wife.

She was taller than most of the women in the village and kept her long hair in a thick braid. She was the girl he would marry as soon as the seasonal harvest was brought in and the traditional celebrations began. He had admired Saphellia on many occasions during political fallouts. The reserve she practiced while handling difficult situations was amazing, and she had bested him many times. No one in the village would make a better wife to the chief's son than her. There was no fear in her voice when she wanted to be heard, and as the daughter of a lead diplomat, courage was expected of her. Saphellia stood tall at her father's side.

It was the tribe's duty to train the diplomats who would return to their home villages. It allowed peace to prosper among the thirteen nations. The other twelve tribes had sworn to God to send every tenth first-born child; in exchange, the same number was returned to them in the form of trained priests and diplomats. That was the way of life for generations, but as of late, the number arriving had dwindled, despite the reported increase in population. Talib's father expressed his concerns, but his ailing health forced him to turn his focus on preparing his sons to lead the village.

"Is it true the work in the fields will be finished today?" Looking into her hazel eyes felt like staring into the skies of heaven. They held wonderful bursts of color; blues, greens, and silver collided and fought to push above one another. "If so, we will be married tomorrow, right?"

She did not realize I was nearly breaking myself in two trying to finish the work in the field. All the older men teased me as I pushed myself to clear my assigned area, trying to move my wedding day up, often finishing more than my share. Sometimes I wonder if they told me the work was done that day just to make sure I did not kill myself in the fields. Either way, it was worth every drop of effort to make her mine as soon as possible.

"Maybe even tonight. It depends on my father, I suppose. Is there something wrong?" His smile faltered, and she laughed over his concerned look. "Do you not want to be married?"

I scared myself, thinking that I had rushed it without considering how she felt about the arranged marriage. Granted, Saphellia was just as excited about it as I was, and she let me know in no uncertain terms in this stolen moment together...

"No." Her cheeks were red, but she allowed herself to come closer to him. "I am excited to hear I don't have to wait any longer. To be yours has been a secret wish of mine, my Talib."

Sighing, he took her hands, marveling at how soft and elegant they felt in his calloused ones. "I cannot wait to spend our days together as husband and wife."

Her lips met his, and he was stunned by her boldness as the caressing warmth of her mouth flooded his own. Breaking from it, he stared in amazement at her sudden expression of love. Gathering her into his arms, he returned her kiss with equal vigor. Again, the hot flood of their lips meeting was electrifying. He could feel her heart thudding within her chest as fast as his own. She pulled away; her face was flushed as she ran out the door, looking back to catch his amorous gaze.

I will never forget that first kiss; it only added to my excitement to make her mine. She left me aching and wanting her more than ever as I watched her run away. I will spend eternity feeling as if I am chasing after her.

The sun rose over the hillside as he made his way to what was left of the harvest. After he finished reaping this section, preparation for his wedding and ceremony could start. Children chased one another around the village as the women made quick work of producing flour and milling the grain brought to them in massive bundles. Tonight, he would marry the diplomat's daughter, and Hotan would be wed to the war general's daughter. It was a good fit, and no one could protest that the pairings wouldn't grant good fortune. Surely, tying the ruling bodies together would strengthen the inner alliances of the Levite village.

But Hotan and Liora were so horribly young at this point. Our fathers rushing them into marriage the same night as my wedding to Saphellia was a horrible decision. I still blame the impeding illness for obstructing my father's judgment and fueling his panic. Then again, who would dare oppose the chief's commands? It was a dying man's last wish.

Their father feared what was to come, suspecting all was not well between the thirteen tribes of Israel. Talib and his father had discussed his dying wishes. He wanted to hand control over to both Hotan and Talib—one large spearhead to ensure the council did not lose sight of what was important. Once the boys were married, even if Hotan was only ten years old, they would take over their father's duties. Only one could take on the title of head of the village, and the council would eagerly accept Hotan for the role. They would hope to make him a puppet, so they could do what they wished with the village. As chief, he would become the mountain that reminded the council of the concerns of the people and their needs. As for the other tribes that relied on them, it would depend on how well they followed through with their promises. As much as his father would prefer Talib to rule solely, he feared pitting him alone against the council would be too much for him.

They spent several nights discussing a plan of action and what would be the best compromise. Together, it was decided to allow the council to appoint Hotan as chief, but Talib would serve as his permanent advisor. His father demanded that the brothers serve each other in such a way that peace could continue after he was gone. Unlike their father, they hadn't fought in wars or battles to earn the level of respect he carried. Their path in life would be difficult; challenges would be thrown at them from even those labeled as trustworthy.

If he only knew how right he was about all his suspicions. Perhaps he should have challenged it before he passed, but his want to care for his sons took precedence. The events that transpired would have been different if he had been well, but we cannot choose when and how we become ill. Still, I wonder if my mother had been alive or if he had taken a new bride for himself, would all this have shifted? I have enough questions to last millions of lifetimes. What matters is how you continue on with the cards you are dealt—a lesson I am still learning.

Sweat tickled his back as his thoughts soared over everything he would face tonight and beyond. He carried a great burden on his shoulders for the future of the people in his village. With the scythe still in his hand, he stood up straight and wiped his brow, taking a minute from the slouched, dirty work. Hotan approached with another basket for him to fill, but he carried a sad expression. Furrowing his brow, Talib waited for the silver-haired boy to come closer.

"What is the matter?" He sat down on the ground, leaning on the handle of the scythe to catch Hotan's attention. "Why is my little brother so sad today?"

"It's about tomorrow." Flopping down, Hotan picked at the ground in front of him. "Talib, if I marry tomorrow, I will be expected to, well … perform in bed."

He burst into laughter.

Hotan was so innocent at the time. It is heartbreaking still; even as I look this far back, I remember it as if it happened yesterday.

"Dear little brother, you are not expected to perform on your wedding night at your age. Our father's health is poor, and he fears missing such an important day of your life." Rubbing the top of Hotan's head, he managed to work a smile from him. "Liora will wait for you as long as you wait for her. You both have your entire lives ahead of you, *alef chet.*"

"I hope so…" His green eyes were bright like gems as the sunlight refracted off his irises. "You always know what to say, Talib. I hope one day I can be like you."

Pulling Hotan to him, he chortled, "You only need to be yourself. Never wish to be the other man; it leads to bad things, trust me on that one, Brother. Until that important day comes, simply take care of one another."

Smiling at him, Hotan lugged up the full basket and hurried off. Talib fell onto his back, and snippets of grass and dust filled his nose. Laying on the warm ground, he watched the clouds glide over the blue sky. Once more, he found himself alone in the field. Hotan's concern was admirable, but his focus should be on the drastic change their lives must take to fill the gap created by their father's invetable death. No longer would they have the leisure to lay in the fields and let the hours pass them by. Once the festival ended, they would take on their roles as leaders and lose most of the freedoms they had grown to love. Taking in a deep breath, he rolled back to his feet and continued the task before him.

Deep down, I wanted to get rid of the looming fate that awaited me. Perhaps I was foolish to rush myself into the next stage of life. In fact, I had not stopped to realize that my eagerness would drag Hotan helplessly behind me. Then again, while I was pulling him behind me, my father was pushing him closer on my heels. There was always a phantom sensation urging me to blaze a new path to carry him down safely.

Talib was exhausted, but the excitement of his wedding helped him catch a second wind. Scrubbing the sweat-soaked dirt from his skin, he grinned like a drunken fool. The nerves in his joints tingled at the thought of waking up every morning next to Saphellia with her amazing rosy scent. Dunking his head into the water, he rubbed his hair clean. Joy overwhelmed him as he burst from the small tub of water, gasping for air before continuing laughing. He had never worried so much about being clean and polished for someone. Leaning over the rippling water, he stared at his silver-eyed reflection, wanting to see the excitement on his own face.

He no longer missed the boy he used to be; he felt pride in the man he had become. It seemed as though his broad shoulders, strong jawline, and the wrinkles coming into existence were all earned in just the last year. Looking back at Hotan, who sat behind him in silence, was a bitter reminder of the huge gap in their ages. He had been the firstborn boy, and his mother endured several miscarriages until her death during Hotan's birth. After seven years of failures, she died smiling as the cries of her second child reached her ears. She had been given a miracle before leaving this world.

Talib thought to himself, *Perhaps if mother had survived, Hotan would have had a better life. Not this one, where father was filled with fear and forced him through the years too soon. Was this the point when it all went wrong?*

"Talib?" He jerked from Hotan's voice as thoughts of their mother stung his eyes. "What if Liora doesn't like me?"

He scoffed and peered over his shoulder where Hotan sat on the bed, moping. "I thought you two were friends?"

"We are, but…" Hotan's bottom lip quivered as tears trembled on the edge of his eyelids. "Being married is different. What if she doesn't, well, *love* me?"

Sighing, he broke away from the water basin. Hotan looked down and fiddled with his thumbs. Despite his own excitement, he had forgotten how terrifying this was for Hotan and Liora. Talib decided to do all he could to make sure their impending wedding night would not ruin them for the rest of their lives. They had played together so often, chasing one another, and even getting into trouble side-by-side; there was no reason for their arranged marriage to fail.

Crouching in front of Hotan, he took his tiny shoulders into his hands. "*Alef chet*, friendship is a seed for love. Like the seeds in the ground, you must take care of it so love can continue to grow. This is why it is possible for friends to feel as if they were brothers, and in your case, two friends may become husband and wife. Do you understand?"

A tear fell, but he nodded with a smile as his green eyes sparkled with newfound hope. "I suppose I need to help my friendship with her grow, so I can be a good husband."

Laughing, he patted his brother on the shoulder as he walked away. "Let us get dressed and meet our brides!"

The sun had fallen, but a warm breeze brought scents of the awaiting feast; breads, meats, and spices mingled and teased his nose as they made their way through the maze of people. As they shook hands and exchanged a few words with friends and family, they were pulled and pushed ever closer to their destination. A large fire whirled high into the sky, and in the heat of its light, they would be married; it was a gorgeous night.

The celebration in honor of the chief's sons and their new brides would carry on into the morning. As they ventured past the last ring of homes and tents, their father stood waiting. His eyes were sunken as he leaned heavily on his cane; his illness was no longer hidden with his occasional coughs. The rate at which he had withered away in the last year was frightening for everyone. It stained them all and left them with one haunting question: When would he take his last breath?

Taking his sons in his embrace, tears streaked Father's face as his feeble voice shook in their ears. "Thank you for allowing me to witness this glorious day, my God, my sons."

"I suppose I was overdue to take a bride." Talib felt the rattling in the chief's lungs resonating through their touch; it was a marvel that he managed to get around or even speak with them in this state. "Sorry for taking so long, Father."

"You have nothing to be sorry for, Talib. It is I who feels sorry for being called away from this life before I can address the surfacing concerns." Breaking their hold, he peered down at Hotan, who furrowed his brow. "Please forgive me for rushing you along your journey, my little one."

Tears fell from Hotan's chin as his father kissed his forehead. It wasn't the first time these emotional gestures had been exchanged between them. Often, Hotan had looked at their father and immediately panicked and sobbed. All their father ever could do to soothe his terror was simply kiss his forehead, expressing his affection for the small boy.

Hotan's voice was shrill with frustration. "Please, Father, don't talk as if you won't be here to see me tomorrow."

"You are right." A smile stretched across the worn, sickly face, and he urged them forward. "This is a time for celebration! Your brides are waiting, my sons!"

He was so young and heartbroken. I do not think I ever noticed it then, but the pain of his burdens already weighed him down. I should have seen Hotan's heart drowning, but I was blinded by my own bliss at this point in my life. Is this why I am seeing this now? Am I recalling Hotan's fall from grace?

Breaking his focus on his brother's tear-filled face, he stumbled to a stop. His eyes were gripped by Saphellia's presence as she stood by the head priest. The fire glowed outward from behind her like the fiery wings of an angel, washing her in a golden warmth. Her white cotton dress swung in the breeze and her hazel eyes caught his stare. The world went silent as she smiled at his enamored gaze, and his heart swelled. During the previous years when their fathers had pulled them together, love had grown between them, but it had not made itself tangible to him until this very moment. Remembering to breathe again, he took his place beside her, marveling over her hands in his own as the priest's words faded away; everything about her was so beautiful.

"Talib." The priest cleared his throat, bringing him out of his daydream. "Do you accept?"

"Y-yes!" he stammered. "I do!"

"And do you, Saphellia, take Talib as your husband?"

He held his breath as he waited for her answer.

"I do." Joy exploded through him to hear her words.

Before the priest could say another word, he pulled Saphellia to him and returned her surprise kiss from earlier. She started giggling, and he couldn't stop himself from joining her laughter as their lips were still pressed together. Yelps and whistles rang out as flowers pelted them, but the priest bellowed out to regain order. The ceremony was still in progress, and he turned his attention to the smaller couple standing before him.

Hotan shifted nervously and bit his bottom lip. They were so young, and neither of them understood this overwhelming excitement expressed by him, Saphellia, and the crowd. Stuttering as they answered the priest's words, they turned and stared uncomfortably at one another. Talib smiled even though his heart ached for them, and he took pride in walking over to Hotan.

Leaning down, he whispered his first real advice to his younger brother, "It is okay to simply hug her. No one is expecting the two you to kiss, *alef chet*."

Swallowing in relief, Hotan nodded eagerly to him. "O-okay…"

There was no mistaking the tension as Hotan hugged Liora, firm and stiff at first. Her green eyes were wide; she had never felt such a tight hug from her friend in their years of playing. Tears fell down her cheeks as she dropped her bouquet and hugged him back. She buried her face in Hotan's shoulders, and he looked back at his brother, bewildered by her response to something they had done so many times before. Before he could explain, a tiny, muffled voice hit both their ears.

"Thank you." Liora's whisper was almost lost in the shouts from the village. "I wasn't sure what to do, Hotan."

Hotan's cheeks flushed, and he whispered back, "Don't worry, Liora. I'm not ready to grow up either. I will wait for you if you promise to wait for me."

Ah, I remember the swell of pride I felt to hear him speak my words of advice with such a loving tone. It was the first moment that I realized how much my advice was needed, not politically, but in a brotherly sense. Father was not there for him much by this point, and it was then that I realized I was already filling a gap left behind. I was advisor, brother, and father from this day on. Maybe my reluctance to accept the role of father for him led to what happened later...

Saphellia grabbed Talib's hand and pulled him away from the tiny couple. He watched with a pang of sorrow in his heart for them as he was rushed away. Their marriage at such a tender age was strictly political. Before he lost them to the enclosing crowd, he watched little Liora reward Hotan with a kiss on the forehead. An endearment reminiscent of their father, now given by his wife, would serve as a much-needed crutch.

"You will make a fine advisor to him, Talib!" Saphellia's father said.

"Thank you, Tzadok." Talib's hand seemed small in his as they exchanged crushing grips. "I promise to take care of Saphellia. There is nothing in this world I would not do for her, even putting her life before my own."

"Careful..." A grave look crossed Tzadok's face at the words from his new son-in-law. "Let's hope the Devil didn't hear you say that."

Tzadok's baritone voice shook the air from your lungs when he spoke, but it served its purpose in taking authority of any situation. The lead diplomat was built like a bull, but despite his muscular looks, he was passive at heart. His black beard carried more lines of grey in them, and his face folded on itself more than Talib remembered in his first meeting with the man. The dark brown eyes did a grand job at intimidating most men, but Saphellia had inherited her looks from her mother. Unfortunately, like many others within their village, Saphellia's mother returned to her home country after she was trained in the art of tending to the tabernacle.

The night was long, and they barely managed to enjoy the feast in front of them. Numerous times, Talib attempted to grab a bite but was forced to abandon it due to an important figure demanding to congratulate them. He gave up keeping track of who had approached them or what had been mentioned while in conversation with them all. His father, and even Hotan and Liora, took leave from the celebration well before Talib would be allowed to do so.

He and Saphellia knew they were obligated to stay until the fires were low and the food almost gone—their first task as leaders. Finally, he managed to get a few bites into his mouth, hushing his grumbling stomach. Washing it all down with the wine, he looked over to Saphellia with heated cheeks. Despite not paying him any attention, her face reddened in response to his captivated stare. Talib couldn't decide if the warmth in his cheeks came from the alcohol or his feverish thoughts about her.

Oh, it was the alcohol. I was growing braver and more fiendish both in thought and in action by this point.

Tiring of the politics, he leaned over to Saphellia and whispered in her ear, "I think we are safe to call it a night, my dove."

Her hand found his, and she squeezed it tight in response. "Forgive me, Lillianna. We will have to finish discussing your concerns on supplies needed for metal working tomorrow."

The muscular girl nodded. "And call me Lilly. Tomorrow, you can find me helping my father recycle some metal scraps for horseshoes. You two have a wonderful night, Saphellia!"

Without further hesitation, Saphellia turned her full attention to Talib.

Kissing his cheek, her lips tickled at his ear as she pleaded, "Take me away from all these politicians and worries, my husband."

"Forgive me!" He stood, showing his excitement as he called for the remaining group's attention. "My new bride and I would like to take our leave now! God bless and may we forever prosper in peace!"

Drunken whistles and cheers rang out as he pulled Saphellia away. He refused to stop for anyone else as they weaved through the enclosing group. Bursting into his tent, they were in tears with laughter from their escape. Pulling her closer, he held her face as he kissed her. It felt impossible to gain another moment to themselves during the feast, but here, in this quiet spot, she was his and he was hers. The warmth of her arms excited him as they wrapped around him. He fumbled backward, knowing his bed wasn't too far from where they stood. Both tumbled down, still kissing, and Saphellia's laughter sent his soul soaring as he gazed over every detail of her face; this was the face of his wife, and it brought him unimaginable joy.

"Please, tell me I am dreaming…" Her eyes were captured by his, and her smile faded. "Are you really my wife?"

"I hope it's not a dream, my Talib." Pressing her soft lips against his, their kiss was lustful and passionate as the heat of their bodies echoed off one another. "If it is, may we never wake from this moment."

3

SUICIDAL DREAMS

928 BC

"Talib." Hotan's voice broke his daydream as their father's dying words echoed in his thoughts: *You shall be Hotan's advisor and protector.* "What should I do? I can feel it deep down; it's not a dream but a warning of what's coming."

I remember this day far too well. This is where it all started to fall apart...

"Remember what you told me the day before father passed?"

Staring over at Hotan, Talib couldn't help but miss the little boy he had been ten years ago. "You had a dream then, and you came to me, like now..."

Looking back, it all happened so quickly. There was nothing I could have done to prepare myself for what unfolded.

"But everyone could see he was on his deathbed, Talib. This time is different." Rubbing the back of his neck, Hotan furrowed his brow. He said assertively, "If I insist a dark army is coming to burn the village, the council will not take it lightly. They will label me mad, and worse, push to remove me as chief."

He was right, but I had no advice to fix the situation we found ourselves in. Even if we had marched down to the council and screamed the information out across the village, no one would have believed something so insane was coming.

"Just in the ten years since he has been gone, we have seen the corruption in the council. Father had suspicions, but if he witnessed the things we do now..." They both tensed, exchanging glares about the crimes they had seen. "He left their lives in our hands, Hotan. You are not facing this by yourself; I will not let you stand alone against such ill-willed men. Which weighs heavier on your soul, attempting to bring this up to the council or remaining silent?"

It was not bad advice. He had to make that judgment for himself. I could have easily told him to be silent, but I needed to know how real of a threat he believed it to be. After Father's death, he became eerily quiet, reclusive in comparison to the brotherly relationship we held prior. At this point, I was excited to be asked for advice, yet terrified of what was being put on the table. How long had I ignored the signs after Father died? Maybe I was partly to blame for not pushing for answers the moment he stopped being himself.

Breaking their stare, Hotan searched the air in front of him. The intensity on his face told Talib he was digging out everything in his own mind to decide the best course of action.

One of those weights was the unborn child in Liora's belly. It would be their first child, and more importantly, the heir to take leadership after them. As for himself, Talib and Saphellia had not been blessed with a child. They had not even a miscarriage like he had seen with his mother growing up, which only led to him blaming himself. They assumed that they were both sterile. Many of his generation had suffered the same fate, though no one confessed openly to it. An illness had struck the village during their father's younger years, and sadly, sterile men and miscarriages were the plague which followed in its wake.

Instead of lingering on this sour note in their lives, they poured their efforts into helping manage the village's affairs. The problems within their village had increased as their numbers dropped. Over the last three months, they had not received anyone for training or even heard back from the other villages. Something was happening beyond the reaches of the tiny thirteenth tribe of Israel.

If we had heeded Father's advice, perhaps we would have known this was coming. Again, looking back, the signs are so much clearer than when I lived in it. Answers seem so obvious when one is a spectator and emotions are set aside.

Hotan paced the room, still haunted by the dream as he weighed the question. Talib noted how much he had grown into a man. He was almost as tall as Talib, but far stockier in the shoulders and arms. His personality had grown away from its innocence and evolved into something beyond intelligence. His ability for seeing through lies was impeccable, and it was rare that he needed Talib's advice. Their conversations took a drastic shift when their father passed. It was as if Talib spoke to the deceased through Hotan; the knowledge he held flowed forth from the unknown. Whether it was a curse or blessing was yet to be seen.

No, it was a curse that not only plagued him but all that remained. In fact, he became a darker person, falling ever deeper into that emotionless abyss until it swallowed him whole.

"I will try to tell them." Swallowing back his concerns, Hotan grabbed Talib's shoulder, bringing his attention back to the present. "Talib, they will remove me. I do not know if they will announce it as a permanent decision, but know that I will not give them the pleasure of hearing you had a hand in this. Promise you will feign ignorance about my dreams."

"I do not think it woul—"

"Promise!" he barked, his fingers gripping tight, his muscles aching under the pressure. "Trust me this one time, Brother. Do not acknowledge them, or we will lose what little ground we have to keep the village safe."

"Fine, Hotan." Huffing, he pulled the hand off his burning shoulder. "I promise."

Talib stomped out of the tent, frustrated by the demand. In all their years, they had never needed to disregard their actions in one another's eyes. Talib struggled with whether he could he keep his promise. He took pride in being honest and fair— that would be damaged if he followed through. He marched on, heading to the fields where no eyes could see the internal conflict raging inside him. *The council has acknowledged and praised me on my judgment multiple times, but how could I ever convince them that I am unaware of Hotan's dreams?*

All the viable options he could think of would force him to break his promise to their father. *I am supposed to protect Hotan, even from himself if necessary. It is admirable for Hotan to want to shield his older brother for a change, but he gave up his childhood for our father's wishes. I owe him my best judgment; it is the only way to repay him for asking a child to get married and become an adult after our father's death wavered on the edge for eight agonizing years.* Looking to the clouds, he couldn't decide on a clear answer. None of them were compromises, and all of them weighed harder, one way or another.

Indeed, I was cornered at that very moment. Amazingly I found an unexpected friend when I needed one most...

"You doing okay, Talib?" Jacob, the youngest son of the Shepard, stumbled upon him while walking back home. "Coming out here to clear your head?"

From this point on, Jacob would always be there during my weakest moments…

"You could say that." Sighing, he realized there was no girl accompanying him as usual. "No lady friend today?"

Blushing, he smirked as his purple-toned eyes sparkled. "I am trying to quit that bad habit. Sort of got my eye on a girl these days, and I don't think she cares for me due to my reputation for lustful behavior."

"Lustful?" Talib raised an eyebrow; it was odd for Jacob to be so honest about his downfall.

Jacob was handsome with tanned skin and dirty blonde hair. All the girls swooned over him, which fueled his promiscuous habits so much so that it became expected of him. Often, he was caught with a girl, disappearing into the fields or out of sight of the herds. Rumors about his passion and taste for women was always on the tongues of the women in the village as well as the angry minds of fathers.

Laughing, he confessed to Jacob, "And I am sure there were many broken hearts upon hearing this news of your new way of life. So, who is the girl who has brought about such an important change?"

"I'd rather not say." Jacob joined him in staring at the clouds. They were each fighting their own internal battle of judgments. "Until I clear my reputation, I want to keep her name silent. It's not fair to drag those we love into chaos we make for ourselves."

That is the wisest thing I ever learned from him, though he also firmly believes in protecting and standing up for those you love…

He looked over at Jacob's taut face; his smile was gone, and his eyes were still on the sky. "It is a very valid point. I respect that decision of yours, Jacob."

"Talib!" A young girl ran toward them, her cheeks flushed as her dark hair stuck to her face. "The council! They are demanding you come at once!"

"He could not have..." His heart felt the tight grip of fear squeezing around it. "Did they say why?"

Panting, she shook her head. "No, just that it was urgent."

The march back was too short to predict what he would be walking into. Each step tightened his muscles, and when he reached the council's building, he reminded himself to take a breath before entering. A heated argument went mute as the glares turned to him. Scanning the room, he could see a few of the councilmen were sweating from their mental efforts, and there were no signs of Hotan.

It fell apart so horribly fast...

Standing tall, he took his seat at the massive table in the room and weighed the expressions before him. Some showed fear, others deep concern, and a select few were nervous. It was the sweaty, fidgeting men he paid the closest attention; they had made the mistake of showing their disloyalty toward his father after his passing. Something had these men scared.

"Where is Hotan?" Having a meeting without the chief present was considered taboo, even a form of betrayal or rebellion against the village as a whole. "What is so urgent that only I am present?"

"He was asked to leave." One of the white-bearded diplomats who had attempted to remove them from power multiple times in the last two years wiped sweat from his face. "Hotan made quite the show of himself before he was forced to leave. We want to know your involvement in this."

"Involvement?" Many shuffled and whispered a few words, but Talib's demanding glare silenced them as he prodded for more information. "Exactly what was he attempting to do? My brother does not lose his temper so easily over nothing, Elam. What in the world was so important for all of you to discuss without me present? Perhaps my absence was the cause of unnecessary aggression?"

"He accused Elam of making deals with Salah to overthrow—" Elam shot the young diplomat a look of warning to still his tongue.

Talib leaned forward in his chair, entertained to hear that Hotan had addressed the suspicions head on during his absence. "Salah was exiled by my father for his violence and disregard for women in our village, Elam. It is forbidden to speak to the man, let alone make agreements with him on the village's behalf."

"You know nothing, Talib," he hissed, but the sweat sliding down his cheek told everyone that the accusations held some truth. "You and your brother were handed a broken legacy, and now you think you can patronize me. I have travelled outside this village and seen the world, and we mean nothing without these agreements."

"And when did you consult the council on these agreements, and what was promised on our behalf, Elam? Does anyone else here know the terms?" The room filled with panic as the council realized what he and Hotan had already known: Elam had made deals for his own protection, leaving the village open for attack and manipulation. "No one knows what was promised on the village's behalf?"

"This is not about me!" Elam stood, slamming his fist on the table as his face reddened from his rage and frustration. "Your brother has gone mad if he thinks we are making a decision based on a childish nightmare!"

And here was the first slice of destiny's sword that struck me down.

His eyes widened; Hotan had let everything loose: conspiracies, traitors, and even his dream. If he was going to be removed, Hotan wanted to pull all the dark secrets from their corners to be resolved. None of these men could deny what was happening, but Elam's lack of response aided Talib's plan. He had been given a chance to put doubt in any trust the rest had in Elam. Still, Talib's inability to respond to Hotan's so-called madness from nightmares expressed a lack of awareness to those weighing him against Elam. This meeting was to decide who would take Hotan's place.

"Did you know your brother was suffering from nightmares, Talib?" Tzadok took control of the meeting; his beard was white with age, and his voice was sincere. "That he sees the destruction of the village? He even went on about dreams involving your father's death, his marriage, and he wept here, stating he knows that you will never be given a child. Worse, he sobbed about knowing that he would lose his own child to a raging storm. Has he spoken to you about any of this?"

Ah, the second slice. Hotan had known and spoke nothing to me about it. I wonder if he ever realized the sting I felt when my own father-in-law exposed such news to me. A couple as in love as Saphellia and I should have at least carried a child once, but to be told I was doomed to sterility was soul shattering. Even then, it must have broken Tzadok's heart and twisted his soul to hear from Hotan that his daughter would never be blessed with children of her own. There are not enough words in the world to express the heartache and betrayal I felt with so many eyes staring down on me, knowing more of my shortcomings than I had willingly accepted at this stage of my life.

He opened his mouth, but the words failed to make it to his lips as his emotions pulled them back. Hotan had never once spoken to him of these horrible predictions. The room spun as Talib tried to grasp how his little brother had held such frightening enigmas from him. Knots twisted in his stomach; a dream predicted he would be childless, but worse, Hotan predicted the death of his own child. *How long has he endured this curse and are there more predictions he still keeps to himself?*

Desperate to regain his composure in this moment of judgment, he swallowed and looked Tzadok in the eyes. "This is the first time I have heard anything of it." Taking a breath, he readied himself, preparing his next words to secure Elam's failed ascension to leadership. "And I cannot say whether my father knew. If I had known, I would have pulled Hotan from his position in fear that his … madness would put the village at risk. Sadly, I cannot disagree with removing him immediately, but I can assure you, I would not make backdoor deals with the exiled as Elam has already done. This council makes those decisions; I am simply its voice and the mountain that holds the village's well-being in place."

Elam gritted his teeth and snarled at Talib's sharp stare. "How can we trust you to see issues if you didn't see that your brother had gone mad?"

"Then we were all blind to his condition." The authority in his voice and body had returned, and his words made Elam sit back down. "All of us have advised him as members of this council, not just me. If I am guilty of not seeing it, then you are as well, Elam. Lord knows you would have pulled this issue into the light the instant you suspected anything."

Elam would suffer a fate far worse than this embarrassment created by someone whom he considered inferior. Far worse…

A wave of rumbling escaped the remaining diplomats as they took in his words. Elam had proven he had his own interests in mind, but Talib was blunt, leaving them with no fears of hidden agendas. He should have been listening to the comments being batted between the rest of the council, but all he could hear was the list of Hotan's predictions. He felt detached from his little brother and blind that Hotan had been suffering for so long. Tzadok's heavy hand shook his shoulder, spooking him from his worries.

Looking up, Talib stared up at Tzadok's furrowed brow as his booming voice washed over him, "Please go see your brother. See what else he is not telling you. As for now, we will need several days before making any decisions on what to do with him, you, or Elam. I'll do what I can to see it is kept peaceful, my son-in-law. Just so you know, I will push hard for you to take the lead, especially after doing so well against Elam's diplomatic attack under so much distress."

"He has been hiding something dark from me, and I never saw any signs of it, Tzadok." Standing, the two hugged and exchanged heavy handed pats on the back. "I do not know if I will get anything from him. He never once hinted at any of this, and it terrifies me to know I do not know my brother as well as I thought."

Elam's voice shrilled as he cursed the other councilmen who encircled him. They pried about the agreements he made with Salah; after his angered confession during Talib's questioning, this was no longer a conspiracy. The chance of the exiled Levite war general keeping true to his word about the village's safety was non-existent. Talib's father had driven the man out, and with Talib and Hotan in charge, he would rather see the village burn. Salah was the one who pushed to break their agreement with the other twelve tribes, but it was his actions which led to his exile.

He was caught forcing himself on one of the girls who had been sent to be trained as a tabernacle caretaker. As their father and several others drove him out of the village, he swore to return. Growing up, Talib lived with Salah's shadow looming over him, waiting for him to take out his revenge. Talib was apprenticing alongside his father when word reached them Salah had been given a high position in one of the neighboring armies. That was one of the events which started their father's suspicions that the treaties were failing.

"Go on, go see Hotan, and report to us what you make of his state of mind." Once more Tzadok's voice pulled him out of the drowning thoughts. "We will deal with Elam."

He felt lost as he took the arduous steps toward Hotan's home. Looking up, the sky was a deep maroon color as the sun began to set, and the icy fingers of night scraped themselves across his skin as the wind blew over him.

It was as if nature itself was trying to warn me; Death's chilling breath on the breeze and the sky painted in the color of blood…

Outside the door, a warrior named Geliah stood. He was a bull-sized man, thick muscled with dark-brown dreadlocks and amber-yellow eyes, much like a cat. He was a tyrant when he was younger, but nowadays, his strength was put to good use serving the village and council. As children, Talib remembered how Geliah would push him about, yet once he married and took on his title, it all stopped in an instant. Nodding in respect, Geliah did nothing to impede Talib from entering Hotan's home.

Hard to believe he was once so caring. Once a man is given power, his soul becomes vulnerable to corruption. Geliah would fall ever deeper into a lifetime of corruption.

Nothing Talib had ever felt compared to the estrangement created in a matter of minutes between him and his brother. Anger and grief pulled at one another in his heart as he felt their conversation earlier in the day was meant to be a distraction, not a confession. Even then, Hotan had only revealed a very small portion of what was cut loose to the council in his absence.

Hotan sat slumped over in a chair with his face buried in his hands. Liora's frowning face met Talib's eyes, and the concern about Hotan's mental state was clear. Talib wanted to say something, but nothing came to mind. Staring down, he watched his little brother sob. Looking to Liora, he wondered how much she knew about the dreams, the predictions of her unborn child's death, and what he had done just a few moments ago. Sitting down in the chair across from Hotan, he waited. There were no words to fix or undo what had been put into motion. Nothing would soothe his own turmoil or the unknown abyss churning within Hotan. The crying man in front of him felt like a stranger, and everything he had known about his little brother no longer meant anything.

I remember thinking the Hotan of our childhood no longer existed...

"I'm sorry, Talib," Hotan mumbled, still holding his face with his hands. "I assume they shared all of it with you. I did not intend for you to hear all the things I have predicted."

"How long has it been going on, Hotan?" Anger seeped forward as Talib looked away from him. "When did this all start?"

"As long as I have existed..." The whisper almost failed to reach its destination.

It wasn't the answer he wanted to hear, so he pressed on, "And did our father know?"

"No." A heavy sigh escaped Hotan as his voice began to shake. "I tried to tell him a few times, but I already knew what little time was left before he would be bedridden. I thought to tell you, tested it with father, but..."

Closing his eyes, Talib guessed what ceased it, "You had a prediction involving me."

"Y-Yes…" Hotan began rocking; his nerves ate at him as he spoke. "I couldn't tell you. It hurt to know it, and then to watch as each year passed and no signs…" Hotan choked on his words, afraid to speak them any louder.

His fears were coming to life and to look me in the eyes was too great of a risk. I sometimes wonder if it was not fear, but the anguish brought on by having each year prove the nightmares were true…

He had no desire to look his little brother in the eyes, not until he could resolve his own feelings. Anger surfaced more and more as he thought about it. An ache in his heart cut through it when a thought ripped across him. "Does Liora know?" Swallowing, he could not dodge her frightened stare. "Hotan, have you—"

"No," he breathed, his eyes wide as they pulled away from Liora's frightened face. "No, I can't. Don't… you don't understand, I… Talib, please."

Furrowing his brow, Talib understood. If the tables were turned and he had needed to tell Saphellia, he could not follow through with such a horrible prediction.

Liora fell to her knees in front of Hotan, grabbing his face, demanding he look her in the eyes. Tears fell from her chin as she gritted her teeth. Her words struggled to climb up her throat and out of her lips. Her body shook with such ferocity that it turned his stomach. Liora was the one person who knew how accurate his predictions were, and she was scared to think she had been in one of his dreams. She shook his head in her hands as her voice came back to him.

"Tell me, Hotan!" she pleaded. "What horrible fate awaits me, my husband!"

Hotan's bottom lip quivered and tears streamed down his cheeks as his eyes fell to her belly, betraying his sealed lips. Chills rippled across Talib's skin to see the havoc twisting Hotan's soul. The weight of the escaped words revealed the unbearable prediction and deafened the room. Muscles grew tense as panic filled Hotan's eyes, but it broke when someone jerked open the door, and the tiny home flooded with the clatter of pandemonium.

"TALIB!" Geliah rushed into the room. "I need to get you all some place safe, now!"

Both he and Hotan paled. They knew what was happening as screams multiplied to a deafening level. A nightmare had come to life as the sun left the sky. Under the cover of night, the other tribes had launched their attack; no longer would they keep their promise or allow the thirteenth tribe to thrive. Based on the direction of the chaos, Talib knew they had hit the council's house first; Salah would have insisted on such a tactic. Instincts assured him the leader of this massacre was the exiled one, Salah, and his next targets would be the brothers. Salah planned to gain his revenge from banishment from the village. Regardless of how much they knew of the opposing force waiting outside the door, with no army to fight back, they could only run for their lives.

"How long ago did you predict this, Hotan?" Talib pulled Liora to her feet, wasting no time following Geliah out the door into the smoke-filled darkness. "How long have you known?"

I never did get an answer. Looking back, I can assume it had been years, and he knew we were getting close. From the look on his face, I do not think he thought it would be that very night. Still, he should have told me sooner, and just maybe, somehow, we could have stopped this… or so I keep telling myself.

Hotan averted his eyes, and his jaw tightened as they ran past the houses. The thudding of horse hooves mingled with screams of terror all around them as they headed for Talib's home.

Bursting through the door, he was relieved to see Saphellia. She was digging out his falchion and had a pack full of bread thrown over her shoulder; she was never one to waste time. Gripping her hand, he pulled her out as smoke stung their nostrils; the village glowed with an orange hue. The invaders had set the buildings on fire, cutting down anyone who attempted to stop them as they weaved through the huts and tents.

Saphellia's fingers dug into Talib's shoulders, and he paused to look back at her panicked face. "What about my father?"

Swallowing, he looked past her to see horses flying through the houses and the ominous glow of torches bouncing in the darkness. "He was in the council's house where the attack started…" Clenching his jaw, he grabbed Hotan. "Take Saphellia and anyone else you can find and get them far from here. I will see who else I can save."

"Talib, let me go with you," he protested.

"No. You are the only one who can lead the others to safety." Breaking away from the group, he raced through the flaming homes.

The night air was distorted with dancing shadows from the burning structures where the living no longer resided. It goaded his resentment; he hated how everything crumbled away so fast, so easily. He made it to what was left of the building where the council had argued moments earlier. Bodies were strewn everywhere; the foul smell of burnt flesh and the iron sting of spilled blood made breathing nerve-wracking. Several council-men's throats were slashed, and others still burned under the fallen building. His eyes caught the colored sash he was seeking; Tzadok lay on his back; his throat was ripped open, and his eyes were wide and lifeless. As he thought, they were the first ones killed per Salah's guidance.

Swallowing, he looked away in time to see Hotan sneak up next to him. Before he could scold him, Elam's voice pulled their attention back to the other side of the massacre. He groveled on the ground by a horse and its rider, blood soaking the front of his clothes and his hands painted red. There was no need for imagination as a dagger glimmered beside him. Elam had turned on the council and assisted in their murders. Knots tightened in Talib's stomach. *If I had still been here, Elam likely would have slit my throat first out of frustration.*

"Salah! I have done everything asked of me! I overthrew the chief's sons; I killed the council! Where's my land? I kept my promise! Where's my gold? I did what was asked of me! I earned my place!"

Elam...

Those were the desperate pleas of a man filled with regrets as he stared up at the Devil holding his soul. Salah laughed as his horse sidestepped away from the broken traitor at its hooves. Tears streamed down Elam's face; his mistake stared down at him with a wild grin. Talib had warned him Salah would not honor his word with anyone from the village, and he was right. Elam jumped to his feet, tugging at Salah's leg and begging to be taken away from the carnage which surrounded them.

He should have known...

"Where are the chief's sons?" Salah's smile faded as he scowled down at the pest which clung to him. "Where are they, Elam!"

"I don't know..." He pleaded, "Please at least give me some of the gold promised..."

"Worthless!" Salah growled, spurring his horse into a gallop toward a group of his men deeper in the village.

The Devil never keeps his promises.

"We need to go." Talib grabbed Hotan's arm, but he broke free. "Hotan!"

He scrambled after him, but his fingers fell short of grasping the back of his shirt. Charging forward with the heat of his anger pushing him, Hotan hit Elam with a thud and tackled him to the ground. Talib flinched from the crunch of Elam's nose as Hotan's fist locked with it, then another, and another. Hotan punched him repeatedly; the outburst of physical violence was the first time Talib had witnessed him lose his temper. Tears streamed down Hotan's face as he panted from the explosion of brutality pouring onto the man under him. He stopped as Elam fell limp, losing the drive to take his last swing when he heard the rattled, shallow breath. Elam wasn't dead, but his fate would be left behind with the village he betrayed.

Talib managed to pull Hotan away and hurried to catch up with Saphellia. As they ran and dodged through the heaps of fires and what little was left of the buildings, the village was thick with warriors from the other tribes. The emblems and armor styles identified their former allies who had indeed turned on them. Talib eyed Hotan as they worked their way through the maze of chaos. *This is not the little brother I grew up with. Instead, I am in the presence of a cursed man. Hotan risked everything and made the difficult choice to reveal his prediction, and still nothing changed for the better.* Talib's anger fell away, replaced with empathy.

Looking back, I would have remained angry if I had known his plans for those who endured and survived. Now, knowing what was to come, I wish I could have screamed and shaken it out of him. But it would not change that we were left with no other option than to flee. Unlike Father, we were not trained warriors. We were men who had devoted our lives to being diplomatic, and at times, I resent it.

The halted when they heard a nearby girl screech. He gripped the hilt of his falchion, daring to look around the burning building while keeping their presence hidden. Jacob wrestled with an attacking warrior, and his shoulder was bleeding; the blacksmith's daughter, Lillianna, sat on the ground behind him. Her face was mottled with ash and tears as she clung tightly to her dead father's robes. She was torn between the living and the dead. The haze in her eyes told him she could not hear Jacob's pleas for her to run. Jacob was losing his grip on the blood-covered warrior who had sent many to the dark beyond.

Nodding to Hotan, they knew their roles. Sucking in one last stream of air, they broke from their cover. Talib headed for the warrior, praying he had stayed within the man's blind spot; Hotan served as the decoy. Unarmed, Hotan moved to pick Lillianna off the ground, breaking her hold and forcing her to her feet. Jacob gained an inch in the distraction. The blood-thirsty warrior stifled a step back, but his ribs felt the unexpected sting of Talib's blade. Another slice across his knees allowed the muscled brute to fall away from Jacob, who gripped his shoulder in relief as he leapt back. Without another word, they left the man howling and gurgling, and they weaved through the flames of their former home.

They picked up a few other villagers along the way; some were fleeing, and others had been fighting for their lives. Survival was the only thing they had in common as the roar of the fires replaced the screams. Behind them, the army's snapping jaws had finished its rounds of slaughter and collected the spoils it came to claim. As the glow of the burning village lessened on their backs, they found Geliah, Saphellia, Liora, and several others waiting in the thin tree line. Fear and shock rattled every face as they looked to one another's soot-covered and blood-splattered forms. Barely a fifth of the village stood there.

And this was only the start of the deaths we would witness…

Whistles and shouts of celebration broke their thoughts, bringing sour looks back to the hell they had escaped from. The flaming village looked like the fiery wings of a demon lashing into the night sky. The wavering shadow of a man on a horse shouted after them; his words were inaudible, but they knew who professed the grave warning: Salah. All eyes fell on Hotan and Talib as they stood, looking back to the primal taunts with furrowed brows. Salah would chase them to the ends of the Earth until he confirmed that the sons of his enemy were dead. Regardless, the brothers were responsible for what lives had been spared.

"We need to keep moving." Hotan's words slammed across the tired and broken survivors who winced at the bitter truth. "Salah might humor us by waiting until the morning to chase, expecting us to rest. We cannot afford to rest until we no longer see them or the smoke of the village."

"But what about the injured?" An older woman did her best to wrap Jacob's shoulder as she spoke. "They may not be able to keep up; worse, many of us are young or old. What if we cannot make this journey?"

Talib swallowed as Hotan's dejected tone and stare hit them all. "This is an exodus. Lives will be lost whether you stay here or push forward. I recommend you make peace with reality now."

It stung to see how easily he spoke in this very moment, yet back in his home, he could not even whisper the truth he knew...

Saphellia's fingers weaved themselves with his, squeezing them hard. Her cheeks had prominent streaks where tears had washed away some of the ash. Flashing images of her father on the ground reminded Talib why he had broken away from her side during the chaos. His lips were met with her fingers, and her frown told him she didn't need his words to confirm what she already knew. Pulling her into his arms, he squeezed her tight as he watched Hotan and Liora begin walking west. There was no advice he could give to smooth over a harsh truth. If anyone managed to survive the slaughter and remain in the village, they would surely become slaves to the army and the tribes who once saw them as equals.

They had broken their promise to God. My brother put a plan in action which he had already resolved from years of haunting premonitions. I suppose we were doomed from the start.

Salah's menacing shadow no longer stood between them and the massive glow, but his hatred stung at their heels. No matter which way they chose to flee, they would face a grim truth; their tiny slice of fertile land was bordered by harsh desert and hostile inhabitants. Heading west might give them some reprieve, but it would end at the sea. A few decided to remain in the trees for various reasons. Most were too old to take on the journey which awaited them, while others feared facing a slow, agonizing death. Talib and Saphellia wished these brave souls the best before following the back end of the marching tribe. The exodus had begun.

Those left behind became slaves for the people who took Salah off his leash and gave him the power to destroy an entire civilization. At least this was a better end compared to those who never made it out of the ashes of the village. Eventually, as the generations went by, they found their freedom and continued their legacy through religion. Foremost, they inherited the task of caring for the tabernacle and temples. With this honor, they were able to preserve some of our history, though most of it is still missing within those faithful pages.

4

HOPELESS

928 BC

It took two days before they reached the edge of the sand dunes, where not even the scrubland plants would grow. This was the first time Hotan allowed them to come to a full stop and sleep. There were no signs of Salah and his army, but at the rate they were going, his horses would close the gap in half a day's time. Fatigue made tempers flare, arguments became a constant occurrence, and morale was dropping. Many felt the first fits of hunger, and the water supply dwindled as people went against advice to preserve it for the sand dunes.

Talib walked through the sleeping heaps, staring at the faces as his thoughts grew grim. He knew many would not make it to the sea in their current physical state. Shoes were failing, so many ripped scraps from their clothes to wrap their blistering and bleeding feet.

I was not wrong. I just did not realize none of those faces would ever make it beyond the sea.

As he walked onward, he found Hotan standing alone in the roasting wind, glaring at the dunes blocking their way. His eyes were disconnected as if he saw something no one else was aware existed. Talib took in the orange waves made of sand, bright against the blue skies. The contrast of the horizon before him was stunning. Heat swelled out from the landscape in a frightening, visible form, twisting and distorting the world behind it. He looked down to the tiny shrubs at his feet. *Perhaps these are the protectors who kept this malicious desert from reaching our village all these years.* Sweat crawled down his forehead; wiping it, he looked back to the west. Somewhere over these scorching hills was the sea and, possibly, their salvation. Several minutes passed as he observed the taut face of Hotan.

Did he even acknowledge me standing there? I think this was the point when he started breaking his power apart. Watching my life play out like this, I realize there was no reason for him to even allow us to rest, not with the plans he had for us. The sensation of time pausing, taking a breath as I watched heat rise off those dunes was all surreal to me. Seeing how tense his expression was, I think this is where he made his decision to make us immortal.

Hotan's chapped lips parted. "No signs of Salah?"

"None so far." Talib paused to look again where they came from. "But we both know he is following on horseback; he will be on the horizon by morning. What are you thinking, Hotan?"

"I'll give them the night to rest." Giving a mournful look over his shoulder, he was reluctant to continue. "But no fires. There are enough people here to huddle and stay warm during the night. I fear we will see Salah's dust trail as the sun rises. Again, I'll give those a chance to stay behind or continue across the desert with me. But it's what happens when we get to the sea… I…"

Yes, that was it. He hoped only those he needed would cross, but he did not want to condemn them either. Some part of him hoped more would make it through to the island, but can I really be angry with him wishing for better odds? If I were standing there, I too would have feigned ignorance. What did dreams really know about the lives we were responsible for? How accurate could a vision be in the physical world? For my brother, it was painstakingly on point, without fail, numerous times.

Talib watched as Hotan paled and stared back to the west. Hotan's worst nightmare had yet to come true; it waited for him some place beyond where they stood. He had lost the ability to speak, and his eyes glazed over from haunting visions. *He must be repeatedly replaying the prediction in his mind. Hotan was unable to stop the slaughter, and he is running out of time to prevent the next prediction.*

Powerless to help his little brother, Talib felt he had failed to carry out the duty bestowed on him. No man in the world could stop it. They had to leave it in the hands of destiny and pray for a better outcome. A harsh wind scraped across, and sand bit at them. The temperature stung at their skin; their clothes failed to keep the heat at bay. His nose was greeted with the earthy scents of hot clay and a hint of the fading sweet aroma of the sedges at their feet. Rain had graced this land not long ago, but the water and flowers faded at a disheartening rate. As he snorted the dust from his nose, he shuddered, feeling relieved the wind had slowed at last.

"I am sorry that I cannot help you, *alef chet*." Talib left Hotan to his thoughts and went to inform the group of their options.

Almost half of the group decided to stay behind; many of them were injured or broken from their attempts to flee their attackers. Some spoke of attempting to travel back, hoping to skirt around Salah and his army that followed them through the dunes. It was a good plan, but it would only work for the smaller groups of people still able to travel at a solid pace. Besides, Salah was only travelling this far for the lives of the brothers; he likely wouldn't bother with the old and sickly when his targets were still out of reach.

The older woman from before shed tears as she informed him of her plans to stay.

"I am sorry, Talib. My path stops here with the sick and dying." Swallowing, she took a deep breath as she continued, "I cannot watch anymore of us drop dead trying to keep this insane pace. Hotan is not wrong with this decision, but as he stated, not all of us will make it. Crossing the desert is something I know my body cannot survive. Please forgive me for abandoning you."

Ah, I miss the old woman. She never formally introduced herself, but she often came to care for Father late at night. We spent many nights engaged in warm conversations, learning much about wound care and how to soothe symptoms of all kinds. She was a skilled healer, but what ailed my father was beyond anyone's ability to cure. All she could offer was aid to ease his breathing, his pain, and help bring sleep. Often, he woke in soul shaking coughing fits that brought blood to his lips. I hope she found peace or someplace to call home after we left her there. Someone with so much willpower deserved a better end than what I left her with.

"You have no reason to be sorry." Hugging her, he felt guilty knowing there was no way for him to aid her once they headed over the dunes, "Please be safe in your travels. I will miss your company..."

"I doubt Salah will want to kill us. He is more likely to leave us for dead and continue his quest to destroy you and your brother." Sighing, she broke away from him, motioning for Jacob to come to her. "Regardless, I will look after everyone's injuries and do what I can to see they make it as far as possible. Though I feel like I am only prolonging death for most of you."

She always had uncanny instincts. I wonder how she would have felt if I could go back and tell her she was right: death was coming regardless of her efforts.

"Thank you for your compassion." Talib watched as she unwrapped Jacob's shoulder, revealing the festering slice. "Are you staying behind as well, Jacob?"

"No way in hell," he grumbled as she pushed out the putrid puss from his wound; the smell made Talib's stomach tense. "I may be hurt and burning a fever, but there is no way Salah would allow me to live. Don't forget, it was my father who reported his whereabouts on the outskirts of the village when he was first exiled. He helped keep the bastard out, gave his banishment the final push, and kept the walls up."

"Salah's hatred for our fathers' actions is what has driven him to this madness." The intense silent stare they exchanged confirmed they knew staying would be death for them both. "How is Lillianna?"

Grimacing at the tightening of the bandage on his arm, Jacob sighed. "In another world."

"Perhaps it will help her endure what is still ahead." Thanking the old woman, Talib walked with Jacob to where Lillianna slept. "Each passing day adds more fuel to the nightmares carving themselves into every soul here. Even if we make it through this, we may never see the end of the sleepless nights it will cause."

"Wherever we end up, it will be best that we all start new lives." Jacob furrowed his brow as his purple-toned eyes scanned the broken people surrounding them. "Most of these people are now widowed or like Lillianna, the last surviving member of a prominent family."

I do not think Jacob ever realized how badly that stung to hear out loud. Perhaps it needed to be said, but I was guilty for many reasons, including having most of my immediate family still intact. I had my brother and my wife; I had lost most of my relatives at an early age. Maybe this is why the attack seemed so surreal instead of painful like it was for the rest of the gaunt faces which looked to me for strength. Seeing it all like this, I was spared from feeling the full force of this tragedy.

"If you need anything, let me or Saphellia know." Shaking hands, he left Jacob to rest and headed to his wife's side. "Are you okay, my dove?"

Sharing water with one of the younger girls, she frowned. "None of us are okay, Talib."

Closing his eyes, he hid the grimacing sensation ripping at his heart. "We are moving at daybreak."

Her forehead folded, knotting her brow under fears and concerns. Falling into him, she buried her face in his shoulder. The warm trickling of her tears hit his skin, and he wrapped her in his arms. He fought back the shudder begging to be released. As she shook in his embrace, his eyes jumped from one tear-streaked face to another in this sea of despair. She was right; no one had the strength to hold back the tears any longer. They had not stopped to rest but to mourn those left behind.

Perhaps we even needed to mourn those who were desperate to see freedom for one more day, but we knew would not make it across the desert.

A chill on the wind made him squeeze her tighter. The sun faded away on the horizon. It was eerie how fast the desert shifted its nature—blistering by day and freezing by night. Nowhere to go, they slid to the ground where they stood. He rocked her as his own tears started to fall. In the shelter of the night, he caved to the emotions. Looking over his shoulder, he saw Hotan still standing, glaring at the dunes. It was hard to say when his little brother had last slept, but it was apparent he would not be doing so until they reached their destination.

A place only he was aware existed…

"Talib." Jacob shook his shoulder, waking him. "We've got to get everyone moving now."

The sun had not crawled over the land just yet, and morning hadn't arrived. The sky, dim with lavender light, struggled to expose the world which the night had shaded. Jacob pointed to the east where a distant plume of dust was visible even in the lack of sunlight. His heart sprinted as his eyes locked with it. Adrenaline renewing his energy, he jumped to his feet and joined Jacob's urgency to wake everyone in silence. They needed to keep any clues of where they were from Salah and his army. Carefully planned movements had gotten them this far. From what they could tell, they were in luck because Salah was much farther south than where they planned to cross the dunes.

Salah was closer than I had even feared. He was growing impatient and had ridden through the night to be near where we rested. We were up against horses and well-supplied soldiers who were not tired or dropping dead. All we had was the drive to survive biting at the back of our necks, threatening to down us like a wolf to a yearling deer.

Hotan and Liora were in the front of the group while Talib and Jacob pushed the last of them to catch up. It took every nerve Talib had to hold back his tears as they left behind the sick and dying. He grimaced with each hand that shoved him away and shake of the head from a refusing survivor. His own sense of morale faltered with each person. People were ripped from the arms of their last loved one; farewells were a luxury with the army nearing. With the sun lighting the dust plume like a fiery pyre, Salah's army was nearly parallel with them from where they rode in the south.

Jacob pushed Lillianna and a few others over the first dune, allowing Talib to stop at the top and look back toward the group who chose to remain. The old woman, her brown eyes tired, gave him a grim expression. His throat tightened as her silent message burnt itself into his core. They had no intentions of travelling anywhere. Her last will and testament was to stay with them to make their last few days on Earth as peaceful as possible.

Every day I think back to this moment and pray I can be as strong as she was. Can I truly achieve the selflessness which she ascended to in those last moments? A saint with no name. Is that what I have always dreamed of becoming?

Afraid she would see his panicked thoughts, he turned away to follow the group. Even if Salah found them, he would leave them as they were to save time. Knowing this brought her solace to stay behind rather than risk travel for the slim chance of making it to the sea.

A saint—no, a martyr—whose name would be lost from the memories of mortal men but forever tattooed on the backs of angels.

The blaring heat burnt at Talib's skin, pushing for him to let the tears fall. Dehydration was settling in, and what little tears he had were swiftly eaten by the dry heat of the desert air. At the very least, he could take this silent moment under the rising sun to mourn those who had been lost and those who would be joining the dead before they found a safe haven.

When I recall this nightmarish moment in my life, I can still feel my skin bubble under the heat of the sun. Each tap of the breeze I so wished for felt like the bite of a million bees. My cheeks and shoulders cracked open like the dried clay we had rested on days before. Lips became nothing more than bleeding shreds of flesh, and eyes sunk deeper into the skulls of everyone around me. So many fell. Some just sat down and gave up, begging for death to come and take them away from this hellish purgatory we found ourselves shuffling through.

Days of searing heat baked their skin into blisters and boils. Sweat no longer graced their skin, and even when it did, the desert air licked it from them with startling efficiency. They had barely spent three days crossing the scorching landscape, and many had fallen over, dead. It was hard to distinguish if it was from the heat, wounds, or just their souls breaking from the lashes of their hardships.

Hotan had not faltered once as they worked ever closer to the sea, still hidden beyond the sweltering horizon. They used the last of the food, and their water was depleted not long after they headed out into the orange, fiery land. It was a grim reminder of how desperate their situation had become. Ghastly thoughts took hold of what was left of their morale. The cloth on their backs had thinned, leaving holes which exposed more skin to the scorching sun. Their sandals were broken or gone, and their skin faded, leaving charred fissures of decaying flesh. The motivation they had used to push into the hell fires of the desert was gone, leaving them nothing to pull them out of this place.

Screams woke him from his unfeeling gait. The morbid throng of villagers stumbled to a numbing stop, and Talib looked to the back of the group where the shrieks had risen. His pupils focused on the blurred shapes before him, and his eyes grew wide as his mind slowly registered what he was seeing. A pair of juvenile male lions, manes brown and not yet at their full boom, had started following them at some point, and they had gained the first reward for their patience. Their muscles were lean and chiseled under their golden fur. Though panting, the heat did not seem to eat away at them as it had done for their prey.

One of the older survivors had fallen over dead, and his brother had dragged him along since. It became increasingly hard for some of them to let go of those who could no longer be here or bear another step. The man's primal screams did nothing to startle the lion which tugged at his dead brother's legs. As the lions ripped open the body, the lack of blood from extreme dehydration was startling. Despite this, the beasts continued to fillet the sunburnt flesh, growing excited at the smell. Dehydration took its toll on all of them, mentally and physically. Talib took a step toward the man, but Jacob gripped his shoulder, stinging his flesh from the touch.

"Leave him, Talib." Looking over his shoulder, Jacob was pale despite the blisters freckling his face and arms. "His brother wasn't even injured like I am. Perhaps his death will help keep the lions off our backs for some time."

Swallowing, he took a long, woeful look; the man cradled his brother's lifeless face as the lions began to devour his feet. "I suppose nature will continue to dominate us..."

"Once they've lost their will to live, they fall to the Earth in an instant." Jacob mustered a half-hearted grin as he continued, "But I am too stubborn to leave behind so many who still love and need me. Lillianna is only alive because I am. If I fall here, I could not bear the weight of guilt knowing she would fall with me."

"You are right." They all started the grim walk again, knowing there was nothing they could do to defend themselves from the hungry lions trotting at their heels.

If it were not for the lions, the vultures would have come to us, and shortly after that, Salah and his army. Nature had swept up our tracks in the most unforgiving manner. I remember taking one last long look at the brother. He was on his knees, arms wide as if embracing the end of his life. The lion stood, jowls red with blood. The golden beast paused—an offering of respect for the man before him. It was a trade between man and beast to bring him swift salvation. The lion lunged, and I looked away, sour yet numb. All I remember was a sickening sensation of envy. He no longer had to take another step or take on another blister or feel the agonizing scraping heat of the occasional breeze. Jealousy was all we could feel in that moment of a fellow man's death.

It was like waking from a nightmare-filled coma when the salty air came across his nose. Relief from smelling his own flesh baking and rotting under the heat brought him back to life. Climbing the next hill would have brought tears to his sunken eyes if he hadn't been starved for water. Not many of the Levites were left; the small group was nothing more than skin and bones. Despite the stinging of the saltwater in his wounds, it was refreshing to cool down as the waves washed over him. The wind no longer carried the heat of the desert but the soothing stroke of cool moisture of the sea. Looking at the water in his hands, he fought the urge to drink it; saltwater would do nothing to quench the haunting thirst squeezing his throat. There, on orange and grey colored beaches, they still had no water, but at least they could wash away the cruel touch left by the desert.

Splashing his face, Talib felt alive again until he saw Hotan helping Liora to the shore to sit and soak her bleeding feet. His own feet had not faired very well. Some of them had shredded their clothes, hoping the frail wrappings would save what was left of the skin on their feet. Walking across the desert with nothing to shield your feet from the burning fire of sand was not an option. A flash of green eyes hit him, locking onto his own silver irises. It was a silent sign that a talk was needed between

Hotan and himself. They hadn't spoken one word to each other since they started their trek across the desert.

Leaving behind the cooling saltwater, he followed Hotan far away from the rest of the group. Talib was shocked at how much energy his little brother still had as he climbed the sand dune. The aching of his muscles and wounds made the ascension slow, and he marveled at Hotan's effortless climb to the top. This whole time, Hotan had kept to the front of the group while Talib lingered close to the back. At some point, Liora had lost the strength to walk; her feet were split open by the searing sands after her sandals gave up. Hotan had carried her on his back, her swollen belly goading him to keep moving, fueling his willpower to stay strong. Talib nearly knocked into Hotan as he came to an abrupt stop and twisted to face him. The frown on his face failed to hide his panic.

Hotan's face had been taut and pale while crossing the desert despite the sunburn it carried. His pupils were maddeningly wide, and a terrified and painful expression broke his face in ways I had never seen before. I nearly forgot to breathe when he turned to face me on top of the dune at the beach.

"I cannot promise what happens beyond this point, Talib." The pain in his eyes warned his last prediction would happen soon. "I fear this is where—"

"No need to explain it to me, Hotan. Your eyes speak volumes of the fear building within you." Looking over to the sea, the setting sun was no longer in view, and dark clouds gathered over the water where lightning danced between the water and sky. "Now that we are here, what is our next step?"

"We will rest tonight. With the incoming storm, we can try to capture water and search for food to regain our strength." A shudder rattled through him, and he struggled to continue his next words. "But by morning, we will have to piece together a raft and head out to sea. It is the only place where Salah will not follow us. Both man and beast will overrun us if we don't take this path. No one will survive if we stay on land. At least at sea, some of us will live…"

This was his way of hinting what was about to happen. He already knew only a select few would live. It was as if the sea was the gateway of truth for who would be allowed to inherit his curse. Or had he given it to us before crossing the desert? I wonder if that is the only reason Jacob outlived so many others despite his wound. Those words, "some of us will live" still haunt me. It is so clear now. He had already given us the immortality, but not all of us…

Hotan's last words trailed off as his eyes shifted focus to the approaching storm. It had grown darker; the lightning continued to flash in and out of existence, and the rumbling of its strike made it to their ears. Some place out on the water, his last prediction awaited its final victim. The wind from the sea grew stronger and colder as the growling storms floated closer to them. Everyone gathered large shells and other items which could hold water. Talib left Hotan to his haunted thoughts and found Saphellia sitting with Lillianna.

The two girls were unwrapping Jacob's shoulder. It was the old woman who had last touched this bane, and she had given them instructions for when they met the sea. They grimaced at the sickening smell of the wound and covered their noses; the putrid decay stung at their nostrils and eyes. It was a miracle he had made it this far with an infection burning through him. Wounds like this should have claimed the healthiest of men, or at least forced the removal of a limb, yet Jacob had miraculously worn this life-leeching demon in a death walk through the desert.

The slash ran partially over his collarbone, so amputating the festering flesh was not an option. Sweat poured across Jacob's ailing frame, and his eyes were dark and sunken. He wailed over the harsh scrubbing as saltwater washed over it. Lillianna held onto him; her blacksmith's arms hooked in his to keep him from pushing away. Watching him struggling against the pain of it made Talib's heart leap into his throat. Saphellia pursed her lips, sealing her mouth tight as she pressed on the maroon and purple mass. An eruption of gangrenous fluids spilled forward, and with it, came a deeper, gut-wrenching odor. She desperately washed it away with the sharp bite of saltwater before the next push. Screams did nothing to relieve the choking agony rattling through Jacob. Tears fell from his eyes as they bulged from each wave of pressure she applied until only blood flowed from his arm and collarbone.

Talib looked away, his eyes stinging from the sight and stench. He clenched his fists as he held his stomach, not understanding how the two women stomached the hands-on treatment. All he could do was beg his stomach not to dry heave.

"Jacob, you should have had someone change this sooner." Saphellia winced as he gritted his teeth; more saltwater poured over the rotten flesh. "How on earth are you standing?"

"This is all my fault." Tears streaked down Lillianna's face as she desperately scraped away the dead, infected pieces. Jacob was too exhausted to fight them while they continued to work. "If I had been stronger…"

"Stop it." Again, Jacob miraculously mustered a sparkle in his purple eyes and a smile across his cracked, bleeding lips. "I'll be fine. I've made it this far, and if you two help me, we can keep this thing clean. We can just keep flushing it out with saltwater."

"But your arm…" Furrowing her brow, Lillianna stared at his arm, thin and atrophied. "You'll never be able to—"

"Stop it!" he barked, holding the side of her cheek with his good hand, pulling her eyes to his own. "One arm is a small price to pay for saving the life of someone I love. I don't regret it, and more importantly, you should never feel guilty for being that person to me."

I swear his words made the Heavens weep. I see why he was placed as the element of Lust… more importantly, of Love.

Cold, icy drops of rain started to slap against Talib's face and arms. The tapping sensation freed him from his nausea. Everyone fell silent as they peered up into the dark skies, rejoicing in the rain. It grew thicker, falling faster in large pearls of savory water. He opened his mouth, and the few drops that landed on his tongue were an elixir of life. The girls finished wrapping Jacob's shoulder; all three of them were eager to join the celebration of rain. Within a few hours, angry waves from the sea grew taller. The storm chased after them, lashing up from the base of the hillside. Not one soul dared to fuss over their shivering bodies in the cold. They all held up containers, desperate to fill them with drinkable water. They may have lived through the desert, but deep down, they knew the sea was no more than a wet version of the hell they had shambled through. No one wanted to sleep that night. Each raindrop slamming into their broken flesh reassured them they were still alive. Hotan's gaze remained fixated on the storm over the ocean as lightning flashed in his pupils. The sparks of it expressed he did not—could not—share in their excitement. One prediction still haunted him, and it waited in the dark.

Did he sleep once during all this? Then again, I wonder how long had he already been immortal at this stage? Was he even my brother? Or was this Hotan I look back on now really a fallen angel who wanted a human life?

The gentle light of sun crept over the eastern horizon. On the beach, the storm had scattered debris and washed ashore treasures of sea life. Hotan quickly put the strong and willing to work. He tasked them with gathering wood and pulling together the scraps which had miraculously found the shore overnight. The rest of them combed the beach for edible and useful items. Every few hours, they rotated scouts to sit on the two highest sand dunes to watch for lions or, worse, Salah. Their cracked skin and malnourished bodies begged them to stop exerting so much energy, but they all felt the knot in their stomachs. With each passing hour, everyone's instincts drove them to work faster. Hotan had told them, but now, they felt his knowledge in their cores; Salah was closing the unseen gap with great speed.

The girls crafted several rafts with braided rope, using what little supplies they had among them on the beach. With daylight fading, it was all they could do. Food was rationed out, but the energy it provided was miniscule compared to what had been lost to get this far in their exodus. Desperate shouts called down from the hilltop; the lions had been spotted, but they had come across the last of their dead and would be satisfied for a little while.

Worse, the man at the other dune looking to the south whistled, showing fear in his body motions. Salah's dust trail loomed in the distance; it was a reminder of how easily he kept pace with them on horseback. Unlike Salah, their feet and bodies had been blistered as they watched those around them die. Morale was low, but the desperation for survival gave them another burst of energy. Swallowing down their panic, they focused on finishing the semi-seaworthy vessels. As the sun sank into the blackened ocean, they pushed the rafts out into the obsidian waves.

The sea was calm, but the gentle swish of the waves rolling across the beach was unnerving. So much had gone wrong in their escape. The ocean's sweet whispers would eventually turn sour after they drifted out under the cover of night. They could at least enjoy the few hours they would receive from the sun if their rafts held together long enough to see it rise. It was agonizing to watch the glowing moonlit sands of the beach fade away. They found relief in not having to walk across the searing sands any longer, but they were at the mercy of the currents. Out there, they were vulnerable, and nature would not show compassion. Fears swirled in everyone's minds. They had survived the desert, but in fear of dying under an army's blade, they risked still falling under the heat, drowning in the salty sea, or becoming prey to the grey lions called sharks which hid from their eyes just under the water's surface. A delusional smile crept across Talib's face. In the end, no matter their fate, Salah would be left ashore in the storm with nothing more than the footsteps left behind from ghosts.

Were the powers of Fear and Judgment at work? Was my brother manipulating us to push beyond our physical means? Seeing it again without the cloud of emotions, I cannot help but question it all. A man who was riddled with nightmares, did not sleep, and had not eaten thus far in such a journey would have gone mad. Hotan could not have been making sound judgments, but would I have been able to do any better? I felt so broken, sick, exhausted… I only valued my wife, who slept so soundly on my lap, despite our pending doom. Had Hotan already become immortal and these needs no longer a concern or factor in his life?

The slapping sound of the water against the logs was torturous as an occasional wave crept over them, icy and cold. Talib fought the urge to sleep. Waves rocked the raft like a cradle, lulling him to rest. His eyelids were heavy, and his chin dipped quickly, startling him back awake when it hit his chest. Saphellia nuzzled her head in his lap. Not everyone knew how to swim, but no one attempted to stay behind with the lions and army fast approaching. Talib wondered, *Did fear drive us to the rafts, or do we no longer value the idea of survival?* Maybe the idea of drowning was more pleasing to the broken soul than death by sword or fang. Shuddering, he clung to Saphellia for warmth as a cold breeze trickled across them.

Looking down at her, he thought, *I'm so sorry, Saphellia; we've been with one another for so long. Will my death break you?*

She furrowed her brow as if she was disapproving of his morbid thoughts, and her fists clung tighter to him. A wave of guilt washed over him for even assuming he would not make it through this. Geliah, the soldier who aided their escape from the village, was next to him. He kept a firm grip on the rope which connected them to the neighboring raft. The wind shifted as they looked out to the bleakness. The smell of rain teased them, whispering hauntingly of the storm it would bring. Straining his eyes into the black abyss, he couldn't distinguish sky from water.

His heart raced as flashes of light gave hints of where the horizon hid. A storm was building at incredible speed and drawing closer. Like an army of skeletons, the waves' white caps glowed brightly as they crawled closer. The loud slapping water reached farther across the raft's planks. Terror crept into his heart. Lightning laughed, shouting to him that it was the sister gale to the one they had witnessed on the beach the night before. The once gentle, smooth rolling hills of water turned violent and sharp. The hills grew wider and taller as the broken shards of the water's surface began to collide with itself. Even the waves seemed panicked; none of them marched in rhythm with one another but elbowed and slammed into each other.

"This may not go very well if it storms like last night," grunted Geliah, tightening his grip on the rope. "In fact, we will get separated if these waves kick up anymore."

Geliah's face was taut but lacked the frightened expression the rest of them wore. His body didn't tremble like the others. Even Talib fought to remain calm as the thunder shook his ear drums and the lightning struck blindingly close. Talib's heart hit his rib cage, leaving it aching, while Geliah remained stonewalled.

"How do you stay so calm, Geliah?" Talib admired the solidarity in Geliah's voice in the most frightening moments. "Through it all, you show the utmost control over your fear."

The toothy glow of his smile snaked across his face as he answered, "I was once told I had become fear itself. Perhaps it was true."

Unfortunately, it came true. Geliah becoming the element of Fear was one of several mistakes made in this chaos.

Thunder cracked overhead, mocking Geliah's words. Flashes of light struck all around them, announcing the arrival of the storm now pressing down on them. White-capped fangs sprang from the dark water, and a wave thrust the raft upward. Everyone woke, startled by the sudden sensation of falling as the raft fell between the passing waves. Each passing set grew taller and angrier in its game of tossing them to the sky. Their fingers dug into the wood, desperate not to fall. Startled screams rang out with each motion as everyone clung to one another, hoping to stay on their only salvation in the booming roar of wind and water. The raft was pitched between the waves as their rise and fall increased in height and speed. The slick rope was slipping through Geliah's hands. Scrambling over, Talib reached out to grip the slack. Gritting his teeth, his sunburnt hands stung in rebellion.

Women shrieked as the raft dropped, twisting their stomachs. They gained a small reprieve before being thrown to the top of the next passing behemoth. The wind howled through them as it tried to shove them off. Foam crawled onto the raft as everyone clung to the wooden logs, unable to stop the violent bobbing. The fraying ropes hissed, threatening to break. The raft under them was falling apart. Wind yowled as if laughing at their futile attempt at survival. Nature had toyed with them long enough and had finally come to claim them. Hope was lost. Screams rung out as the icy water slapped, promising to pull them under. As they reached the top of another wave, Talib held tightly to the rope as it dug into his fingers and squinted over to his brother's raft.

"This is it." Hotan's words hovered over the panicked rumbling of the four rafts like a phantom's whisper. "The last prediction has come…"

The rope ripped the flesh apart on his fingers. Each braid tore another piece of hope from him until he was left with nothing but the bloodied hands of failure. Tears mingled with rain and saltwater. Clenching his fist and grinding his teeth, he turned back to his wife. *Saphellia is missing!* Icy water wrapped around him before he could call out for her. Clawing upward, he was already starved for air. Breaking back into the roaring winds of the storm, he gasped and struggled to stay afloat. The raft no longer existed. Choking saltwater filled his senses, dragging him under the white-capped water.

All I could think about was finding Saphellia. I had to save her, even if it was the last thing I did…

5

HEAVENLY

928 BC

The heat of the sun and screeching of seagulls jolted Talib back to life. Saltwater still lingered on his taste buds as he rolled onto his back and squinted at the glaring sky. A rush of cool water pushed up around him, but quickly retreated as if welcoming him back to the world of the living. He had made it through the raging storm, but he wondered who else found themselves half-buried in the sand?

Sometimes I wonder if I really did die that night.

Suddenly, he was gripped by uncontrollable coughing; each gasp for air stung his lungs. It took every drop of energy he had to sit up, still gagging on saltwater. Muscles aching, he managed to catch his breath. The turquoise waves caressed the white, sandy beaches like a baker rolling dough with gentle skill. His mind struggled to right itself, still foggy from the swirling chaos of being tossed around in the waves.

His memories were fragmented. Images of him waking Saphellia, sea foam glowing in the flashes of lightning, and the mountains of water swallowing them all raced through him. A nightmarish blur of repeatedly drowning in the monstrous waves made his lungs ache with the memory. Every time he fell under the surface in the brutal currents, he was left confused about which direction was up. At some point, he started diving into the abyss, hoping to find Saphellia and avoid the weight of the breaking waves.

All I remember was thinking over and over, Please let Saphellia make it…

Breaking his exhausted glare from the calm waters, he looked down to the palms of his hands. The burning sensation that still haunted his mind had no wounds to match. When he fell off the raft last night, he felt the sting of the rope digging into his flesh. It lit on fire when it contacted the saltwater, but now, no signs remained—not even a scar. One thought rushed forward: *How long have I been lying on the beach?*

Examining his skin, he discovered the sun-scorched blisters and boils left by the desert were all gone. The scratches, and bruises from malnourishment, and the calluses gained from working the fields were no longer in existence either. The gulls and ocean were silenced by the weight of his fears. *Am I dead?* Talib thought, and the horrifying question echoed through his mind.

If I had died, the life events which would come to plague me for eternity would be nothing more than a forgotten nightmare. I used to look back on this memory and wish I had never made it ashore.

Flopping onto his back, the cold wet sand underneath him brought no comfort. Another wave rushed up the shore, engulfing him in its chilling touch before being pulled away by the ocean. Staring up into the sunlit sky, white clouds floated through the endless blue like any other day. His muscles throbbed, and he felt heavy lying there as the weight of the world pushed down on him. Pumping his fists a few times, he was sure he felt his heart beating; the blood in his veins was still connected to his soul. Drawing one slow, deep breath, he held it until he felt like bursting.

No, this is far from death. From what I can judge, this is something miraculous. Sitting back up, he continued his deep thoughts while watching the peaceful rhythm of waves drumming at his feet. *Where is the debris? The bodies? Did anyone else make it here at all?*

A sharp ache stabbed into his chest, and the frightening words hit him—*sole survivor.* Closing his eyes tight, tears worked past his eyelids, and he caved to the drowning sensation of grief. Cupping his face with his hands, all the mental and emotional exhaustion boiled over inside him. He clenched his teeth and sobbed at the thought of his recent hardships, from the moment Hotan revealed his visions to the raging storm. *I endured all that pain and misery, only to end up sitting on a heavenly beach, miraculously healed, and left all alone. Where are my friends, family, and fellow Levites?* It all seemed like a cruel taunt from destiny.

It was a horrible sensation. I had never drowned in my own emotions as I did in that very point in time. Sitting there in a serene environment did nothing to brighten the darkness which swallowed me. To think I had lost everything besides my life was soul shattering.

Talib's despair rattled every part of him as he gasped between the choking sobs wracking his body. *All this effort to make the right judgments has only brought me pain.*

The wind pulled at him like the gentle hands of a lover, whispering for him to look down the beach. Swallowing, he calmed himself and wiped the tears from his face. Shading his eyes, he sat up and looked to where the breeze blew further down the shore. Two figures in the far distance were fast approaching, one waving excitedly. He jumped to his feet and waved back, feeling a sense of relief. His heart leapt when his eyes focused enough to recognize the familiar forms. He wasn't alone; others had made it to this place too.

"Talib!" The last of his tension faded at the sound of Saphellia's voice. "Thank the Lord, you made it!"

With newfound energy, he sped across the sand. He snatched up Saphellia, laughing as he swung her around. After kissing each other repeatedly, he set her back on her feet, and they hugged firmly while their fears of losing each other melted away. Pulling back from her embrace, he looked her over in amazement. With his thumb, he gently wiped away the tears on her cheeks and sighed. His heart fluttered to see that she too was free of the injuries and marks from their horrendous battle for survival.

"What's wrong?" She furrowed her brow at his bewildered look. "Are you okay?"

"Where are the blisters from the desert? The cuts on your hands from building the rafts?" His ran his thumb across her bottom lip, and his voice faded to a whisper. "Even the deep bleeding cracks that were on your lips are gone…"

She looked back at the tiny, old man next to her, confirming they had noticed this miracle of healing as well. "Peter and I saw the same thing. Everyone we've come across is healed, but there are only twelve of us so far. Some are combing the beaches for survivors while others try to build shelter, but we all seem to have miraculously recovered."

"Is Hotan or Liora among you?" His voice quivered from his wavering nerves. "Did they make it?"

Saphellia's brow knotted, and her voice softened. "No signs of them yet."

We would have been better off if Liora had survived and Hotan died. Then again, what is the chance we would have survived without the aid of his powers healing us.

Her lips parted, but instead of speaking, she inhaled, swift and short. She found herself at a loss for words; nothing she could say would bring any comfort to Talib. He took a long, silent stare at the horizon where the sky met the dark blue, deep waters. It felt like the same stare he and Hotan had made from the dune at the edge of the desert. Somewhere out there was the aftermath of Hotan's last prediction. Reluctantly, he followed them back to where the rest of the survivors gathered. In the shade of a few palm trees and an old oak, they found refuge from the heat of the day. The island was large; the other side could not be seen through the dense forest, but exploration would have to wait until later.

As they climbed over the last round of sand dunes, he could see the number of survivors had grown to eighteen—nineteen including himself. Scanning the broken remains of what once was a grand exodus of villagers, he was relieved to see Jacob and Lillianna among the few. A sense of guilt hit him; *I had focused my hope more on my friends' survival than for the whole group.* Swallowing down the wave of emotions, he mustered a hopeful look as everyone paused from their activities to stare at him. Relief washed over each face to see one of the chief's sons had survived the storm.

They managed to get halfway through building a decent shelter for the night. A red-haired boy was starting a fire while some of the girls gathered wood and anything recognizable as food. Geliah and another blond-haired man set up the next wave of logs while others waited their turn to cover it with palms to cut out the wind and rain. Everyone eagerly jumped in where they felt they could do some good for the whole of the group;

Talib's presence seemed to have added to their energy as he noticed small smiles on their faces.

It was good to feel wanted. To see my presence have a positive push on the group was something I needed. My confidence had been whittled away more and more with each step I made from the council's house, through the desert, and even as I approached the survivors. Sometimes life gives us something to help keep hope and faith alive.

Taking in a deep breath, Talib refocused himself; he walked around, approaching each person to assess their mental and physical states. He tried to be calm and stable, despite the rolling panic of wondering what happened to Hotan and Liora. The oldest survivor was Peter, followed by himself and Geliah, who easily fell under Peter's age by twenty years, if not more. The youngest was a small girl with long black hair who had lost both her parents during the massacre. She couldn't be any older than twelve; her hands were still small, and her body lacked any curves or signs of puberty. She fought amazingly hard, and the young blonde-haired girl who accompanied her kept her spirits high during this travesty they called life.

Without Metsy, we would have certainly lost Abigail, and without Abigail, we would have lost the reborn Hotan.

"Talib!" Jacob ran over to him. Relief was on his face as he said, "You made it!"

"Your arm…" Knotting his brow, Talib marveled over the bare arm which was previously infected; the skin looked as if all Jacob's injuries had been imaginary. "How in the world…"

Grabbing his shoulder, Jacob pumped his fist a moment before he whispered, "I know. It's unnerving that we all experienced an abnormal amount of healing overnight. Even after being thrashed by the ocean and storm."

There was an unsteady aura among the group as the others paused to listen in on the one disturbing detail which everyone avoided. Pondering over it, Talib eyed where he had noticed injuries on some of the survivors before setting sail; all of them lacked traces of the struggles from their travels. *Is this part of Hotan's predictions and why he did not hesitate to rush us across the water?* Saphellia's fingers caressed his shoulder, but he flinched in response. Wincing, he regretted giving a noticeable physical reaction of his paranoia.

"I am going for a walk," he huffed. "I need some time to focus my thoughts."

Indeed, I felt so lost and afraid at that point for what our lives meant... What the meaning of my life was going to be.

Marching across the beach, he had no idea where to start. All these years, he had been Hotan's advisor, and now, he was lost without him. His life had been one unbelievable instance after another, and nothing he knew seemed to fit into this surreal existence he stumbled through. The gulls screeched in annoyance as he spooked them from feeding on the pile of seaweed up ahead. Taking a few steps closer, his body froze as his mind registered what lay tangled within the debris.

This was the first time I started to doubt...

Blinking a few times, he was sure it was a body covered in seaweed. He dared a few more steps until it shifted. It was unclear if it had been something in the heap of debris or the body itself. Waiting, seeing no more movement, he finished his approach and crouched over the mess. Pale skin and the deep reds and blackish greens of the sea plants only made its presence look more otherworldly. The body had washed ashore rather recently; tiny crabs and snails ran around in the seaweed, and tiny shrimp flicked their way off. Talib's fingertips jerked away from the icy sensation of the skin; he was frightened that there were no signs of goosebumps or shivering. *This person has to be dead.* It took a few tugs on the cold, stiff shoulder to break the person from their fetal position. As the face rolled upward, he gasped. Violently, he shook the lifeless heap as fear squeezed his soul.

"Hotan!" he pleaded, "Hotan, wake up!"

I started to doubt Hotan was ever human.

Despite his lifeless complexion, Hotan began coughing up water as if the sudden movement brought him back from death. Talib pulled him into a sitting position, but Hotan began swinging his arms about, wild and angry. Seaweed flew off him as he pushed Talib away and climbed to his feet, hacking up saltwater from his lungs. Wide-eyed, Talib realized he was marching back to the ocean. Scrambling to stand, he ran for Hotan, who had managed to get knee-deep before Talib wrapped his arms around him. Hotan squirmed loose, knocking him to his butt with a great splash. Determined to stop the madness, he tackled Hotan and dragged him ashore. His brother kicked and screamed, furious over the action.

"Let me go, Talib!" His blow hit its mark on Talib's jaw and cheek, knocking him to the ground, busting his lip, and dripping blood across the white sand. "She's still out there!"

Again, Hotan made the mad dash to the water.

Panting, he watched his brother in bewilderment before his thoughts urged him to give chase and stop the madness. *This is why he is covered in seaweed; how many times has he swum out, diving and searching for Liora? Has he lost his mind?'*

Once more, Talib chased after Hotan.

"Hotan, she's gone!" This time, he secured Hotan's arms from behind and lifted him off his feet as he shuffled them both out of the waves. "LIORA'S GONE!"

"No!" Hotan's struggle ceased as he sobbed, "Why wasn't she allowed to come with me…"

"I'm sorry, Brother." Confident they were a good distance from the water, he let Hotan go. "I understand your pain."

"No, you don't!" Enraged, Hotan turned and shoved both his palms into Talib's chest, sending him stumbling back and knocking the air from his lungs. "You still have Saphellia! And Jacob has Lillianna! And Geliah has Cassandra! You all have what you desire! I get nothing but pain and nightmares!"

I forgot his predictions about the relationships before they came to blossom. How far did his predictions go? Did he know about my encounter with Death as well?

"What on earth are you talking about?" Neither Jacob and Lillianna nor Geliah and Cassandra were a couple, but it seemed more secrets were hidden deep inside Hotan's broken mind. "Are these predictions? Things to come?"

Sinking to his knees, Hotan couldn't hear his questions as he pounded at the sand. "I just want to be left alone! No more visions! A peaceful life! Not this life! I want to be free of this!"

Sitting in the sand next to Hotan, Talib did not try to quell his brother's rage as he physically fought against the beach. While he listened to the outburst, he leaned on his knees and watched the sun come into view and fall toward the watery horizon. Haunting predictions entangled with the ravaged remains of his brother's soul flew from those torn lips with chilling animosity.

Hotan didn't even acknowledged him sitting there as he flung sand and punched the ground, but Talib could not bring Hotan back with him in this state. Until he reached a point of calm, he was a danger to the morale of the group. For now, he would let Hotan wear himself down until he either exhausted himself or hit a point where he would be more willing to listen.

It was here that I realized we were becoming immortal. We were changing away from mortal men, as our healed wounds had already whispered to us all. We were all afraid to hear the notion as true, but it was a fact, even on that first day on the island.

Through Hotan's crazed mumblings, the words spilled forth of immortality and it frightened Talib. If what he heard was true, all twenty of them on the island were now immortal. *Why us? Perhaps we all possess, or even lack, something compared to those who were left to their fate under the waves.* Hotan stopped his thrashing as the burning orange sun touched the water. In his current condition, there was a slim chance Hotan would reveal what he had spent decades hiding. Deep down, Talib hoped he would continue to keep those dark scrawlings hidden from him.

He wasn't ready to take on the burden of an element neither of them could comprehend, let alone feel they could grasp its purpose.

With a sigh, he flopped on his back on the warm sand as he listened to the muffled sobs next to him. He watched the orange sky fade to pink, then lavender shifted to a brilliant purple, and before long, a deep blue as it bled darker. Stars peeked through the night as his thoughts sorted through all the comparisons and differences between the living and dead. The longer he worked over the details, the more numb he grew to the morbid task performed within the privacy of his mind. His blood chilled his core as one conclusion kept surfacing; *It is a matter of being able to procreate.*

He and Saphellia were sterile; perhaps Geliah, Jacob, and the others fell into this category. Much of his father's generation had been sterile due to an illness that had swept through their village—something that happens on occasion in the world. Often, the remnants of the illness would carry on into the next generation—his generation. After rumors of his failed attempts for a child, he had heard they weren't alone. Unfortunately, none had ever been named, but it wouldn't take long to uncover if it rang true. As for Hotan, he would never fathom being with another after losing Liora. Moving on from her death was impossible for him, especially after the trauma caused by the predictions. Hotan was a key element in this obscure logic, but his purpose was unknown.

Hotan fell onto his back next to him, panting from his fight with the phantoms that plagued his mind. He reached over and gripped Talib's upper arm tightly, making it sting as his skin was twisted. Glaring over at Hotan, he could see his eyes emitting a green glow as he slowed his breathing. The look on his face was pure desperation as he knotted his brow at his older brother.

"I'm sorry, Talib. Thank you…" Swallowing, his whispers continued, "thank you for allowing me to grieve and keeping me from harm."

Talib snorted and returned his stare to the stars. He felt nothing but bitter hatred for Hotan at this point. Deep down, the last sour thought gripped his core with such ferocity it sent his blood boiling; *Hotan has control over whatever is happening to us, but he has no idea how to control it. Everything is his fault.*

Yanking his arm free, Talib pulled himself to his feet and shook off the sand. At the far end of the beach, a faint, dancing, orange light waved in the bleakness; the others were waiting for him and had a strong fire rolling. Looking over his shoulder, he saw the pain on Hotan's face but had no desire to offer a helping hand as he started for the camp.

Fists tight at his sides, he fought the tears pushing to be released as he heard his little brother's footsteps closing in behind him. *If he had figured out how to control this power sooner, maybe we could have saved the village. We would not have had to face the nightmares that will haunt our minds for eternity.*

"Wait." It was a weak plea, but it was enough to make him pause and listen. "I know it's there inside me too, Talib, but it's too much for me to control."

"Is that why you dragged us here?" Talib growled. "Sacrifice hundreds just for a select few?"

"I tried to use it to keep them alive." Tears streamed down Hotan's face; he looked to his hands as if they were dripping with the blood of his guilt. "If I had any real control, I would have been able to save Liora…"

"And what would have become of us if you had drowned?" Anger spilling forth, Talib gripped the front of Hotan's cold, wet shirt and shook him. "If you die, we die! Do not tell me it is not true!"

"It's true…" Hotan avoided Talib's rage-filled glare as he gritted his teeth at the confession. "I am already immortal. I cannot die! I simply drown and come back again! Five, ten, maybe even twenty times I dove back into the sea looking for her. The sensation of drowning is frightening—saltwater stinging and aching in my lungs as I painfully struggle to stay awake through the lack of oxygen as more of my body dies. The worse part, the very nightmare of it all, is waking up alive without her and marching back in to die all over again."

"Why us? Why did you choose us?" Talib released his grip, but he had no more sympathy to give. "Is it because we are sterile?"

Hotan's eyes met his, and the grim expression confirmed his suspicions. He forced them to become immortal. If his plans to relieve some of his power failed, at least no children would be born into the chaos. It was both logical and cruel. Talib's stomach twisted further as his rage became nauseating. The thudding of his heart in his ears was the drum to the war of emotions exploding within him.

"Say it," Talib commanded Hotan, a haunting tone in his voice. "I want to hear you say it."

Straightening himself, Hotan swallowed as his eyes started to glow with his own frustrated anger. "It was because you were all born sterile."

Another twist of the stomach made Talib's abdomen tighten. "And what are your plans for us?"

"Relieving most of my powers into you." The glow in his eyes grew brighter as Talib could feel the pull on his own soul. "I have already begun the process."

"Begun?" Talib's nausea weakened and shifted to anger. He asked Hotan assertively, "With who?"

"You." Wind started to tug at them both as Hotan's glowing eyes peered over his own shoulder and started to fade away. "And Saphellia of the Wind, all of you, in fact…"

Looking back to the camp, three people started to cross the beach in their direction. *Not now, not until I finish getting my answers first.*

The wind ceased as if his thoughts—his desire—had been heard; they stopped and turned back to camp.

"I see Judgment suits you just fine," Hotan said, his eyes eerily glowing green again. "Everyone has been given elements that suit them, it was the least I could do."

Every muscle in his body went taut as his fist smashed into Hotan's left cheek, sending him to the ground. "How dare you decide for me! For her! For them!"

Seething, he forcefully kicked Hotan in the ribs and sent him rolling. Talib marched toward him as Hotan coughed and hacked on all fours. Consumed by rage, Talib failed to hold back on his second kick to Hotan's side. Much to his surprise, the physics of the feat were all wrong. He watched in astonishment as his brother skipped over the ground a few times before sliding to a stop thirty feet away. As his anger faltered, he realized a glow surrounded them. Looking down at his hands, blue fire crawled across his arms, up his shoulder, and wrapped itself around his entire body. There was no heat or pain, but black lines wrapped around his skin as if painted across him by some unknown artist.

Hotan held his side and wheezed, but he shared the blue flames and stripes across his skin. Baffled, Talib waited for him to stumble back as he watched the flames on his fingers flicker in the wind like candle's flame.

"When I split the power, it created a physical tell." Coughing, Hotan managed to stand straight again as his injuries and pain faded. "I suppose I encouraged it, but it seems dependent on how much power used. Just now, with the others on the beach, you used it to turn them around, didn't you?"

"I do not know." He closed his fist, pushed his anger away, and watched the flames die. The markings slithered away from existence, and he failed to keep up with them as they slid over his shoulders. "Maybe I did…"

"Perhaps I made you stronger. It seems extreme emotion ignites the flames when it comes to you." Hotan tried to rest a hand on his shoulder, but Talib jerked away, still stinging from betrayal. "Just know, the others will always have the marks on their skin when they start to use it. I will need help keeping track—"

"Help keeping track!" Another wave of fury sent the flames back into existence as he gripped Hotan's shirt once more, lifting him off the ground. "Are you insane? A power you could not control has now been thrown into nineteen others without warning! Worse! These people have just lost everything they knew! I may still have Saphellia, but I am far from calm and stable after the things I have seen!"

"I'm sor—" Hotan started to say, but Talib dropped him to the ground with a shove. "I… I can never apologize…"

"You need to set this right, Hotan." Turning his back to him, Talib took deep breaths, pushing his emotions down so the fire would recede. "You have put us all in more danger, again. You expect me to know what to do with something you could not control. You are putting too much faith in my abilities; I am only human."

"Faith in you is all I have left," Hotan mumbled in a heart-wrenching tone. "You're all I've ever had…"

Gritting his teeth, Talib weighed everything filling his mind. He struggled to keep the lid tight on the emotions he was forced to bottle against his will. His fists tightened as he took slow, deep breaths, begging his blood to cool before he spoke. He closed his eyes, having no desire to exchange eye contact with his little brother.

"Fine," Talib huffed, "but you better pray I figure it out before one of them does. Every day, you will take time to tell me everything you know about whatever this is that you have willingly plagued us with."

The sand was cold and hard under Talib's bare feet. He didn't bother to look over his shoulder to see if Hotan followed him to the flickering campfire on the hill. His chest was tight with his frustration and anger; his jaw ached under the pressure of his gnashing teeth—an attempt to keep himself from saying anything further. The rest of this fight could play out in the privacy of walks when he intended to draw out all the information and knowledge Hotan had on this inhuman power. For now, all Talib had left was time. Time was all everyone had now since they were immortal against their wills.

His legs ached from marching up the steep hillside, and he paused in the warming glow of the fire. Eyes bore into him, and his heart fluttered from the gasps which followed. They shifted ever so slightly, and their stare fell behind his shoulder where

Hotan had also paused. Talib had brought back a ghost, someone many of them assumed—or possibly hoped—had died after driving them through a maddening trek across desert and ocean.

Saphellia's eyes gripped Talib's, and he frowned. Without words, her expression told him she knew something was not right. Breaking away, he headed silently to the other side of the hillside as the rest murmured their words of comfort to Hotan. Sitting, he rubbed his forehead, lost in thought as the heat of the fire trickled over his back. Warm fingers slid over his back, and Saphellia rested her chin on his right shoulder.

"So Liora did not make it," she whispered cautiously. "But I cannot help but see something far worse written on your face."

Leaning his head against hers, he sighed. "It will be hard to keep him from harming himself. He is a broken shell of what once was Hotan. I do not know the man standing there who shares my brother's name."

I had no idea how accurate my words would prove to be. Even now, hearing those words fall from my lips leaves a bitter taste on my tongue. If I had known what would unfold ... I still do not think I had the power to change any of it.

Each day after, we would walk far away from the camp. We claimed we were staking out the island, but that was only partly true. I tried to force Hotan to tell me everything he knew about the powers he gave all of us. As I learned to use them by pushing my power onto him, it became very clear he had not relinquished even half of his own. He had simply given us a small portion at this point. I wonder if, with the passing years, he slowly gave us more, draining himself in a slow drip.

In my attempts to shift Hotan's judgment and manipulate his decisions, it was clear he could disconnect or even repel it. There were times when I felt an invisible hand within my soul, guiding the flow and direction of how I used the power. I remember in those chilling, terrifying waves, I could see that eerie green glow in his mournful eyes. There was never a doubt in my mind that Hotan could reach inside me, tug at my soul, and turn the powers of Judgment against me; he could force my hand, my actions, against my will.

Adding to the chaos were the physical repercussions of using it in those early decades. The powers affected us then just like they are all experiencing it now: the breaking of the body, building of endurance, and the fight to keep one from falling into an endless sleep. Yet, there was never the cold sensation so much like death. Back then, there was a warm glow which brought us back to the surface. Perhaps Hotan constantly guarded us from the freezing horror the powers kept in the darkness of our minds and souls.

For the first several years, it was physically destructive. Talib's muscles were bruised from attempts to manipulate Hotan's judgment. He mostly tried to force him to perform miniscule chores like sitting, walking, turning, and similar tasks. Part of the injuries were a recoil from trying to control Hotan, but the other half was the struggle to suppress visible markings or flames. They concluded it was crucial for Talib to be able to persuade others in secrecy in order to maintain peace as powers unfolded.

Often, he would return home to Saphellia's concerned face over his weak and feverish condition. She questioned whether his health was failing. A walk on a beach would leave him drained, shaking and weakened to the point of being unable to hold a ladle to his lips as if an old man on his deathbed.

If she only knew how I tortured myself for the sake of her and the others. In fact, I let that secret out only once when I cried over her comatose body. I let out a lot of my deeper and darker moments. Maybe it was the start of changing my ways...

As they verged on the twenty-year mark, Talib mastered keeping his powers of Judgment hidden. He was still limited to smaller judgment pushes, but there were no flames or crawling of his tattoo to give away his usage. As for the others, they developed the ability to communicate without the need of parting lips or the tap of a tongue on their teeth. At first, it happened so softly that it went unnoticed. The simple request for something when not facing someone or the sensation of reading another's mind came into play. It was very obvious, and he and Hotan could sense when the others used this ability. It pulled at them like a lightning strike in the deepest of nights; it was light, sound, and even the rumbling of their souls which all pointed to one location where it rang out.

"Do you think this whole time they have felt my usage?" They watched the fiery red sun sink into the darkening horizon as he pondered out loud. "All these years of pushing and I had not thought of the recoil felt by the others."

"Don't worry, Brother." Hotan sighed. "You were sick because I didn't link you to them. My goal was to make you my equal; no one ever feels my powers, and only I can feel yours."

"True. Otherwise, we would have known what was happening." Looking down at his hands, calloused from aiding Cassandra with tilling the soil, he clenched them in frustration. "I like to think I would have been able to stop you. Stop this curse of immortality and madness you have set in motion."

"Would you have been willing to kill me?" Hotan's green eyes were distant as they met Talib's silver glare. Hotan's eyes showed the mournful agony of existence which grew with each passing decade. "I like to think you could have ended this misery for all of us if I would have at least asked your advice. There was a reason Father chose you for that task, and not following his guidance has only aided in my torture."

"Like Father, I would try the peaceful way first." Breaking the painful stare, Talib watched the last sliver of red slide down into the black sea. "How much longer until one of the others discovers their powers?"

"It won't be long." Hotan started to walk back, and Talib followed close behind. "I pray they don't attempt to use it against one another."

"They will not at first." Stopping, he looked up to the deep blue and purple sky with the few strong stars peeking through. "But we are humans given endless time. Just as generations can cut the ties of those before them, I fear things could happen to change their hearts and minds away from being so kind to one another. Deep down, you still have the heart of a child, don't you, *alef chet?*"

"Perhaps my heart is to blame." Silence took hold as they continued their walk.

6

SOMETHING I CAN NEVER HAVE

900 BC

"Does it scare you?" Talib stared at Hotan's tense face, hoping to see a reaction as he pushed the point again. "What if they cannot control it or, worse, understand it? They could harm themselves or each other."

"I can only have faith—"

"Faith!" Anger seeped forward; pushing down the rise of power, he spoke his frustrations. "Do you not take any responsibility for the dangers and torment you have, and will, put them through? We have been on this wretched island for over twenty years, and Abigail has not aged! The girl is doomed to be a child for eternity! Do you feel any guilt?"

"Perhaps..." Hotan's eyes dulled as he looked down to his hands and fell silent.

I wish I knew what he was thinking in that moment. My guess is he thought about using his powers to age her but was too afraid to trust it. Could I really be angry with him for his fear? To be scared to hurt an innocent any more than he already had?

"We are all stuck as we are, Hotan. How do you expect Paul to endure this power in his elderly state? It has nearly killed me to master it in peak physical condition." Hearing no response from Hotan, he continued, "Did you take any of that into account?"

"No…" Tears fell into his open palms as he whispered, "All I think about is Liora."

Grimacing, Talib closed his eyes and said steadily, "I understand, but we need you to lead us. You have given us this power, and you cannot abandon us without some guidance. You must take responsibility for what you have put in motion, Hotan."

"I've done something…" he mumbled, lips trembling and barely audible as the tears fell heavier into his hands. "I did something far more devastating…"

Wait, I do not remember this…

"What have you done?" Talib's heart raced as his brother's terrified eyes met his own. "Please tell me you did not…"

Why do I not recall this moment? I remember walking back after telling him… no. I do not remember after that. The next morning, I woke up in my bed and never questioned it. Dear God, what did you do Hotan? This is where it all started to go wrong, was it not?

"I tried to bring her back." Hotan shook, frightened by his own words. "I don't know what came back. Something woke up in those depths, but it wasn't my Liora."

"Why would you…" Furrowing his brow, the confession rattled him. "When, when did you do this?"

"Last night." Hotan paled as he spoke. "It caused the storm which ripped off some of the roofs of the huts."

He did try to bring her back, but what did he summon? How do I not remember any of this?

"You're too reckless!" Fear and anger wrestled inside Talib's heart. "You will be the death of us all."

Both turned, feeling the heavy aura of something approaching. Looking to the waves, they saw the shadowy heap of a naked man as it crawled out of the water. Neither could will their legs to move. Talib's eyes grew wide as the drenched man looked to them. His eyes and hair were blacker than the night; his skin, paler than the sand at their feet, glowed in the moonlight. His face was eerily like Hotan's. The resemblance was breathtaking as he peered confusedly at them. Talib's mind raced for answers and sought all the possibilities, but no villagers, kin, or anyone he could recall matched the man before them.

This man—naked and broken on the beach—was Iapetos. I have met him before, but why do I not remember? He didn't seem to remember me either. What did you do, Little Brother? What did you set in motion to cause such hatred?

Hotan sank to his knees as he wailed to the heavens, "This is not what I wanted! GIVE HER BACK! GIVE ME LIORA!"

The exhausted man in the waves looked lost; it was heartbreaking to behold. He reached out, pale and deathly, his mouth opened but only produced a rasping sound. Talib was frozen by uncertainty as he witnessed the exchange. Ignoring the angry sobs from Hotan, he focused on this new person. Hotan had brought this man back from death, but Talib did not remember him from the village. There was no denying the resemblance between him and Hotan. Every joint in his body unraveled as the answer gripped him, and he looked from one to the other.

Could he really be? Talib thought.

"I wanted her," Hotan choked. "Why give me this stranger… I wanted my Liora!"

"Hotan." Talib swallowed as he knelt next to Hotan and fixated on the tear-filled eyes of the washed-up soul before him. "Do you not see who this man really is?"

It must be! It could not be anyone else!

Hotan struggled to catch his breath as he glared at the man who reached out to him from the sand and waves. "No, I do not know this man."

"It has been over twenty-eight years since Liora drowned, pregnant with your child." The reminder made Hotan wince. "You have made it clear to me that you do not know the full consequences of your powers. This outcome is a result of that unpredictability."

"Are you proposing…" Hotan paused before he sourly hissed, "Are your proposing this man is my son?"

Hotan begets Iapetos; in turn, Iapetos begets Hotan. Rebirth completes itself. But, were we not all sterile? No, but why was this memory taken from me? From us?

"Yes." Talib jerked Hotan to his feet. "And if you are the man I pray you are, you will find the compassion to welcome him here."

"I would have to tell the others…" Hotan gripped his shirt as he begged, "They will know what I have done."

"Yes, but you need to tell them." His grasp on Hotan's arm tightened as he failed to keep his markings from crawling forward. "You must tell them. They need to hear the sins you have committed and how you intend to set it right."

Wait, this sensation... It was not anger pulling my markings out. Hotan was affecting me, and I did not know the difference back then. I did not know the dissimilarity between me using my powers and Hotan using my powers through me. What did you do, Hotan? What have you hidden within me all these centuries?

"No." The cold answer slipped through Hotan's lips. "I will cast him out of paradise and make this all disappear."

Talib screamed as he erupted into flames against his will. As he fought through it, he saw Hotan, also covered in flames and his own markings. No longer in control of his own body, he was dragged by Hotan toward the frightened innocent on the beach. Hotan's grip on Iapetos' hair was rigid and cruel as he heartlessly looked his own son in the eyes. Talib's greatest fear came into existence before him, and his powers were utilized to carry it out.

"You will leave here and never be able to return." As Hotan spoke, Talib felt his own lips voice this command. "You will not remember this place or who we are. Go, leave here now."

NO! YOU FOOL!

As if in a dream, Iapetos turned to face the ocean again. Talib filled with dread as wings ripped outward from the man's pale shoulders, black-feathered and broken with decay. He took to the air as if it were natural and instinctual to do so. Hotan jerked him away from the sight of the pale figure flying to his doom, and Talib was met by his crazed stare. Hotan's icy wrath was now aimed at Talib; his little brother was nothing more than a powerful monster in the wake of chaos.

Once more, Talib's lips echoed the command being forced through him, "You will never remember that man or my connection with him. Walk home now, go to sleep, and wake tomorrow like any other day. You are right. I need to make amends for what I have done, but I am not ready. Please forgive me. If you ever remember this moment, please understand I am afraid. The taboos I foolishly performed turned you all into tattooed angels. Hear me now; in this moment, I am terrified, but a day will come when I leave this childishness behind and find a way to make this all go away. I just need more time..."

He knew it was wrong, and he still went through with it. Worse, he used me, his own brother, as a tool to do something so unforgivable! How many times has he done this to me! What other memories are stolen and hidden from me!

Anger woke him from his sleep, and he was sore. Memories of his talk with Hotan on the beach last night echoed in his mind; his final plea was, *You must take responsibility for what you have put in motion, Hotan.*

Talib's head swam. He knew he must have pushed himself too hard again to be so sore. It had been a few years since he had dared to use his abilities to this extent, but he couldn't remember what he had attempted to do.

"Are you alright?" Saphellia came in the door, carrying a bucket of cool water and cloth. "I didn't think you would wake with that fever returning."

"I, I feel fine." The words were unconvincing even to him. "Did Hotan come back with me?"

"Yes, he walked with you." She felt his forehead and cheeks. "You don't remember?"

I do remember this day better than I thought...

"I suppose I was not feeling well." He forced a smile. "Where would I be without you, my dove?"

"Dead," she scoffed. "Or at least still passed out on the beach somewhere."

He erupted in laughter as he gripped her in his arms, knocking the bucket of water across the floor. She laughed as she wiggled, failing to free herself. Holding her tighter, he kissed her shoulder and neck. Suddenly, he froze; a shudder rattled through him, shaking them both.

"I know what you're thinking." Her voice was soft as she pushed open his arms and held his cheeks with her loving hands. "We were fortunate to be able to keep one another."

"I'm sorry; I did not mean to ruin the moment." His eyes looked away from her shining face as he whispered, "I just feel..."

"Guilty." Saphellia's smile faded as she kissed his lips before speaking for only him to hear. "I feel that way often, but how much longer will we need to carry this guilt before we are allowed to reclaim some of our lives?"

Looking up at her, he admired the words of the wisdom she showered upon him. "Then let us start living it today."

His lips pushed hard against hers as his hands sought a way under her shirt. The thrill of his palms sliding across her ribs and over the muscles in her back sent chills across them both. The tips of his fingers followed the divot of her spine as it led his hands down and across her buttocks. Her tongue pushed his mouth open, luring his back to her own mouth, sucking playfully. Hands fumbled at his pants, and once more, they laughed at their desperation. Husband and wife acting like wild youngsters, eager to take one another in the bed. Grabbing her by the waist, he flung her down on the bed, and she squealed in delight. Her heart raced from his weight on top of her as he kissed her gently across the neck and shoulder again.

Nuzzling at her ear, he smiled and whispered, "I have the most amazing wife in the world."

She truly is the most amazing person in my life.

"You look surprisingly happy." Hotan shifted nervously as Talib entered his hut, flinching as he spoke to his elder brother. "Are you feeling okay?"

"It's a good day so far. Why the sour look?" His brow knotted, and he noticed a cold sweat forming on Hotan's cheek. "Are you feeling ill?"

"Very much so." Hotan diverted his eyes. "Glad you are well. Last night was taxing, even on me. I expected you to be down most of the day."

He felt guilty; I see that now. Then again, he was surprised I recovered, and looking back on this moment, I cannot help but question my own recovery here.

Rubbing his forehead, Talib closed his eyes. "Exactly what were we trying to do last night? It is all a giant blur."

"An experiment to see how strong your Judgment truly is." He held his breath. Hotan's eyes glazed over as his words faded away. "You've gotten so strong…"

"I suppose it has been a while since we tried pushing beyond the small attempts." Sighing, he grinned to himself as moments with Saphellia danced in his mind. "Do you think the others are starting their lives over? Moving on?"

"Some." Hotan stood up and walked to the doorway to look out past the small assortment of bungalows. Together, they watched the others work in the fields. "Do you ever forget to eat?"

He opened his mouth but paused. Thoughts flew across his mind before he corrected, "You mean to ask if I feel hunger like I did before coming to the island?"

"Perhaps that is the better question." Sighing, Hotan looked over his shoulder. "I drink and eat only for the morale of the others. It has been a very long time since I felt the need for it, felt the pangs of hunger, as you pointed out."

"To be honest, I try not to acknowledge it. Like you, I think we are all eating for the sake of normalcy, humanity even. These are things we are losing at an alarming rate." Stretching, he said, "I think that is why Cassandra and the others are pushing so hard to maintain some sort of crop. In the back of their minds, they know they have no need for it, but as human beings, it is a frightening component to lose. Maybe hunger is one of the many things which reminds us we are still alive, still breathing, and capable of dying."

"Alive ... for eternity." He returned his glare to the fields where Cassandra fell to her knees. "Are you ready for them to find their powers?"

"I have no choice," he snorted. "It has never been about what I want or what I am ready for."

"I'm afraid our follies from last night may have broken down the last wall for them." Cassandra screamed her frustrations as she pounded her fists at the dirt around her failed attempts to grow a viable food source. "Today, they will all find their elements unfolding."

Using his powers to that extent hindered his ability to keep everyone's powers bottled up. I always knew he had a tight connection to our abilities and elements. Even after the night when the reborn Hotan used Peter as a conduit, I... of course! He repeated the technique, and thus broke my brother's last hold! All this time, he was still holding up the walls and using Rebirth to call upon a person's power! This has broken everything including the barrier blocking the powers! When and who did he use that caused the reincarnation spell he cast to crumble? Does the answer lay hidden here in my memories as well?

A breathtaking wave of power hit everyone in an instant. There was no flash of power or flames, but the heat of it made them all look in the direction where it had exploded from— Cassandra. Her rage and fury of emotions triggered her element. Pounding her fist, sobbing and screaming, her last strike to the barren earth caused it to explode before her. Green vines reached upward; monstrous stalks sprouted taller than they were ever naturally designed to do. The earth at its base pushed upward, filling itself with nutrients as it shoved her backward. Wide-eyed, she looked from her fist to the swaying stalks of wild asparagus which she had failed to tame numerous times over the last several years.

Talib rushed out of Hotan's doorway but stopped a few steps from him. His eyes locked onto the bright green stalks, amazed her power could produce something so wonderful. Jacob and several others stood behind her, looking upward at the overgrown plant. Even from this distance, her markings painted her skin. She did not produce the flames he had grown accustomed to seeing on Hotan and himself. He looked to the stern expression on his little brother's face, but no signs of surprise could be found on it.

Hotan, Iapetos, and I all have flames. A few others started to show signs of it at their peak. Exactly what is the significance? Is it the amount of power? The level of mastery? Or signs of something else? If it was simply a tell, would we not have immediately seen it in Cassandra and the others? How have I not taken notice of this? What other lies have I been fed by you, Hotan?

"It has finally happened," Talib whispered, shocked by the sensation flowing through him. "One of them has managed to call out their element."

"Cassandra." Hotan shuffled, his body tensing as he readied himself for what chaos was to follow. "She has become the element of Earth."

Jacob was fast approaching, and his nearing footsteps ended their conversation. They watched his approach, waiting to hear what words would follow the event. At the field, Cassandra failed to stand; the feat had physically exhausted her, and she fell heavily onto Geliah. Talib thought to himself, *Indeed, they will all have to overcome the cruel whiplash of using their powers. It has taken me over twenty-eight years to get this far, and even this morning, I felt the whiplash. How long will it take them to master it? Easily fifty years or longer for the oldest, Peter, and youngest,*

Abigail. Their bodies would suffer the most, depending how hard they pushed themselves.

"Talib! Hotan!" Jacob's face was flushed. "You have to come see this! Cassandra… she's performed a miracle!"

"Indeed," Hotan replied coldly. He turned his back to Jacob and Talib. "Talib, I leave this to you since I am not well."

Hotan glanced over his shoulder to Talib; his green eyes were sharp with an animosity, sending it across them. "Is everything okay, Hotan?"

"Please go with Jacob and make sure Cassandra is well." He walked farther into the shadows of his hut, sitting on his bed, staring endlessly at his hands. "I have faith in you, Brother."

Talib winced; he knew Hotan was falling apart. "Let us go. Geliah is having to hold her up."

"R-Right." Jacob paused as he took one long look at Hotan, tears now falling from his face. "You loved her so much, and you also love those here, Hotan. Don't pain yourself with guilt when you can do so much more with it."

Talib felt the power emitting from Jacob as he spoke.

He gripped Jacob's arm, pulling him away as he whispered, "When did you start using that ability?"

"Huh?" They stopped; his silver eyes burned into the wide-eyed purple of Jacob's. "What are you talking about?"

"It is subtle, but I know you feel it." His hand still gripping Jacob, he pulled on his own element of Judgment. "Just go ahead and tell me."

"I… it started sometime last night." His face reddened. Huffing, he failed to keep it in. "All day, I have felt an overwhelming sense of love and care from everyone. I even felt the joy and pleasure between you and…"

Talib released his arm. "You are like me, someone who can manipulate emotions. An element of the human mind."

"What the hell was that?" Jacob rubbed his arm where Talib had gripped it. "Did … did you just force me to tell you that?"

"Sorry." Talib hung his head, regretting the move. "I will never do it again."

"How long have you known?" They started their march toward the others as he dodged Jacob's questions. "Apparently, you figured this out."

"No, far from it," he hissed as they approached Geliah. "How is she?"

"Cold and shivering. You'd think she came near death." Geliah looked over to the plant, amazed by her feat. "I don't know what's happening to us, but at least we aren't all terribly afraid of it."

"She needs rest." Sighing, he glanced at Jacob's still fuming expression. "Let us not jump to assumptions until she recovers."

Nodding to Jacob, he motioned for him to follow as they headed back to Talib's hut. Despite the questions he pressed for, he remained silent until they reached the privacy of his hut.

This is when I realized I was on my own. I had no idea what to do with what Hotan had shoved onto my plate. Naturally, I turned to the two people I trusted more than anything else in the world.

"I, I cannot do this alone." He paled as he knotted his brow and looked from Jacob to Saphellia. "This, this is beyond my ability to control."

I was so afraid. Did Geliah feel that from me in this moment? Is that why he saw me as weak shortly after?

"What happened?" Saphellia sat down on the bed, startled at the sudden intrusion. "Does it involve the wave I felt?"

"Yes." Jacob softened his expression as he whispered, "You know what's happening, don't you, Talib."

"Yes, in theory." He was beginning to understand that no one else felt the strings which pulled within his own soul. "I wish I could say I had the ability to stop it, but I do not."

As the silence took hold, he realized he had indeed torn down walls last night; he had become eerily aware when others used their abilities. Some used the powers unknowingly; others, like Jacob, could feel the rise and fall of what their element entailed. Regardless, each usage pulled at him, making him painfully aware. *Did Hotan unlock this door on purpose, or did he push it on me to relieve himself of it?* At this point, Hotan was lost in his own guilt and remorse, and it fell on Talib to help them master their abilities.

Sliding to the floor, he failed to keep his anxiety at bay. "I do not know where to begin. Do I start with what you all know deep down? Or should I focus on what has been uncovered today?"

Saphellia gasped, her hands covering her mouth. "Talib! Your face and arms!"

"It's just like Cassandra!" added Jacob.

"It is attached to our emotions." Holding up a hand, he swallowed back his feelings, and they watched in wonder as the tattoos slid away. "This will reveal who is using the full spectrum of their powers or feeling overwhelmed by their emotions. The two go hand in hand."

"Powers?" Saphellia squirmed as she looked down at her hands. "What sort of powers?"

"Human emotions. That I can attest to." Jacob blushed, dodging her eyes. "But Cassandra seemed to have commanded the earth. She made a plant grow to monstrous proportions in an instant."

"Could someone control the wind?" she asked meekly. "If so, perhaps I have been meddling with this longer than I thought…"

"It would be a fitting element for a dove." Closing his eyes, he pleaded, "I need both of you to help me. Something has happened, and everyone's powers are coming to life. Our goal is to encourage them to practice it with caution since it is physically taxing. I have had my abilities for quite some time."

"All those nights…" She paled. "Every night for nearly twenty years, you walked through this door near death. Was it all for the sake of mastering your powers?"

"Yes." They locked stares. "It is dangerous to push too hard. I do not know if it will kill anyone, but they may find themselves in a deep sleep for some time in order to recover."

"What exactly is your element?" Jacob tensed, recalling the moment when Talib had used it on him. "You made me tell you something I never intended to reveal."

"Judgment." He looked away from their faces, fearing the expressions he would see. "But I have not used it on anyone else. I have practiced it on Hotan and, regrettably, used it on you today, Jacob. Please understand, I was panicked and had to know."

"What is Hotan?" Jacob was determined to uncover everything. "Is it safe to assume all of this is happening to us because of him?"

"Yes, he is at the very center of this." Looking up, he gave him a grave stare. "He is the element of Rebirth. All things start and end with him. Every time you use your powers, he feels it."

He paled. "Then there in the hut, he knew I was…"

Talib's sigh answered Jacob's fear. "We will have to help everyone learn at a slow pace. There is no limit to the time it will take to master their elements; it could take years, decades, centuries."

"Centuries?" Tears welled up in Saphellia's eyes. "So, it really is true?"

"We are immortal." He covered his face, but a weight was lifted by openly making the claim. "We will not die from old age, that is for certain, and food is no longer a necessity."

Saphellia and Jacob looked to one another in astonishment. After several minutes of silence, they gathered their thoughts. Hours went by as they asked him questions, and the three of them tried to sort through the sensations Talib felt. It wasn't long before they resolved that they all felt the new sensations, but he was far more sensitive to it. In all the instances, he used judgment to intervene, therefore denying anyone the choice to use their power.

It took months to figure out everyone's capabilities. As I had initially feared, Peter had a harder time with his abilities due to his elderly body. The old man had inherited the element of the Mind. Unlike Intelligence, he manipulated more of a spiritual resonance to create calm and clarity. It allowed someone to dig within their own mind, call forth memories, and sharpen their perception of the world around them.

As for the element of Intelligence, Fae embodied this. It worked differently than Peter's powers. She pulled information, languages, and more from an unknown pool of knowledge. It created a restlessness in her thoughts and behavior as the years went by. It seemed her knowledge was limited to her experiences and information she had access to, and it did not take long before she exhausted everything she had accumulated up to that point. Later, when she set foot back on the mainland, her powers grew to massive proportions.

As for Abigail, she never felt the physical recoil like the others. Her element was Body, and with it, she could change into any animal she wanted. It still did nothing to free her from the haunting obstacle of being forever trapped in a child's body. Saphellia and I took her aside to discuss our immortality. When it was made clear she would forever be trapped in that body, she disappeared for weeks. There was nowhere to go, but occasionally, she would lurk back into the village in the form of a black cat or bird of some kind.

Fears grew as powers unlocked, and physical struggles began. This only fueled Geliah. Obtaining the element of Fear was just as dangerous as Judgment; his ability to feel the tugs of everyone around them was as strong as mine. There were so many times when Hotan, I, or even Jacob noticed him using his powers to toy with others. Fortunately, he never mastered hiding his tattoos until the reincarnation spell broke centuries later.

Jacob's element reflected his promiscuous and romantic habits from before the massacre. It caused him much inner conflict; he knew everyone's romantic feelings, about whom, and when certain physical interactions were happening. This struggle became maddening later in his life before he found enough inner peace and strength to put himself back together.

In fact, I can still see the day we sailed out...

7

ABSOLUTION

4th Century BC

"A ship?" Heidi, the element of Sound, repeated after Hotan. "Am I hearing you right?"

"Yes, I am proposing we leave." Hotan eyed all of them, weighing their reactions. "We won't be able to come back if we do, but we can't possibly stay here for eternity and not do something good with our gifts."

"You know this frightens some of them," grunted Geliah. "Not the idea of leaving, but the matter of exposing our existence to a world we haven't been part of for hundreds of years."

"He's right though," Fae interjected. "We cannot possibly stay isolated here any longer than we already have. This is the most we've interacted with one another in years. I dare not say how many."

Lilliana pushed herself to the front. "I want to leave, but what skills do we have? Between all of us, we have limitless materials, but none of us are shipbuilders."

"Yes, let's not repeat the raft ordeal on our way out…" Jacob rubbed his shoulder as chills from painful memories crawled across him. "We can agree on leaving, but let's at least make something truly seaworthy."

"Agreed." Talib nodded. "Who here has the most experience in building boats?"

"What if Fae takes time to study different ideas and materials?" Lucius, the element of Light, rarely spoke, and his voice caught everyone's attention. "We can all pitch ideas or even materials to her in the next few weeks, and surely, she can develop something from that interaction."

"I will help her," Peter chimed in. "Between the two of us, we can come up with something."

"Do it." Hotan walked away, making it clear he wasn't giving anyone a chance to disagree with leaving. "I'll check in on your progress in a week."

"Hotan, what of their fears?" Geliah huffed, grabbing his shoulder. "Are you not going to attempt to soothe their worries?"

"Why should I?" The animosity between the two was no longer hidden as Hotan addressed Geliah. "You are not to interfere with those fears either. They should be afraid. We have no way of knowing what waits for us on the other side of the ocean, and we cannot anticipate the impact our powers will cause."

Geliah gritted his teeth, gripping him tighter. "Do you know how terrified they all are of you? Every day, I wonder what sort of monster you are—"

"Enough!" Talib tore Geliah's hand from his little brother's shoulder. "Walk it off, Geliah."

"Or what?" he spat, jerking his hand free. "You'll do what, Talib? Make me? You can do that, right?"

"If you keep this up, one day you may find out." A smirk crawled across Geliah's face at Talib's threat as a wave of fear washed over everyone. "Thank God you never ended up with my ability, Geliah. You are constantly throwing Fear into others to manipulate them. It would be disastrous to see you force Judgment in the same malicious manner."

Frustrated, Geliah stomped away angrily, and no one dared to stop him. With each step he took, their sense of fear lifted, and tense shoulders relaxed. They all looked to Talib with expressions of trust and relief. Obviously, Geliah had been abusing his abilities to scare the others into a mutiny, but it failed. For now, his threat of using the element of Judgment would keep the element of Fear from trying anything more. He hadn't used his own element against anyone since the incident with Jacob. Staring into their watchful eyes, Talib could see the unrest they felt toward him and his brother. They controlled a greater power and could overcome anyone who dared to oppose them.

Within a week, Fae and several others had put their minds and resources together to build a seaworthy vessel. Cassandra's wood, Lilly's metal, heat from Kyle's flames, and the hands of the rest created a monstrous ship. Fibers were woven together to create the great sails which Saphellia's Wind would fill. They built the ship on the beach in a trench dug to hold it level. Once everyone was ready, Callan would bring the tide in and whisk them away. Thankfully, Peter had previously spent time with another tribe which built boats in a similar fashion, and after much research, Fae was able to improve on the basic river vessels he had encountered in the past.

They resolved to leave at sunset, confident their ship was as strong as it could be. At the bow of the ship, Talib looked to the tree line and watched the growing shadows in the forest. Jacob stood beside him, knowing the weight on his shoulders. Handling what would come fell onto them. Together, the two of them had managed to teach and keep track of everyone's growing power. Out on the mainland, it would become overwhelming to keep pace. They would not be able to go in every direction and follow every immortal to all the corners of the Earth. They would have to carefully pick and choose who to keep close.

In fact, it was naïve to think we could keep anyone in check at this point…

"What about Abigail?" Jacob looked over his shoulder, counting the faces on board. "Are we really going to leave her behind?"

"No." With a sigh, Talib gave Jacob a grin. "In fact, she has been in Hotan's personal care since she chose to hide away."

"That girl has a lot of love for a broken man." Leaning against the railing, he confessed his knowledge through his element of Lust, "Hotan will never be capable of loving anyone but Liora. Does she know this?"

"Yes." His smile fell away as a shiver ran through him. "She is very aware, and sadly, it is the reason for her affection for him. I think it is a way for them both to live out their days in the company of someone who understands what it means to never be able to love another. Abigail is imprisoned by her immortality. Even as the element of Body, she has no ability to age herself beyond the little girl she came here as."

"It's so horrible." Jacob sunk his chin into his resting forearms. "Can't Hotan fix this?"

"Part of me thinks he can." Talib peered into the growing starlight above them, trying his best not to choke up. "But he has no control over his abilities and would not, could not, live with himself if he unintentionally harmed her. I think he wants to go back to see if he cannot uncover a way to fix all of this."

"Fix this?" Straightening himself, Jacob glared at his hands. "Do you ever wonder if we are being punished?"

"Sometimes…" Talib's voice trailed off as he paused. "Then I look back and realize we must have a greater purpose which requires us to wait a very long time."

"Are you two ready?" Hotan's voice startled them as he walked between the two. "Everyone is here; it's time for us to leave."

"Everyone?" Jacob blinked and realized Hotan was cuddling a black cat who purred in delight, rubbing its petite head against his chest. "Abigail?"

The cat paused and opened one sleepy yellow eye. "Mew?"

Hotan smiled, winking at Jacob as he walked away.

"That man scares me," shuddered Jacob.

Huffing Talib replied, "Me too, and I am his older brother."

The familiar tug at his soul turned Talib's attention to the beach at the keel of the boat. Callan pulled the waves up and around the hull of the great ship, lifting it from its sandy cradle. Like a mother passing her newborn babe into the arms of a grandmother, they gently flowed out to sea. They stood shoulder to shoulder and watched the night wash away all sight of the glowing sandy beaches of the island paradise which they had called home for centuries. Tears fell from their faces—except for Geliah and Hotan—as they moved into a new fearful era full of more unknowns.

As the sun climbed back into the sky, land could be seen in the distance. Seeing it brought them no joy or reprieve. Once again, they found themselves on the beaches with the desert looming before them. No one spoke a word as they stood, recalling horrific memories. Many spent the first few minutes digesting the searing heat of the beast that had devoured so many friends and family. Others stared down at their hands, memories of their torn state washing over them. Unlike Talib, they had failed to recognize their immortality when they first reached the island. It had been placed on them somewhere between the storm and the beaches of paradise. Paled faces wore eyes that wrestled between rage and frustration. It wasn't hard to determine their thoughts. They all wondered: *Where were these powers when those dying needed them the most?*

I know that was the question I had asked myself many times before we left the island. We broke apart the ship, and after much debate, we split ways. Spreading out seemed appropriate since a group of power-wielding men and women might be perceived with alarm. Some headed north, others went south, and I decided to travel east in hopes of uncovering what had happened to the survivors who stayed behind. Much to my relief, some lived through the massacre. Most were enslaved; they were made permanent servants and cared for the tabernacle for several generations. Sadly, the tribes were no more; they were torn apart by betrayal and civil war between one another.

Honestly, we were lost children desperate to do right for our fellow human beings. We possessed skills and knowledge which could improve the quality of life around the world. What more could you want from miracle workers and saints? Were we not taught to treat others as we expected to be treated? Peace, love, and compassion conquer all... it would prove to be a horrible mistake.

As each of us shared a new element to improve life, its immediate abuse followed. Again and again, I watched as a good deed led to wars and destruction against my fellow immortals' wishes. Most of the time, the misuse was something I could not have predicted. The desire to rule and gain power and riches kept undoing the good we offered.

"You are a strange new face!" Talib paused in front of the wooden building to look in the direction of the voice. An enthusiastic man in black held a new emblem of Christianity in his hands. "Welcome, stranger! Our great ruler, Constantine, has brought the blessings and miracles of Christianity to this land! Please come inside! See for yourself the glories of God!"

Furrowing his brow, he looked at the elaborate gold and silver crucifix with disdain. "Why the need for gold. Would a wooden crucifix not be more intimate? Crafted with love and devotion by the hands of man versus this trinket of wealth?"

"Don't be ridiculous," scoffed the priest. Frowning, he gave him a heated glare. "Does God not deserve the very best this land has to offer?"

Talib smiled and closed his eyes; he spoke from memory, "Lay not up for yourselves treasures on earth, where moth and rust does corrupt, and where thieves break through and steal. Matthew 6:19."

He opened his eyes to see the red face of a now outraged follower of this church of treasures and power. "H-how dare you quote God's words to me in mockery!"

Laughing, Talib replied again in quote, "How much better is it to get wisdom than gold! And to get understanding rather than silver! Proverbs 16:16. Did you not recently add this scripture, my dear priest?"

Veins pulsed from the man's forehead and neck. "BLASPHEMER!"

"Calm yourself." Talib placed his hand on the priest's shoulder, instantly melting the rage as the element of Judgment pushed away the violent intentions. "We are all here to worship God."

"Y-yes…" He paled, confused at his own reactions. "Service will start soon."

"Ah, how about you run the service today and take your followers out into the field." He still used his element to imprint the suggestions as final decisions. "Nothing more holy than preaching in the light of the sun."

"Y-yes … that should appeal to the pagans…" He pocketed the crucifix and entered the church.

Talib followed close behind but immediately sat in the back pew. Losing interest in the priest, he looked at the crude carvings of monsters and demons. Images of angels and demons fighting over souls, even impaling and devouring humans, were all meant to scare them. This was not what having faith was about. Sighing, he looked outside to the far side of the building where the man directed his followers to go. As the congregation flowed out the doors, the old priest scooped up the massive book of scripture and followed behind.

After a few minutes, only Talib and one priest, still kneeling and praying at the altar, remained behind the closed doors.

"Talib, you astonish me with your ability." The priest did not turn around to face him as he spoke. "I cannot thank you enough for rescuing me from this situation."

"Lucius, it is my duty to be at the aid of all." Sighing, he took a moment to relax and relish in this chance to simply sit and converse. "You are not the only one I have done this for."

"Did you really push Judgment on the whole congregation?" He stood, doing one last Hail Mary.

"No." He tensed; pulling on so many people at once would have had a whiplash he wasn't ready to face. "I simply moved one core person, and the rest merely followed without question. Sometimes, the smallest pebble holds back the boulder on the mountain. It is a tactic many have put in motion as of late, and I am coming to practice it myself."

"I see." With a sigh, he smiled. "Let me gather my things and change my clothes."

"I will be outside waiting."

Standing up, he walked out the doors and leaned against the building. It was a sunny day, and from where he stood, he could see the group crowded around the priest. Constantine had used Lucius in the worse way possible. The ability to emanate light from anywhere not only invoked fear and excitement, but many took this as a light from God himself. Lucius never intended it to be that way, but he did what he could do to rectify and redirect it. He had become a priest, but even that didn't stop Constantine's misuse of him. He pushed his army through his enemies wearing the symbols of Chi-Rho, the first two Greek letters for Christ, paired with Lucius' miraculous light.

At first, it probably seemed like a harmless assist on Lucius' end, but Constantine spilled blood from any who opposed him and his churches. For the first time in history, the lines between state and church were officially smudged. Corruption took root, and Lucius could no longer convince Constantine his actions were unholy. Instead, he was stationed in the middle of nowhere, surrounded by the most relentless group of mercenaries any king could hire. They had one task: to keep Lucius here. To Constantine, he was a holy object to possess, not a man whom he befriended in Milan years ago.

The door creaked open, and Lucius stepped out. He no longer wore his priest garments, instead, he donned a hooded arrangement which matched most of the low-class beggars and farmers in the region. Nodding, Lucius tightened his grip on the satchel on his shoulder, and they headed out. He stayed on Talib's heels as they approached the gates which led out of the central village. Without hesitation, Talib walked past them; his power had already reached the guards by this point. Lucius looked at the unmoving mercenaries in awe. They stopped everyone from coming and going, but they acted as if Talib and Lucius were merely ghosts passing through—a breeze even.

After several miles, Lucius finally asked, "Any word of your brother?"

"No." It was enough to make him pause in his steps. "I imagine at this rate, it will not be long before he comes out of hiding and calls for us all."

"Can he really do that?" Lucius dug into his satchel. "Summon us?"

"I think so." Lucius offered him some bread, but Talib shook his head in refusal. "My instincts tell me he can. Even I do not know the full extent of his powers."

"Exactly what is his power?" Lucius took a bite, sitting on the ground to rest. "All of us seem to have some sort of focus, but he's something entirely terrifying."

"He controls life itself … or life controls him." Sighing, Talib sat alongside him, welcoming a conversation. "We may be terrified of it, but it haunts him. Hotan has never been in control of whatever gripped his soul and dragged the rest of us into this aimless wandering on Earth."

"Wandering?" Lucius stared at the bread in his hand as thoughts flooded his mind. "One day, one of us will uncover why this happened. Then again, the book talks about how it's the actions you take in order to move through the world that really decide your placement in this chaos we call life."

"That may be where he keeps going wrong." Lying flat on his back, he squinted into the bright sunlight. "He has a nasty habit of lingering in the past, clinging to it like a babe to a mother's skirt. Maybe this all happened because he was too far into the past…"

"I think you may be right, Talib." Frowning, he lost his appetite and returned the bread to the satchel. "We don't feel hunger, but we desire to eat. He doesn't see a future, but he wants what has been handed to God. Sometimes I wonder if he's a fallen angel who has dragged us into a battle he waged against the Lord himself."

Furrowing his brow, Talib soaked in the concept. "You might be right, Lucius. My mistake is still seeing him as a man."

"Are any of us men anymore, Talib?" A concerned expression twisted his face. "Whose warriors are we? God's? Hotan's? Lucifer's?"

Snorting, Talib sat up, leaning on his knees as he locked eyes with Lucius. "We are lost souls, Lucius. Never-ending until we find our place in the world again. We belong only to ourselves and those to whom we choose to reveal our secrets and share our most intimate moments with."

"Ah, yes." A smile returned to his face. "I like that idea much better. Cursed to walk the Earth until we discover our purpose and make amends with the living. It gives meaning to our immortality."

"Come," Talib said, standing and offering a hand to Lucius, "Saphellia awaits our return."

"Thank you for being strong and caring." Lucius gripped his hand firmly, hugging him as he stood. "Without you, many of us would have lost ourselves completely."

Many immortals had similar experiences as Lucius. Lillianna gave people the gift of stronger metals, but soon after, they made blades to cut down those before them. Fae's knowledge and art for

studying were mocked and used to create wars through manipulation and sabotage. Many of us saw this pattern; they gave men a way to improve life, and they squandered it through violent tendencies. It broke us down. We overcorrected and added to the fall of cultures, cities, villages, and people. A lot of these people were good and innocent. We unwittingly gave more powerful tools to people of malicious intent..

Geliah benefited the most from the unintentional havoc we created worldwide. The waves of fear added to his power, and he made it clear he wanted more. His violence finally peaked, forcing Hotan out of hiding. It was then when we were all summoned to meet. We all heard his call within our souls and felt the tug to return to the very spot where we first landed. To the place where we last walked as human beings...

"We must no longer meddle in mortal affairs." Hotan gave Geliah a heated glare. "I have found a way to restore your mortality."

They whispered to one another in disbelief as tears welled in their eyes. If what Hotan said was true, their nightmare would be over; they could live a normal life once more and welcome the arms of death itself.

"How?" Talib asked quietly, prodding for an answer from his little brother. "Is it a permanent solution?"

"It should be," Hotan replied solemnly. "I will put all your souls into a permanent state of Rebirth. You will remain immortal but will grow old and be born again like a true mortal."

"What a about our powers?" Fae voiced her concerns as some shot glances at Geliah. "And will we remember who we are?"

"Your powers will be gone." Hotan gave a meek smile. "And you will not remember this life. It's all I can do to rectify what I have done. You will spend eternity living multiple lives as men and women."

"What about you?" Geliah hissed, narrowing his eyes. "I take it you will propose to stay awake and watch over us?"

"No." He ignored Geliah's fiery glare and turned to the others. "I do suggest one remain outside this spell in case something goes … wrong. It is no secret you do not trust me. After everything I have done, I would not trust myself with this task. Choose your guardian wisely…"

"Brother…" Talib watched as he walked far out of ear shot, glad he couldn't hear the disappointment in his voice.

"Talib, I want you to watch over us," said Jacob, wasting no time in voicing his opinion. "You have already been a protector to each of us at some point. It saddens me to separate you and Saphellia, but I want you to be the guardian."

And then the most heart wrenching words I have ever heard…

"Me too…" Saphellia's voice shook. "If I had my choice, I would want to know you were watching over me like a guardian angel."

"My dove…" His heart thudded loudly in his ears as more of the others agreed. "But… I…"

"This is bullshit." Geliah gritted his teeth. Fear pressed down on all of them as he approached Talib. "You're purposely rigging this!"

"No, far from it." It took all his inner strength to push off Geliah's overpowered element. "You're the only one using your powers here, Geliah."

"I'll force you all to change your minds." A devilish grin snaked across his mouth. "I'll be left as your guardian."

Looking at the frightened faces behind Geliah, Talib focused his power on him. Anger which he had bottled away so long ago let loose; flames and tattoo markings covered Talib instantly. Geliah flinched as the transition caused him to freeze. With a surge of power, Talib pushed Geliah's Fear out of his mind and broke the rest free. Geliah took a step back and laughed. He had not gained enough power to call forth the flames, and his skin became striped. Everyone backed away, unsure of the consequences of using power against one another.

"I've been using my power while yours collected dust on the island!" His eyes were wild as he sneered at Talib. "I'll win this game!"

"Never," Talib hissed. His body burned with rage as he looked deep into Geliah's amber eyes. "I will keep the promise I made. Now, let me pass Judgment on you, Geliah."

They charged at one another. Geliah swung his fist but missed as Talib ducked. He circled behind the brute and waited for his next move. Growling, Geliah attempted to grab him. Again, he dodged out of reach. Stumbling, Geliah caught his balance and reassessed his plan. He had not counted on Talib being so agile in a fight. In fact, he assumed Talib would have no fighting experience since he always chose peaceful solutions. After a short pause, he came at him again, swinging punches and doing his best to keep an eye on Talib's movements.

"Are you even going to fight me!" Geliah roared in frustration. "You know I'll knock you out in one punch!"

"Fine." Talib ducked under Geliah's blow and rolled forward. "Let me show you what my power can do..."

Crouching before Geliah, Talib pressed his palm against the heavily muscled chest. It wasn't a hard slap; he aimed to simply touch him. Geliah paled and broke out in a cold sweat, unable to move or finish his attack. He knew Talib had snared him before his next attempt; Geliah had lost control of his body. Standing, slow and steady, Talib's stare met Geliah's terrified golden eyes. No one expected the fight to end so quickly or with such ease.

"Stand up straight," Talib commanded, and Geliah straightened himself, arms at his sides, as Talib's palm pressed gently on his chest. "Now apologize."

"I-I am so sorry." There was a spark of anger in his eyes as his words betrayed him. "I am sorry I used my power on all of you."

"What are you going to do with him?" Peter looked worried as he took in Talib's grave expression. "You don't intend on harming him, do you?"

"No." He looked over Geliah's shoulder at the group. "I will hold him here. You are free to make your decision without his influence."

"We've already decided, Talib." Tina, the element of Sanity, spoke up. "Geliah's state of mind is nearing the boundaries of insanity. We fear he will never agree with our decision."

"In that case, I can force his hand to make him comply." Geliah's muscles twitched—a small refusal to what was coming. "Who have you all chosen for your guardian? I will wholeheartedly agree with whoever it may be."

I hoped the display of power had changed their minds. I even thought about using my powers to make them fear me. If I had, then I would have been no better than Geliah. I hated that they trusted me so deeply...

"We choose you, Talib." Peter's words were soft, knowing what this meant. "We want you to be the guardian."

I remember screaming in my head: NOOOOO!

Deep down, I knew it would fall on me. They needed me to do this. Could I really blame my brother for my immortality while everyone in my life forced me to be advisor and protector? I was never the strongest physically or entirely the smartest. My blame lies in the trusting and thoughtful nature of my heart... of my words. My natural talent was observing and making decisions without bias. From this moment on, I could only blame myself for my immortality.

"So be it." He glared into Geliah's eyes. "You are to sit here and agree with the group. Do not move from this spot until Hotan has finished the spell."

Geliah sat obediently on the sand after Talib removed his hand. The only signs of his unspoken refusal were a cold sweat, pale complexion, and the occasional twitch of a muscle. They whispered in astonishment that Talib did not need contact to maintain control. No one would ever doubt that Judgment could overcome Fear again.

Until he manages to sneak up on me and knock me out. I cannot do anything if I am not awake to use it. I have never felt so useless as when Geliah cornered Hotan for the last time. I almost lost him all over again...

"Have you all come to a decision?" Hotan walked back to the group, ignoring Geliah. "Who will not be included in the spell?"

"M-me," Talib stuttered. He took in a breath before continuing his declaration on behalf of the group. "They have chosen me to be guardian. All but Geliah."

Hotan looked down at him with a cold stare. "I see he attempted to sway the decision with his own powers. As a result, your opinion in this decision has been forfeited. You will do as you are told, Geliah."

There was a moment of silence as if waiting for someone to protest this claim.

No one wanted to defend the man who had helped ignite the fire of violence brought to the world from our powers. Hotan showed him pity, despite being aware of the thousands who died by his hand and powers. Honestly, we should have never allowed him to live. He had become much like Salah in nature—willing to pursue meaningless revenge. No living being who had the misfortune of falling before him was ever shown mercy. Even worse, Geliah took pleasure in torturing and building fear in his victims before relieving them through their gruesome deaths.

"Are you all ready?" His eyes jumped from one set of eyes to another.

Each nodded, but some were more eager than others. He motioned for them to come closer and close the large gaps between them. Hands trembled; they had never seen Hotan's power. They had only known its name: Rebirth. A nervous sweat ran down Talib's temple as he turned to Saphellia.

I hate this memory the most. It haunts me every day...

Her hand gripped his jaw, pulling his lips to hers as she tearfully kissed him. As his arms wrapped around her, he couldn't stop himself from crying. She hugged him tightly, gripping the back of his shirt with her fists. They kissed passionately, afraid to let go of one another.

Pausing, tears falling, he gritted his teeth as his voice trembled, "I will only love you, my dove."

"And I will do the same, my husband." Before he could say anymore, she returned her lips to his.

A glow emanated from her whole body. He pulled away and watched blue flames engulf her from within. Along with the others, she disappeared. Their bodies glowed a brilliant blue before dissolving in a burst of flames. What little flurries remained faded; nothing remained but the footsteps of phantoms who once walked this desolate place.

He gave me no warning. I wonder if anyone noticed the fright on my face and in my eyes in that wretched moment...

Panic consumed him at the sudden launch of the spell. He searched through the flames of the disappearing immortals until his eyes met Hotan's disconnected stare.

"I was not ready!" Tears streamed down his cheeks as he screamed. The forceful departure between him and Saphellia fed a bitter rage. "We barely had time to say goodbye!"

"It's better this way." Hotan's voice was a monotone. "It was never about when you were ready or wanted it. Was it not you who said that?"

It hurt horribly to have that thrown back in my face by him.

"Why must you twist things so horribly?" Talib fell to his knees, covering his face. "I am convinced your curse is now my own…"

And this is the last moment I remember before waking up … alone.

Hotan walked over, placed a hand on his shoulder, and squatted down to look him in the eyes. "I'm sorry for all the trouble I have caused you, Brother. Please bear with me a little longer."

Not again, the pull of power, did he really do this to me multiple times? How many memories are locked away inside my mind? Has it really taken death to retrieve these when they could have saved us from Iapetos' rage! You were such a fool, Hotan!

"What are you?" Talib gripped his shirt, angry with him. "Do you even know what you are, Hotan?"

"A tattooed angel, like you." He rested his forehead against Talib's. "I think there's more, but for now, that is all I have. Perhaps when the right time comes, you will remember this moment and realize we haven't blossomed completely."

"What do you mean?" Hotan pulled away, and Talib stared at him, lost. "If I remember this?"

Giving a mournful look over his shoulder, he mustered a faint smile. Talib felt helpless as he watched the last of the blue flames sizzle out in the orange sand around him. Looking back, Hotan had made it to the top of the first dune, where he paused.

Holding his hands out, blue flames erupted from his back, and wings with cerulean blue feathers sparkled in the desert sun. As his brother took flight, his eyes rolled back, and the world went black.

Wings … like Iapetos. He meant it when he said "tattooed angels" are what we had become. Or did he mean they are what we should become? How many centuries has he left me clues and apologies? Oh, dear God, all those disasters… I was there for each one but awoke lost or misplaced. Was he there? Did he find me there in Helike when the first one hit?

8

HEART-SHAPED BOX

373 BC

It was an awkward sensation when they first started their reincarnations under the Rebirth spell. Strangely, I felt the cycle within my soul like the breath of a phantom at the nape of my neck.

They were mortal: able to be born, to grow, even die from old age, illness, or other means. The cycle of life and death had been returned to them, and their immortal lives were forgotten. I grew more curious with each generation. Hotan had instilled in me the ability to feel them when they came in and out of the ever-changing world. Eventually, I was able to recognize who they were through each connection.

A subtle trace of their element attached to these invisible strings. I could only assume Hotan had used their powers to tether them to me … or perhaps himself. These chains allowed their bodies to fall back to their days of creation—as they had been in the beginning.

Hotan had given birth to reincarnation. It was uncanny to see how they grew into the same people I had spent centuries with. Different clothes, hairstyles shifting with the times, scars ever *changing, but their personalities were always left intact. I travelled from one location to the next, wherever I sensed their presence.*

It gave me a sense of comfort to take in the faces of friends who would never know me or who they had been. It also left my heart aching when I came across Saphellia.

The first time I stumbled upon her, I froze. Tears fell down my face without warning. I could not breathe when I saw her face and those eyes that had captured my heart so long ago. Watching her in that new life, I could still feel the warmth of our last kiss on my lips and the grip of her hands on my back. The agony of it was not just in the memory, but that she had never taken another lover. This was the third reincarnation; it could not be coincidental. Worse, it was as if she could always sense when I was near. Without fail, she would pause from whatever tasks she was doing and instantly look in my direction. Each time it sent my heart racing. I would slink out of sight, terrified to accidentally break the spell if she spotted me. I avoided hearing her voice. To hear the voice of my lost dove would have shattered what little willpower kept me sane.

As for the others, there was no indication they recognized me. I had been in full view of Jacob multiple times, and nothing even sparked or tugged at him. What became worrisome was the two people who were unaccounted for: Hotan and Abigail. I felt their presence, but I could never find them. I theorized my brother was still searching for answers without the need of worrying about the others. Regardless, what did he gain by alienating himself from his own brother?

"Excuse me, can you tell me the name of this place?" Talib had lost track of his thoughts while standing in the market when a merchant approached him with the question. "You seem to be someone who would know."

"Helike." Shaking his head free of his frustrating memories and questions, he turned to the weathered man beside him. "This city is Helike, sir."

"Ah!" He nodded, looking at the merchant stalls which clamored with voices. "Is it always so busy? I am a merchant looking for a city to setup a permanent trade line."

"It has grown immensely, sir, since I last visited." Sighing, he looked at the row of buildings, recalling when Lucius, the element of Light, had been reborn into the once small settlement. "It would be a fine place to do business, indeed. There are ten Spartan ships in the harbor among the merchant vessels this morning. It seems this is a favored resupply route for them these days."

"Thank you, kind sir, for your honesty!" The merchant shook his hand excitedly and scurried off into the crowd.

"Strange how they always seek me out for advice like that…" he mumbled to himself. Another flutter of power called his attention, and he walked in toward it. *Now, why do I not recognize this one?* He thought

With each step, he scanned the boiling waves of faces among the bustling market. He was desperate to put a face to the presence he felt here in Helike. Lucius had moved on, reincarnated elsewhere, since his last visit here, but it had remained a quiet place in his route for a long time. Oddly enough, he had sporadically felt this power for some time, but it was neither Hotan nor Abigail. As he pushed through the crowd, he spotted someone who held his attention. The strange, dark-haired man looked so much like his brother; it was uncanny. His broad shoulders, the way he walked, and even how he came to a sudden stop all seemed reminiscent of Hotan's own mannerisms.

Looking back now, I cannot deny how many moments of déjà vu I experienced when thinking I saw Iapetos and my brother. Is

this the result of hidden memories tucked away from me by my own little brother? You went too far, Hotan...

As if sensing his stare, the man turned, and his black eyes locked onto Talib, sending a shiver across his body. The dark-haired man stood motionless; the sea of people were cautious not to touch him as they rushed past. Furrowing his brow, Talib's heart thudded loudly as he could not break his stare from the ghostly, dark doppelganger of Hotan. Swallowing, the familiar giggles of Abigail allowed him to tear his eyes from the cold glare. His heart sped up as he looked around the stalls on his right, hoping to catch a glimpse of her. Another bout of snickering led him the opposite direction, away from the dark stranger. Without hesitation, he chased after the sound, desperate to speak with her or even Hotan. Seeing no little girls matching her appearance, he looked for any moving creature which carried her giggling voice.

Abigail's cat form taunted me several times. I cannot count the number of times I would stare at the stray black cats which came in and out of my life over the centuries. Each time after that gentle meow, I would silently wonder if it was Abigail checking in on me...

Looking over his shoulder, the dark phantom had disappeared in the street. Another round of laughter brought his eyes forward again, calling him down a narrow alleyway between the buildings. Without hesitation, he stepped out of the bustling streets and into the emptiness of the pathway. It was long and silent as he walked farther away from the sounds of the rumbling market. As he neared the corner, a black cat with yellow eyes peered out from behind the wall. Stumbling to a stop, he squinted down at the cat, unsure of what he was doing anymore.

"Abigail?" his voice shook with hope.

"Mew." It rubbed its head on the corner before fading from sight.

Afraid of losing her, he rushed around the corner. Much to his surprise, the petite black cat had not gone far. She sat, licking her paw next to the only door hidden on the backside of the buildings. Looking back over his shoulder, no one from the market seemed to notice or acknowledge he had travelled this route. He calmed himself as a sense of hope washed over him, even though he tried to quiet it with every step he took toward the feline before him. The fear of coming so close to Hotan or Abigail and losing them again clawed at his soul. As he approached only steps away, she did not run away like before, instead, she stretched her tiny paws up on the door as if pleading for him to open it. Placing a hand on the door, he sighed as he looked down at her sleepy little yellow eyes.

I remember following her down the alley but losing her at the corner. What hidden memory will this be? I thought this was the moment when… no. Is this what Fae and I feared? Is this a time when Hotan's presence brought destruction to the place where he hid away? What sort of power could destroy a place like Helike?

Smiling down at her, she purred and mewed pleasantly in reply, and he gently opened the door. She sauntered into the dark hallway with a playful trill. Closing the door silently behind him, it took a moment for his eyes to adjust to the darkness; the light of a candle painted the far wall as it wavered and flickered. The cat waited patiently for him. She cantered a few steps to the illuminated area and looked back, meowing to him, entreating him to follow. Goosebumps crawled across his skin with every step; something seemed misplaced for her to want him to be here. Panic crept in as he recalled the number of years since he had lost sight of them. He wondered, *Why now?*

Abigail sought me out … but why? How distraught or deranged had Hotan become at this point? Am I ready to see this even now?

Taking a deep breath, he begged his heartbeat to slow as he took more confident steps toward the glowing room at the end of the hall. Stopping at the entrance to the room, he watched as she galloped to the desk, leaping onto it to interrupt the writer who sat there, busily writing. Pawing at the arm, she looked to him as if to announce his arrival. The man jerked, slapping the quill down on the parchment in frustration.

"I told you no, Abigail." The voice was raspy but unmistakable—Hotan. "I don't need Talib's help."

Hearing the hiss of disapproval in Hotan's voice, he sunk back into the shadows of the hallway, hoping his presence went unnoticed. Holding his breath, he continued to listen; Abigail brought him here for a reason.

"But he's already here in Helike." It had been thousands of years since he had last heard the pleasant sing-song tone of Abigail's real voice. "Talib can help! He's your brother, and we left him completely alone! Did you not tell me how this haunts you, yet when he's near, you fail to approach him!"

Talib furrowed his brow as he listened to her desperate pleas to his little brother.

"You don't understand, Abigail." The chair creaked under his shifting weight as his voice trembled with a horrendous sorrow. "I've done terrible things to Talib, and facing him now would destroy me. Not until I fix this. I must find a way to undo what I have done to Iapetos, then Talib and the others."

"You do know they are both here…" she pouted. "What do you intend to do with Iapetos this time?"

"I, I can only hide and defend myself." The slap of Hotan's journal made Talib jump from where he hid in the hallway. "We need to move on. After our last encounter … if we fail to slip away, he will surely level this place."

"What did you do to him last time?" Her voice was barely audible from where he stood. "He seemed terrified, and then his face went calm as if he let it fade away."

"He was terrified." The chair screeched as it slid away from him so he could stand up. "I tried to kill him. As the element of Death, he was horribly aware that I was using his power."

"What stopped his fear?" Peaking around the corner, he saw the black cat's fur prickling up as if spooked by the information. "How does one become calm when someone is trying to kill them with their own power?"

"You don't." Hotan leaned on the table, his shoulders heavy as he petted her; the motion seemed like he was trying to keep her fur down. "I realized I couldn't do it, and so wiped the memory from him. Instead, he remembers me making him fall asleep."

"Was it impossible?" Her tiny feline head nudged his arm as he sighed. "Or something else?"

"I've already told you; I couldn't do it." He broke away from her, heading out of Talib's view. "Don't ask again. Ever."

As the tiny yellow eyes locked onto Talib's, she whispered inside his mind, *Iapetos is his son, but he has yet to utter the words out loud. Talib, Hotan's mind and heart are sick. I don't know what to do anymore...*

"Who are you talking to?" Hotan asked angrily. "What did you say?"

Licking her paw playfully, she replied coyly, "Tina."

"Uh, Tina?" Scoffing, he asked, "Does she even hear you?"

She stopped and eyed Hotan with one tiny yellow eye. "I like to imagine so. She is the element of Insanity. It pleases me to think that I am the tiny voice in her head."

Hotan laughed as Talib worked his way toward the exit. Now that he was aware of her concern, he could debate on an answer for her. *Any aid I provide Hotan will have to be through Abigail.*

Hotan's determination to keep his distance from me is from guilt, not an estrangement intended to be hostile in nature. Before he could fully process what she whispered to him, he had to make his way out without Hotan noticing. *A desperate man can do frightening things, even to his own family, and Hotan was no exception to this fact of life.*

Talib was halfway down the hallway when a booming sound reverberated from the ground. The world seemed to freeze from the startling, unnatural sound. Gravel and dust slowly started to dance at his feet, sending his body into a cold sweat. Looking behind him to the room, the clattering of clay pots was followed by the rattling of the chair and desk. The vibrations from the ground escalated as vertigo took its hold on him. He stumbled several steps backward, unable to find a point of balance. The world tilted one way, then the other. The earth rumbled from every direction. He lost his footing, and his back slapped against the shaking walls of the hallway. Gasping, he looked to the room as Hotan grabbed Abigail in his arms. *If I cannot escape, my brother will know that I overheard most of the conversation.* Hotan was rushing; he threw the book into his satchel, slung it over his shoulder, and stumbled a few steps into the hallway. Talib tensed, still leaning against the vibrating and crumbling wall behind him. Hotan froze, his face paling as pieces of the walls and ceiling toppled down between them.

Locking eyes with him, Hotan hissed, "Talib!"

Another thumping *BOOM* rattled the earth and sent the walls and ceiling crumbling down on them. Talib fell backward, and he yelped. However, his fall was cut short as a rafter and chunk of wall clamped onto his right arm, trapping him under heavy debris. His arm was pinned, and everything felt like it had been sent spiraling. Mottled light shone through vibrating gaps, but he saw no signs of Hotan or Abigail. His shouts were muted by the screams of people, screeching of horses, and the roar created by buildings falling all around the city. As the earth started to calm, his ears were left ringing from the sound. Dust clouded the sun, filled his lungs, and painted everything outside his prison in one dreadful, muddy color.

Helike had fallen.

Coughing and wheezing, he struggled to free his arm. His fingers were numb, but the pain let him know that the rafter had broken his forearm. The throbbing and sharp stings added to his frustrations. If he could just lift the rafter, he could unpin himself and heal. Planting his feet on the large chunk of wall, he tried to lift it to relieve the weight on the rafter, hoping he might even be able to crawl out from under the rubble. His efforts failed despite his inhuman strength. There was far too much stacked on the rafter for it to budge from his broken arm. Leaning his forehead against the wooden vice, he coughed to clear the dust from his lungs. He thought about his choices: *I can hope someone finds me, sit here for days—or longer—until the debris shifts or rots away, or tear off my own arm.* Strangely, Talib laughed as he thought about his dilemma. *I am immortal and have lived for over a thousand years, yet even I do not know if my arm can grow back.*

I am likely in the center of a massive debris pile; it will be a while before they are able to dig far enough back to where I sit. Even still, I am relying on the assumption that the last survivors have not fled, and that the city is not being engulfed in flames from fallen lanterns and braziers. He didn't need food or water to survive, but the idea that he would have to sit here long enough for wood to rot was frightening. Again, the pain throbbed through his left arm, and he pushed back the idea of losing it. Swallowing, he sighed as his mind called out to the one person who might help him, *Hotan, if you are there, my arm is pinned, and I cannot free myself...*

Staring up at the tiny holes of weak light, he waited, listening for any signs. The muscles in his back tightened with each passing minute, and hopelessness grew with each thump of his heartbeat against his eardrums. In the distance, he heard cries of the other earthquake victims and the occasional crumbling of more debris. He wondered, *What will I find when I manage to crawl out of this coffin of destruction? Helike is no more.* Seconds turned into minutes; minutes became hours. The heat of his capsule made him sweat, turning the dust on his skin to mud. It only added to his frustration of being abandoned.

The dirt around him started to flow upward, floating in the little streams of light like smoke. Debris crumbled and shifted; an aftershock was hitting. Screams and shouts made their way to him as the shaking peaked. Something nearby shifted, and the rafter responded in movement. The weight increased on his arm, crunching and crushing bones and flesh. Popping and crackling added to the horrific smashing of flesh between wood and building. He howled from the agony, and regrets raced through his mind. *Since becoming immortal, I never carry a knife or sword. Cutting my arm off would be a relief compared to the torture I am at the mercy of.*

Pulling on the debris made the rafter press on him further, adding to the pain. Tears fell from his dirt-covered face as the sting of ripping skin brought his blood dribbling from under the tight gap. His fingers barely fit under the wood and failed to provide any relief to the limb on the verge of being flattened. Thoughts flew through his mind as he pounded his head on the rafter. Finally, the aftershock stopped vibrating through the ground, but his pain remained. His teeth chattered, and he struggled to push back his torment to think of something to do. More aftershocks were coming. If he stayed, he risked being crushed completely.

Swallowing to calm himself, he closed his eyes. Taking in deep breaths, he stilled his panic. He grabbed the top of the rafter, shaking from knowing what he had to do. Knots twisted in his stomach as he stared down at his trembling fingers which dug into the rafter. Blood continued to drip down the wall—never-ending. *If I was mortal, surely this much blood would have made me lose consciousness.* Gritting his teeth, he willed himself to take in one last breath. With all his strength, he closed the last of the gap between rafter and wall. Heels bracing against heavy debris, he shifted his strength. He twisted his torso harshly away from the flattened, ensnared limb. His ears rung from the primal scream that spilled from his lungs. Slamming against the rubble behind him, he gasped for air through the agony only to continue shrieking.

Torn skin and jagged bones were all that remained where his right elbow had once been. The screaming dulled to panting; his eyes were wide as he stared at the ghastly travesty left behind from his actions. He was soaked with sweat, and his breathing was labored as he sat in shock. When he looked back to the rafter, there were no signs of the rest of his right arm. Blood painted the wreckage and ground. Despite the trauma, his wound had quickly ceased bleeding. Swallowing, he allowed himself to relax against the debris around him. Staring at the streams of light, he felt disconnected. The whole moment felt surreal as his nub throbbed.

Finally, his breathing calmed, and he looked over the end of his arm with renewed curiosity. Despite being immortal and stronger than a normal person, he still did not know the complications of such a severe injury. Like anyone else, he bled when cut, and bruised from impact, but the loss of an arm was something entirely different. Rubbing the sweat and mud from his eyes, he wondered, *Will the limb grow back the same or will I spend the rest of my immortal life with only one arm?* His heart jolted as crumbles fell from the debris overhead, and he heard footsteps on top of his coffin. He jumped to his feet and began shouting.

"In here! I am in here, under you!"

The steps paused, and the sounds of heavy rubble being tossed away met his ears. Tears of relief slid down his cheeks. He ripped a piece of his shirt to create a make-shift bandage. No matter who it was, his arm needed to be wrapped. It stung and ached with each tightening wrap, but the increasing speckles of sunlight which rained over him reinforced his nerves. He would not spend eternity buried in the debris of a decimated city. Suddenly, a hand and fingers came through. Tying the knot to his bandage, he squinted through the blinding light. The hand gripped a large piece of wall and ceiling which was far too large to move. This piece should have taken three men to move, but one hand lifted it away.

His heart raced. *Has Hotan returned?*

As the debris was flung away and his prison of rubble was opened, his eyes were met by the black-haired doppelganger of his brother. They froze as the dust settled around them. They looked at one another wide-eyed and surprised. The dark eyes shifted, and he knotted his brow and gritted his teeth in anger. A wave of power, much like Hotan's, slammed into Talib, and he recognized the presence he had felt earlier. This was the power that had brought him to Helike. Neither could deny the uncanny similarities in their own features to one another. *Whoever this dark stranger is, he is connected—even blood-related—to and Hotan and I.*

"Who, who are you?" Talib's voice was raspy from all the pain-filled screams, but he wanted to know who this new immortal was. "Where did you come from?"

"Where's Hotan?" he grunted, ignoring the questions. "Tell me where that immortal bastard went."

"Gone. The building fell on us." Grabbing his throbbing arm brought Iapetos' dark eyes to the injury. "I was pinned, and well, you can see for yourself what happened to me."

"You do know him?" His harsh tone and face softened as he offered a helping hand. "I've been looking for him a very long time."

Reluctant to take the hand that floated down from the opening, Talib asked again, "Who are you?"

"Iapetos." He motioned again for Talib to take hold, so he did. "I need to ask you who you are and how you know him. No one has ever known the man for whom I have spent decades looking. You are the first in over a thousand years."

Taking a few steps on top of the collapsed building, Talib stood in awe. Helike no longer stood tall and proud. In a matter of seconds, the buildings had buckled in on themselves, betraying the lives inside them. Smoke billowed up from various places; fires burned as victims stumbled about, covered in dirt and blood, shocked, and crying. Boats lay tilted on their hulls; the water around them was too shallow for them to float. He looked to where the bustling market used to be, confirming that many people had been crushed or left behind to die.

"Dear God…" He held his missing arm as he stood in shock. "And I thought the massacre in my village had been devastating…"

"How do you know Hotan?" Iapetos gripped his shoulder, ripping him from the sight of destruction. "You look like him. Are you related to him too?"

"Too?" Blinking in surprise, the questions broke his daze. "I am his older brother, Talib."

"Older brother?" The dark eyes grew wide and danced from one side to the other as if reading invisible lines in the air. "Did you know he had a son?"

"N-no." Talib's heart thudded against his aching chest as his eyes wandered past Iapetos to the destruction around them. "Did… did you do this?"

"Is he here?" Ignoring the question, Iapetos shook Talib with a tightening grip. "Was he here?"

"Yes, but the building collapsed when I found him." He continued looking at the wreckage. "He did not want me to find him. I am certain he left me behind."

The pain made it impossible for me to focus. Surely Iapetos knew I was in shock, but this is a far calmer man than the angry one we met on the rooftop…

"Not even his own brother can get close to him." Letting go of his shoulder, Iapetos looked about the rubble, peering under the debris as if hoping to find clues. "There's no way this killed him, but maybe he left his journal again."

"Journal?" Talib's arm ached and throbbed. He grabbed it, willing himself to endure the pain. "He had it when he ran into me as the earthquake hit."

"Damn, I need that journal; it's all I have. He puts everything I need to know in that thing. The last time I found it, I learned a little about him and who I am." He paused from his frustrated search. "But, just maybe…"

His eyes became crazed. Iapetos peered over his shoulder at Talib, sizing him up for a moment. Talib still felt confused and exhausted, but the dark eyes became more menacing by the second as Iapetos marched back toward him. Gripping his throat, he lifted him from the ground; his feet barely touched the debris under them. Their eyes locked, and fear washed through him as he felt the dark power growing inside Iapetos. Black flames and tattoo markings crawled across his skin; there were no more doubts that Iapetos was one of them. A chilling sensation of death and destruction flowed from where he gripped his throat. Talib tugged with his remaining hand—a weak plea for Iapetos to release him.

"Just maybe he will come back to save his brother from me," he snarled. "I'm betting yes."

"But…" Talib gasped for air, desperate to speak. "He left me pinned! I begged for his help and got nothing! Is my missing arm not proof enough?"

"Oh, you were in no real danger before." A smile crept across his face. "But the moment he senses this, he should come. I have no real intentions of hurting you, Talib. You're just as much of a victim as I am."

"V-Victim…" The element of Death was a terrifying power, and it had him by the throat in his most vulnerable moment.

As he struggled in Iapetos' grip, he felt the power wash in and out, as if Iapetos had a hard time making it obey him. The man before him was Hotan's son—left abandoned and broken— and now, he sought revenge. The few centuries he experienced alone had been hard. Talib imagined the difficulties of being cast away without comfort from anyone. The sorrow engulfed him and brought tears to his eyes. *This man is alone to face such a dreadful power.* None of the elements of Nature or Humanity were as dark or dangerous as Death.

One tear landed on Iapetos' hand, and his expression softened. "Why… why are you crying?"

"I feel sorry for what my brother has done to you," Talib stuttered. The grip loosened, and his feet touched the ground. "He wanted your mother so badly that he blindly tossed aside what he was given—his son."

He pulled his hand away, panicking, from the empathy offered to him. "I just want answers. Why would he bring me to life only to cast me out?"

"Because he was a heartbroken fool." He winced as another wave of pain hit his arm. Gripping the remaining part, he fought the urge to curl into a ball. "I pray this will not pain me for eternity."

"Is this the first time you've lost a limb?" Iapetos' face grew stern as he stared at the bloody bandages on the nub. "You seem to be in shock from it."

"Y-yes, I have never been injured this badly before." His chest tightened as he noticed the pale complexion growing on Iapetos' face. "I take it that you have been injured like this before?"

"More times than I would like to admit." Iapetos leaned closer, and Talib flinched at the threat of his outstretched hand touching his injury. "Trust me. It's better to leave the bandage off."

"Why?" He furrowed his brow, hissing as Iapetos tenderly unwrapped his stump. "I would think it would get infected or cause alarm."

He reached the last wrap, and the tug of it sent every nerve reeling with pain. Looking down, he gaped at how the flesh had grown back and merged with the wrapping. His eyes shot upward to Iapetos in terror. Flesh and bandage had become one in the first round of wrapping, explaining the pain he felt. Locking eyes with Iapetos, he knew what was coming. With a taut face and strong glare, Iapetos ripped off the flesh-infused bandage. It was a hundred times more painful than when he ripped it from the rafter. Nerves had fused with the bandage, and he fell to his knees, screaming. Iapetos still gripped the arm; he hadn't been able to remove all of it the first time. Another tearing of his flesh brought tears down his face. Agony rattled through him like a thousand bees in a log.

"That's why you leave the bandages off. It's painful enough when it returns; bandages fused with flesh slow the process and add to the agony of it all." Finally, he released him, and Talib fell to his side, panting and shivering as the pain pulsed through him. "Next time, keep it clear of obstructions."

"IAPETOS!" Hotan's angry voice made him turn on his heels. "Back away from him. He has nothing to do with us."

Brother, wait! Talib pleaded from his mind, praying it reached Hotan as blue flames erupted around him.

His green eyes dropped to meet Talib, and the fiery rage in them made his heart stop. *Silence! You should not have followed me here.*

"I am sorry for what he may do." Talib rolled to stare up at Iapetos' back; his clothes were dyed black, including the ragged hood that lay across his broad shoulders. "If we meet again—"

"Chances are we won't remember." Iapetos replied darkly, tightening his fists as the black flames grew. "He likes to toy with memories, locking them away. He's right; this is our fight, not yours. You have nothing to do with this."

"Locking memories away?" Sweat trickled down his temple as his stump throbbed and ached. "Why…"

I think you know why, Iapetos' voice reached his mind as he approached Hotan, building a distance between them. *I am confident I will fail here, and we will not recall my destruction of Helike.*

You did this? Talib looked to the bloodied limb; his elbow was back, but the gruesome, tangled mix of flesh and bone hung where the rest of his arm should have followed. *Was it necessary to take so many innocent lives?*

The earth started to tremble under his back, and dust wafted around him before being pulled away by the breeze. Birds fled overhead, and there was a dull roar in the distance, unlike the aftershock from before. The growling sound did not boil up through the ground, instead, it shook the air itself. His stomach tensed. These vibrations built with each passing second, slower than before; the shaking of the world only added to the panic in his chest. He rolled to his feet in time to watch Iapetos and Hotan run toward one another.

Black and blue lightning strikes collided. A great thunder erupted as they connected with their first strikes. A wave of pressure blew out from the blinding explosion of power, and Talib nearly lost his balance. Shielding his eyes from the blinding light made from Life and Death was difficult with only one arm. Staggering backward, he marveled over their power and its weight. Each step they took crushed the debris below, leaving flames wherever they touched. He was watching a battle worthy of demons and angels. Their fists locked, and an explosion of blue and black flames scattered like shattering glass. The booming sound was deafening. Blue flames wrapped around Iapetos' arm; black flames raced across Hotan's arm. A black flame snaked across Hotan's neck, and he leapt back to break it. Iapetos snarled and charged at him again.

To think they were pushing their power into each other in such a malicious manner made Talib's skin crawl. Facing Geliah had been unnerving enough, but he did not understand the purpose behind this fight. They exchanged blows, ducking and dodging as they ignored the rumbling beyond the city. Rubble bounced at his feet as buildings further crumbled. Breaking his stare from the fight, Talib looked to the harbor where the roaring sound seemed to originate. The little water that remained before was completely gone. His heart dropped, and his face paled. In the distance, a wall of water could be seen; a tsunami was fast approaching.

Ba-Boom!

Like the first earthquake, a loud cannon roared before the ground tilted and shook. Vertigo brought Talib to his knees again. Debris shifted violently all around Helike. Screams came from the remaining survivors, but they did not see the approaching coffin of water. Pillars of fire painted the distance around the city. Helike was being devoured by Hell itself. The ground dropped again as if the very foundation was being ripped away. Even if they had managed to make it out of the city, the explosion on the outer edge would have taken their lives.

Ba-Boom!

Another drop. Hotan and Iapetos finally halted their fight to look to their feet. Iapetos looked back at Talib's frightened face and then back to Hotan, who was running toward him. Knotting his brow, he held out his hand toward Hotan. A wall of black flames deflected the incoming attack. As Hotan fell backward, Iapetos ran toward Talib. They locked eyes, confusion taking hold in all the chaos. *Why is he coming for me?* Large, black-feathered wings burst into life behind Iapetos as he ran ever closer. Talib froze in awe of the angelic creation before him.

"Time's up; we must leave. NOW!" Iapetos gripped Talib's good arm. With a graceful leap, he beat his wings once, and they were in the air. "I do not wish to experience drowning again…"

Stunned, Talib peered down to the ground as Hotan stared up, shrinking as they ascended higher.

Looking back on this moment, I wonder why Iapetos cared enough to save me? His one goal was to fight Hotan, was it not?

"You need to figure out your powers, Talib," Iapetos grunted, still flying above and toward the approaching tsunami. "You could have flown away on your own, or has Hotan kept that secret to himself?"

I could have flown away? Talib thought. His thoughts still scrambled to resolve what was happening.

"Wh-why?" Talib stammered as the wave rolled under them, obliterating the ten massive Spartan ships before crashing over Helike. "Why did you save me?"

"I…" His grip tightened as if he was just as confused by his own actions. "I think you once tried to save me…"

THUD!

Iapetos lost his grip and started falling. Looking to the sky, a blue-winged Hotan had slammed into them. As he fell toward the boiling mass of water and debris below, he watched as they fought in the sky above him. Lightning bolts splintered into sparks of blue and black. His back slammed into the water, and his bones snapped. His screams were muffled by the swift waters. He banged into the side of a ship and lost his grip. The current pushed him farther into Helike. Talib choked on sea water; his lungs stung, his body was painful, and the sensation to sleep took hold. Drowning was indeed a horrible thing to experience.

I remember none of this! Did Hotan double back after defeating Iapetos and lock this away? Thinking back, I recall losing the little black cat in the alley, then the massive wall of the incoming wave, and yes, then drowning within the city. All those moments were spread further than I had realized, with massive gaps between. In fact, I have no memories of the earthquake and assumed it was the shaking caused by the tsunami. Everything I thought I knew about myself, my brother even, has been mistaken. And Iapetos… how many times have we met and not remembered? Why is he so angry this last time? What happened in the last forgotten encounter?

9

BLACK HOLE SUN

526 AD

Watching my life pass before me like this, I now realize how many disasters I have experienced firsthand. Present-day history books fail to capture the tragedy of each terrible point on this destructive timeline humanity follows. Unlike the text strewn throughout the pages of so-called textbooks, I saw the faces, heard their screams, smelt the burning of flesh, and even felt the crushing of my own bones. Worse, many events have been forgotten or distorted to meet the agenda of greedy, power-hungry men and women for the sake of politics and personal interests. Regardless, this faithful vulture watched silently, unmoved through it all, but I have never forgotten.

I was there in the Qumran Settlement when one of Peter's reincarnations, a monk, aided in writing the Dead Sea Scrolls. Later, in 68 AD, the Romans destroyed it, and the scrolls were lost for thousands of years until the rediscovery in modern times. So many times, when nature failed to devour man, man turned on himself. When Mount Vesuvius erupted, wiping out Pompeii,

I was there in Herculaneum. Rocks riding on the searing heat of toxic gases slammed into the terrified in a blink of an eye. My skin still feels its sharp bite; memories of crawling out of my ashen coffin to see an entire city annihilated and preserved for centuries to come. I can never forget how the ground shook in 365 AD on the island of Crete, and the gut wrenching sensation of nature biting a gaping hole in humanity when I discovered a tsunami had swallowed the great city of Alexandria and, with it, the world's library. After that, written history fell apart, blind and vulnerable, to be rewritten as the powerful saw fit.

Seeing these hidden snippets of memories tucked into what I originally recalled is unnerving. I wonder how many of those horrible events were caused by battles between Hotan and Iapetos. Considering the state Hotan had fallen into, I wonder if the drowning of Alexandria was intentional. Was there information hidden in that library which he did not want found? How far into madness must a man be to want to rip the world of knowledge as precious and rare as what that library held? I once walked its shelves, curious to see this rumored collection of books and found myself humbled. My heart aches to know it is gone forever. Why were humanity's few possessions lost? Natural disaster or my brother's meddling? My gut tightens at the thought, and with depressing confidence, I can only confess the latter makes more sense.

The familiar sensation of vertigo broke his thoughts. Horses squealed, dancing about and rearing up. Talib looked to the merchant he dealt with as tents fell behind him, and he began to stumble. The ground under them shook violently, tilting every which way. Horses tugged on their ropes, and birds took to the sky for safety. They both struggled to calm the animals attached to the reigns in their hands as the earthquake peaked. Sweat trickled across his chin and nerves in his joints tightened—a frightening reminder of how many times he had been through this with grim outcomes. Another disaster of historical proportions had started in this place of trade.

As the shaking decreased, he searched the horizon for further dangers. In the distance, smoke increased in one area; a city had been struck hard and was now on fire. His heart pressed against his aching chest. His horse pawed at the ground, tugging at him, pleading with him to flee. With an assertive pull, he calmed her by rubbing her nose to reassure her that all was well now that the rumbling underfoot had silenced. *I must make a decision; should I leave this place behind or attempt to aid those in the city in the distance?*

"Are you alright, my friend?" The merchant attempted to calm his horses. "That is the worst one yet..."

"It is not my first time, unfortunately." Giving the old man a grave stare, he confessed what truth he could, "I have been in far worse earthquakes, my friend."

"May God have mercy on their souls." The man's eyes caught the smoke which filled the skies behind Talib. "Antioch burns."

"Let us swiftly finish our business." He handed the reigns of his old mare to the man along with a small satchel of gold. "I am in need of a younger horse before I travel to aid those in Antioch."

"Aye, this one is my youngest, though he is not broken in." He pointed to a frisky stallion which still huffed and snorted from the quake. "He may be too much—"

"He will do fine." Talib approached the horse, and as if by magic, it calmed and responded like a well-seasoned animal. "I have a way with horses."

"A gift for miracles!" The merchant scratched his head, bewildered by the instant compliance from the once rowdy, untamed beast. "I pray Antioch still stands by the time you get to its walls."

"If not, it will be rebuilt." The young, lean horse didn't even flinch as Talib strapped on his saddle. "Thank you for the fine horse, kind sir."

"And thank you for your gold, my friend," chuckled the merchant, weighing the bag in his hand again.

Confident that his gear was properly attached, he hoisted himself on and galloped full steam toward the smoke that stretched for miles on the horizon. Indeed, Antioch was burning to the ground; the devastation would be a swift reminder of his time in Helike. By the time he made it to the edge of the city, the horse panted and foamed at the mouth. If he had ridden his old mare half as hard, she would have fallen over dead from a heart attack. Luckily, there was a trough of water by one of the main entrances to the city. He left the stallion there to rest and hydrate in case he needed to escape. Inside, the debris would prove too dangerous for a horse, especially with the inevitable aftershocks still to come.

Much of the debris was on fire as he worked his way through the devastation. He helped those he could, but most were beyond his aid. Many had died—crushed, burned, bled out, or some similar fate. Each glimpse made his arm ache, making him roll his shoulder to relieve the phantom reaction. Whispers of Helike rattled his body. As he pushed deeper into the crumbling burning piles, his eyes caught a flash of blue flames through a wall of smoke. His heart sped up, pounding in his ears, silencing the cries and screams of the damned. A wave of power took his breath away as he felt the familiar tug of Hotan's power. It wasn't the only power that had surged through him. There was something new—someone new—along with the element of Rebirth. He rushed eagerly through the smoke and flames to find Hotan.

As he came out of the other side of the pillar of smoke, he halted. Black and blue flames erupted from Hotan and a dark-figured man. A feeling of déjà vu added to his confusion. *Why is this discovery so strangely familiar?* Talib thought to himself. His stomach knotted as he watched the exchange of blows, waves of power colliding with each hit. The shimmer of blue and black sparks was both menacing and beautiful under the sunlight. The dark-haired man looked so much like his brother that it sent his mind reeling. One thought instantly surfaced: *What has Hotan created?*

Another wave of nausea struck him. *Antioch's demise is the result of this clash between titans.* Each footstep under the blue-and-black-flamed bodies left ashes and dents behind. As his eyes scanned the immediate area, his panic increased. Almost panting, he could see that the dented walls which lay haphazardly among them had fallen from their fight, not the monstrous earthquake he had felt. *Exactly how deeply rooted are our powers to humanity? To the earth at our feet?*

Hotan dodged a black-flame-covered fist, and his hand gripped the man's elbow. Blue flames erupted across the stranger's arm from Hotan's grasp. Terror filled the man's face as he pulled away.

"Raaaggghhh!" The dark-haired man clutched his arm as sweat poured across his face from the pain. "Was that necessary!"

The flames extinguished, and the arm exploded into ashes. Wide-eyed, Talib watched the wind carry it away. Shivers rattled through him; he had never seen the violent side of Hotan's abilities.

"Iapetos, we both know it will grow back. You must stop chasing me down in waves of destruction." Hotan was eerily calm as he stood tall, glaring at Iapetos. "I am trying to fix this…"

"Fix this!" growled Iapetos; his other arm made a wide swipe to refer to the destroyed city they stood in. "How does isolating me help fix this! You cast me off the island! You continue to abandon me despite knowing what you've done to me and to this world!"

"You are not the only one I have wronged." Hotan's green glare shifted, catching Talib's silver eyes as Iapetos also turned.

Talib's heart raced as every muscle tensed. He didn't think his presence had been noticed with so much power exploding from their fight. The world fell silent; both his brother and the unknown man bore their eyes into him as if he were a pest. Belittled by their presence, he turned and stared more deeply at the stranger. The jawline, the broad shoulders, and even the way his hair fell across his eyes were reminiscent of Hotan's features.

"Who ... who are you?" The man looked confusedly at Talib; they both felt déjà vu at the sight of one another. "What else have you done, Father?"

"F-father?" Talib looked from the dark-eyed Iapetos to the cold, vacant eyes of Hotan. "This is… you tried to…"

Hotan looked to the ground in shame as he balled his hands into fists. He marched toward Iapetos, who instantly leapt away in alarm. A few steps closer, another leap back, and it became obvious that Hotan planned to do something unimaginable. *He has already turned one of his arms to ash; does he intend to finish off the rest of him?* Talib's eyes searched the air, trying to grasp the thought which flew through his mind. A realization—no, fear—engulfed him. With a flinch of his muscles, he broke from his dumbfounded state.

"W-wait!" He rushed out between them, shielding Iapetos as he glared at Hotan. "We can work together! Hotan, you should not have to do this alone! This is why it has all gone so wrong in the first place, Brother!"

"Brother?" Iapetos panted. His arm slowly grew back past the elbow as blood dripped across the fallen walls at his feet. "What else are you hiding from me? From them?"

"Move, Talib." The dark tone of Hotan's voice made his skin crawl as he approached him. "I need more time, and you both are slowing me down."

"Wait, what?" Fear squeezed his heart and soul as his brother closed the gap between them. "You do not intend to…"

"Yes, he does," barked Iapetos from behind him. "He would rather we take decades to regenerate, so he may have his quiet time. Who knows how many times he has already done this, and we don't remember."

"No, it… it cannot be." As Hotan reached for his throat, Iapetos gripped the back of Talib's shirt and yanked him back. "Why! Why do this!"

"You fool, don't let him touch you!" Iapetos shouted, letting him fall back onto the debris.

Baffled, Talib looked up at Iapetos. The angry look on his face quickly shifted to one of terror. Hotan came closer, but Talib stood up, determined that he could stop him from this maddening resolve to take on the impossible alone. Iapetos took several steps back as Hotan's fingers dug into Talib's shoulder. As Hotan's power seeped into him, he pushed back with his own—determined to control his decision. Desperately, he tried to sway Hotan's judgment for the better. There was no way to know if it were even possible, but he had to try. *In the end, out of everyone on Earth, I have the best chance to change Hotan's mind and end this madness.*

"Stop it," growled Hotan as he began to sweat from the internal battle. "I have to do this alone."

"No, no you do not." Panting, he eyed Iapetos behind him. "If he really is your son, then you need to take him under your wing, not battle against him. He is of our blood! At least leave the boy in my care!"

"No." The harsh answer held no hesitation.

"You are Judgment…" Iapetos was shocked.

"Yes." Talib grimaced; he was losing his fight with Hotan as the element of Rebirth began to turn his own power against him. "Unfortunately, I am losing. Leave this place! Find me somehow in the next life…"

Large, black wings erupted from Iapetos' back as he took the chance to flee. "Thank you, my uncle."

"No!" roared Hotan as his power broke through, taking his soul and element into its control. "You will not flee!"

As if under a spell, Iapetos stopped, turned, and fell in line beside Talib. Horror danced in those dark eyes, but Talib's own were aflame with rebellious anger.

Hotan's hands covered each face, and his power seeped into them as he pleaded, "Please forgive me for this moment and so many more. I am so close to solving this; I just need more time. Perhaps one day, you two will meet and become the pillars you need from each other. I, on the other hand, simply need to fade from this world. I am slowly destroying it with this unstable power of mine. Please, my brother, my son, understand my intentions when you remember this time."

A searing pain crawled through Talib; his veins felt the blistering heat of the element of Rebirth running through them. Under the heat of his brother's palm, tears fell down his cheeks from the pain pushing inside him. Deep in his soul, he still felt the tangled struggle of his power trying to overthrow Hotan. Regret made him ache further as his fingers grew numb, floating away on the wind. *Maybe I should have practiced using my powers more? Would I have a better chance in this moment?* An aftershock shook his legs apart but was quickly forgotten; Talib was unable to feel through those appendages any longer. He was gone—dead even—as his body became ash and joined the flames of Antioch.

All this time, I thought I had been struck down by debris and was burnt alive. Instead, my power had been used against me! Against Iapetos! How could this have been the better choice, Brother? Killing us to buy time? For what reason! Did you ever find the solution? I doubt it, seeing how all of this is played out. Here I am on my deathbed while an innocent boy who wears your face and wields your power fights a man you destroyed from the inside out. Do you reveal your mistakes somewhere among my broken memories, or will I die realizing you are gone without soothing the rage of Death itself?

Gasping for air, Talib found himself naked on a familiar beach. His head pounded, and he shielded his eyes from the blinding sun. Images of Antioch in flames mixed with the pain of being turned into ashes. All of it was hazy. Clenching his teeth, he was flustered, knowing he had died again. Rolling over, his body stung with its first movement in decades. The whisper of waves and singing of the gulls was far from comforting. He had been turned to ash and, much to his despair, was brought back on the cursed beach where the reincarnation spell had begun. He took three steps before his legs wobbled, failing him, and his knees hit the soft ground.

He gripped the sand in his fists and sobbed. Something lingered in his heart. His soul felt shattered, but his mind was too cloudy from his death to remember why. He was frustrated to be in this state. Blinking a moment and staring down at his arms, he was surprised to see his markings drawn out so far. *Did I attempt to use my powers in the throes of death? There is so much I do not know about my immortality, let alone what the element of Judgment is capable of.*

Cawing drew his eyes to the sky again as he leaned back, sitting on his heels. A satchel fell from the raven's claws, hitting the sand before him with a thud. He grabbed it and searched inside to find clothes and a small dagger. He looked to the black-feathered bird as it landed out of reach, cocking its head. Mustering a sigh, he smiled.

"Thank you, Abigail." The bird cawed once more and flew away. "At least I know you will help when I am in need..."

10

HIT THE FLOOR

1157 AD

The world had turned on itself by the 12th Century. China was torn between the Song and Jin dynasties while Europe and Middle Asia imploded. Countries attempted to show their strength by overpowering their neighbors as well as forcing religion and political views onto the seized citizens within. Humanity devoured itself with every opening it found. Worse, the dreadful crusades were full stride, and the Europeans would soon defeat Saladin by 1192 AD. This only added to segregation and hatred among the different people who made up the world.

None of that was my concern. I had no desire to undo the travesties mankind laid upon itself. I had one task: Be the guardian of the sleeping immortals formerly known as the Levites. For the first time, there in 1157 AD, more than one reincarnation gathered in a single city. It was alarming. I feared if they met, it could cause a complication to the spell. I went to the city of Hama to see what exactly had happened, especially in a place so dangerous as this wartime city.

Hama was under siege; the sting of the crusaders and Seljuks still played out in dark alleys and the underground of the city. Getting around was dangerous, and Talib no longer dared to go anywhere without his falchion at his side. Hood on, scarf over his mouth, he went to inspect why so many had gathered in one area and why he sensed more than three immortals within the city boundaries. The city streets were a battleground between the Sultan and competing rulers who attempted to overthrow him. Talib stepped back into the shadows as a pack of soldiers marched down the market lane. The leader was Geliah's reincarnation, and he carried out his orders with an unusual amount of bliss. They were out to disrupt merchants who supported anyone other than the Sultan, and the fear it created was sparking his element. It was a terrifying observation; this was the first time someone's powers had appeared since the spell started over two thousand years ago.

"You there!" A grin snaked across Geliah's face as he pointed his sword at a merchant. "I do not recall your support to the Sultan!"

Marching up to the stall, the merchant coward in fear. A wave of it hit Geliah, and his muscles tensed as his excitement increased. Gripping the edge of the table, he flung it, and the merchant's wares landed on top of him. Geliah let out a bellowing laugh as the man fell back under the clatter of items. The soldiers shifted uncomfortably at the inhuman strength he had displayed. On the table, the merchant had been selling large clay water pots and iron ingots for blacksmiths to use in repairs; the heavy table should have taken two or more soldiers to flip. The merchant pleaded with Geliah as his brow bled from the heavy wares that had crashed into him.

"Pay tax to the Sultan for safety or leave," snorted Geliah.

Talib sighed and closed his eyes as he thought about what was unfolding in the street before him.

I could not figure out if it was the abnormal, long-term fights and fears in the area that had seeped into him or if there was a weakening in the spell. Seeing the hidden parts of my life, I can confidently conclude that the unfiltered use of Hotan's power disrupted the reincarnation spell. With each misuse of Rebirth, it tore the spell apart. Eventually, they began waking as he increased his meddling.

"You there!" Snapping open his eyes, Talib was greeted by the point of Geliah's sword. "Show your face!"

Without hesitation, he dropped his hood and pulled the scarf down under his chin. As his silver eyes met Geliah's amber-colored irises, he halted his aggression and shifted to fear. Some part of him instinctually recognized that Talib was a force to reckon with. Perhaps a connection remained between them from long ago when Talib passed Judgment on him before his reincarnation started.

"What business do you have in Hama?" Geliah barked, a bead of sweat trickling down his cheek.

"I am here to—" Vertigo struck, halting his words; the ground shook, and they all began to stumble.

Ba-boom!

The earth let out a loud roar as buildings collapsed around them. The people in the city began to scream. Panic hit him, and he started to flee to a safer area, but Geliah's sword dug deep between his two lower ribs. Glaring back at the golden eyes, he gripped the blade and yanked it from his body in frustration. *Even Geliah's reincarnation is spitefully annoying.* As he pulled himself away and off the blade, he stumbled out into the wide market street. As the earthquake peaked, cries of victims and the crashing of walls filled the air. Gripping his bleeding side and struggling to maintain his balance, he looked back in time to watch the walls collapse around Geliah and his men. The buildings that once made up the edges of the alleyway had buried it. Pieces crashed down in loud thuds, swallowing the pack of soldiers under them. All around, the earthquake crushed the screams in this rattling world.

Even being immortal, I found myself horribly vulnerable…

Looking down at his red-stained hands, Talib was losing his ability to stay awake. His lung was punctured and breathing became impossible as he fell to his knees. The earthquake was slowing, but his eyes rolled back, and he fell face first to the ground.

Cool water painted his face and his eyes crept open. His heart stopped when he saw Saphellia's hazel eyes looking down at him. She wiped his face with a wet rag, as tenderly and identically in motion as when she lived a life at his side. Choking memories flooded his mind, and tears welled up in his eyes. He stared up at her, marveling over feeling her touch for the first time in thousands of years.

I had hungered for decades—centuries—to be that close to her. Often, I had dared myself to approach her, even pursue her as a lover, to see if she would take me over the thousands who had failed over her reincarnated lives. Instead, she found me through the wreckage of Hama after I had helplessly hit the ground.

"It's alright; the earthquake has passed, but you need to rest before the aftershocks start to hit." Her voice was like the most wonderful music in the world. Her words echoed in his ears, "Don't cry. You're alive."

"I..." A tear slid down his cheek, and a smile crawled across his face. *She always takes care of me.*

She shushed him as she dipped the rag in the water and wiped his forehead.

"I thought I died, and you were an angel sent to retrieve me," he lied.

"Who are you?" She paused and peered into his eyes as if love-struck. "I feel like I should know you..."

Fear gripped him, and he sat up out of her lap. He scrambled to his feet; breaking her spell at a time like this would destroy him. He glanced around at the destruction. Buildings lay in ruins, and people were digging one another out of the wreckage. He turned his back to her, pulled on his hood, and covered his face with the scarf to disrupt any reminders of who he may be in her thoughts. Panic rattled through him as he looked for an escape route. *This indulgence will have to suffice for another millennia. I hope I have not failed my duty to keep her spell intact.*

"Wait!" She gripped his shoulder, her face filling with dread. "You're bleeding!"

"I am fine." Knowingly, he pulled up his shirt to reveal no mark; his clothes were soaked with blood, and a hole remained where the blade had cut through him. "See, it is not my blood. Thank you for waking me! I... I really must go!"

I was so afraid. It was heart wrenching to be so close to her and, at the same time, frightening that she felt some connection to me. Even thousands of years later, she still had never taken another lover. Generations of lives lived, and she had done so alone with no interest in another's company. It was depressing to watch from the shadows, but what was I supposed to do? Reveal the secret behind her promise to me so long ago?

"But you were hurt!" she countered, shoving a blood-soaked rag into his hand, demanding his attention. "I cleaned it moments ago. What are you?"

"I am… I am…" His mind raced. Afraid to speak his name, he found the only answer he could. "A tattooed angel."

Breaking from her touch, he ran as fast as he could. Tears streamed down his face as he fled from his soul mate through the blood and destruction of Hama. He had found Hell, and he was ready to leave this place behind.

Despite it, I would look back and cherish this moment. She had unknowingly given me the fuel to go on in a time when I was starting to lose myself.

Wobbling over a fallen building, he slid down the other side and ducked behind a piece of collapsed wall. An intact alleyway greeted him. Peering over his shoulder after the next turn, he saw no signs he was being followed by her or anyone else in the chaos of the fallen city. Looking forward, Talib barely back-pedaled fast enough not to smack into the hooded stranger in front of him. He was dressed in rags and wore a Mesopotamian mask—a statuesque face of a bearded man.

Again, destruction matched with unknown memories. I remember running away from Saphellia, but I do not recall leaving the city. As in the many times before, I wake elsewhere as if everything was normal. Why have I not been alarmed by these gaps? Did I convince myself that the days were blurring together after thousands of years? That it was normal or even expected?

The man's scarf dropped away from his face, exposing the assassin-like individual who did not flinch from the near collision. He reached up and pulled the mask away to reveal its owner.

"H-hotan!" His brother frowned to hear his name spoken so loudly. "Why are you here in Hama?"

"It doesn't matter; I need your power." Without warning, he closed the gap between them and gripped Talib's shoulder with uncanny aggression. "Sorry to have to do this again…"

"Again?" Talib muttered before the inner tentacles of Hotan's power took hold of the element of Judgment.

Could it be? Wait, why did I not see it before…

"Iapetos…" There was a fiery rage in the way Hotan's power mingled with Talib's. "You will come back here. Now!"

A shadow appeared over them. Talib struggled against the soul-crushing control of the element of Rebirth within him. Before them, a black-winged man landed in a plume of dust. He turned to face them; he was the same height as Hotan but broad-shouldered, with dark-eyes and hair. Setting those features aside, his face was nearly identical to Hotan's.

"Who is he?" growled Iapetos, flaring his wings and shooting a heated glare at Talib. "Is this how you forced me back here?"

"It doesn't matter; I have no time to chase you." An aftershock caused the debris to creak and crumble around them. Hotan continued in his frustrated tone, "Now, come here, grab hold of Talib."

He could not have done these things without my element, my power over Judgment. His sins, his mistakes, all channeled and performed through me is unforgivable!

Sweat dripped down Iapetos' temple as his body reacted against his will without hesitation to Hotan's command. Talib tried to break the bond but was unable to open his mouth. Hotan denied him the right to talk or protest these actions. As their eyes met, Iapetos' icy grip brought a chilling sensation through Talib's body. He gasped as Iapetos tightened his grip and the strings of the element of Death began to invade him.

"I'm sorry for this," the element of Death said sincerely, looking to Talib with sorrowful eyes as the words left his lips. "I know what he intends to do, and I will not go down without a fight."

Grimacing, Talib felt his soul tangle in a battle between Life and Death. He struggled to push both entities out, wanting to be master of his own soul again. Using their elements in this way was exhausting. Muscles tight, bodies weakening, all three fell to their knees. Talib managed to push them both to the outer edges of his core. His body ached with tension from attempting to overturn both the elements of Rebirth and Death. Panting, he reached over to his brother's hand and tried to pry it from his shoulder.

Hotan dug harder, gritting his teeth and glaring at him. "You don't understand…"

"I am not your tool to win wars." Blue flames crawled across Talib, and his tattoo curled around him like stripes on a tiger. "How many times have you done this to me already!"

Hotan's eyes broke away from his heated stare. The element of Death shifted inside him, helping push out the last remaining shreds of Rebirth from his core. An ache struck inside Talib's chest. *My brother should be pushing out the enemy, not the other way around.* As the last piece of Rebirth left his body, Iapetos dissolved his own power. Before Talib could catch his breath, Iapetos pulled him away, increasing his distance from Hotan. His power surged freely under its own control, and he glowered at his little brother. Breaking from Iapetos' grip, he stood tall, jaw muscles twitching from the rage boiling inside him. Blue flames grew taller and wider with the building of his emotions. Talib needed to know how much of a monster his brother had become.

"Answer me!" Talib's flames shifted from blue to red as he made his demand. "How many times!"

Red flames… I have never produced red flames. Well, not that I recall. And this feeling, this swell of power, is it inside me? Do

I just not know how to access it? To be able to push Hotan out without touching him and force him to do things… was this a fail-safe he hoped would be used against him this whole time?

"This is the seventh time." Again, Hotan avoided eye contact with Talib as he failed to resist the element of Judgment. "If you intend to ask why, I will willingly answer that I intend to kill you both to buy myself more time to fix my element."

I intended to block him, but knowing that, he turned the table. Did he fear that taking the power back would kill me? Or did he think that he would further abuse it if given constant access?

Iapetos shot Talib a look before he spoke. "That doesn't justify casting me, your only son, off the island."

Regardless, none of this could ever be justified. He used me to erase his mistakes. Worse, he cast his own son's life to the side. The way he came into existence was indeed frightening, but was it not the same for you, Hotan? We were terrified when we learned that we were becoming immortal and gaining destructive powers. How is that any different for Iapetos?

"You were a mistake." Hotan's cold and swift reply was painful, even for Talib. "I was grieving, aiming to bring your mother back. Instead, I created the element of Death. You shouldn't even exist."

Unrestrained wrath consumed Talib. Marching up to Hotan, he punched him square in the jaw. *CRACK!* Two teeth bounced across the ground, but Hotan did not flinch. There were no signs of pain on his face, no sound came from his lips, and not even a step back from the impact. Instead, his own markings crawled across his skin as blood dripped down his chin. Hotan had tired of the weight of Judgment and was pushing it from his body. Talib's control ended.

"Back away or he will take—" Iapetos' warning was too late. Hotan grabbed Talib's throat.

Instead of the tangled fight of power like before, he felt searing agony throughout his body. The hand on his throat tightened, and Talib's flames fell away. He gripped onto Hotan's arm, desperately hoping to pull it away. He clawed at him, but his fingers reduced to ashes. Terror filled him as he peered into the wild madness of his brother's glowing green eyes. Talib's body grew lighter, turning to ash and floating away.

"You left me no choice. I cannot have you slow me down here, Talib."

Everything went black.

He was determined to get to Iapetos. He has turned me to ash not once, but twice, possibly more. The huge gaps of time in my memory were not from me being killed in natural disasters. He killed me. He knew it would be decades before I would wake in the desert, physically resetting myself from the same starting point. I wonder if there were times when I failed to notice his presence, and he simply slew me from behind? Were there no limits to the madness which plagued you, Hotan?

II

ANTHEM OF THE ANGELS

1350 AD

Piles of burning bodies filled the streets and courtyards where the people of London once thrived, traded, commuted, and lived out their daily lives. The Black Plague found its way through China and across all of Europe. Death came in huge waves in London; no one was spared from the invisible wildfire which spread from one vessel to the next. He tightened the leather straps of his medical mask and pulled up a black hood to shield his face. Talib took on a foreboding appearance—a hooded crow or vulture intending to brave the chaos outside. With his hand on the wooden door, he hesitated. His stomach tightened in preparation for the sights, sounds, and smells that awaited him on the other side of the wooden shield. Venturing outside required emotional hardening and acceptance that you could not help those who suffered from the illness. No one could help those in the final stages of the beastly infection.

The smells from the pandemic still stain my nostrils. The plague ate away the body in ways never imagined. People died at such an alarming rate; children were left alone with the decaying bodies of their parents and siblings. I started a routine of checking houses at night for children in these homes of death. It was horrible having to pull them away and set fire to their plague-stricken homes. All anyone could do was purge areas with fire, much like the Romans had done to clear their streets.

During the day, the streets were filled with macabre images; bodies of the dead, in all shades and conditions, were brought in wheelbarrows to their final resting place. At night, more grisly actions took place. Terrified of those showing the rosy rings and early signs of rotting flesh, they dragged the sick innocents from their beds. Most no longer had the energy to kick, or even scream, as they were added to the flames. Many met their end this way, but the chance of them surviving was minuscule. Three out of five people fell to the fiendish illness which struck so rapidly that any precautions to prevent its spread were rendered useless.

Talib took a deep breath; the potpourri in the cone of his medical mask would do very little to mitigate the stench in the air. Goggles helped shield his eyes from the ashes floating through the air and the copious amounts of flies that thrived in the fall of mankind. Pulling the latch, he stepped into the dark, troubled alleyways of London at night.

He quickly found the house where he had left off the night before and resumed his search for children in need. He began the monotonous tasks: knocking, listening, opening the door, and checking room by room for any signs of life. After searching three houses, all he found were barren homes or the rotting bodies of the dead. It was numbing to see the twisted faces; the scene felt surreal as he kicked up ashes and watched them float back down before pausing at the next door.

Sighing, he knocked and waited. He listened, but there were no sounds inside the dark building; it was setup more like a business than a home. As he reached for the latch, the door crept open. He expected to see someone as he stared into the darkness of the building. After nothing appeared, he gently pushed it open to peer inside. He noticed ashen, muddy footsteps leading toward the stairs before they faded away. *Indeed, someone has been here rather recently.*

"Anyone here?" he bellowed, sending an echo through the building. "Anyone in need of help? I am a doctor."

No response.

He took a few more steps and closed the door with a soft click and skid of the latch. Turning back to the steps, his heart fluttered at the sight of a black cat. Unlike other pets which had become ill with the Black Plague, her fur was pristine as she rubbed her head against a prong of the railing.

"A-abigail," he muttered within his cone. "Is that you?"

I remember seeing a black cat, empty rooms, and moving on. After that….

The cat paused and opened a sleepy yellow eye. It responded, "Mew."

She turned in a tight circle before bolting up the stairs. He nearly slipped on the wet ashes on the floor as he frantically chased after her. His heart raced as his feet thudded loudly against the creaky, wooden steps. Almost nearing the top, a door opened, and light flooded the landing. Freezing, he waited to see what would happen, when he was struck by a surge of unfamiliar power.

Why do I not remember anything but Roanoke?

"You're not really a cat, are you?" huffed the voice from the door. "But thank you for helping me find this journal."

How have I failed to realize such a large chunk of my memory is missing?

The floor squeaked under the man's shifting weight, and before Talib could move, he was staring down at him from the top of the steps. The thudding of his heart did nothing to calm him as he stared into the dark-eyed man who looked so much like his brother. Familiarity rippled across his mind, and the stranger knotted his brow as he felt it too. Both opened their mouths to speak, but no words came to them.

Of course! Another repeat of clashing with Iapetos and Hotan!

The giggling of a little girl came from the cat as it leapt to the railing. In an instant, it morphed into a raven and flew into the shadows of the abandoned building. Talib looked back to the man in all black, determined to discover why he held power like the rest of them.

"Who are you and what power do you have?" he commanded, hoping he did not need to use his own element. "My name is Talib, and like you, I am immortal."

"Talib." The man peered down at the journal in his hand; its red leather cover caught his eye. "You are Hotan's brother…" There was a loneliness in the man's voice.

"Yes," Talib replied. "Is that written in that book there?"

"That … and more about my father." As if deciding, he looked to him with renewed determination. "My name is Iapetos. Has… has he ever mentioned me to you?"

"No. I have not seen Hotan since the fourth century." Iapetos frowned at his reply. Talib also frowned, thinking about the answer to his own question. "Who exactly is your father?"

"Hotan." He gave another forlorn look to the book in his hands. "But sadly, he says nothing about me in this journal. I see that he has even abandoned you…"

"Y-yes." So many questions flew in his mind about the immortal who stood before him. "Iapetos, what is your element?"

The dark eyes looked back to him as he sat on the top stair and whispered mournfully, "Death."

What a horrible element to possess. How does one accept that they can only bring Death and never be fully in control? Why did Hotan not want to help him or even allow me to help him? If only I could have been there for Iapetos, even for one moment...

He pulled back his hood, unbuckled the leather strap, and removed the plague mask. Iapetos stared wide-eyed at the silver-eyed man with long silver hair. Talib wiped the sweat from his face; he wanted to find out more about this element of Death. His stomach knotted as his logic sorted the information. Instincts rolled through his mind, and he latched onto those sensations for guidance.

"Iapetos, are you responsible for the Black Plague?" Iapetos winced at the question and sighed. "I imagine your element is difficult to control, being a segment of Rebirth itself..."

"The plague started when I got close to Hotan." Swallowing, he locked eyes with him as he explained. "It used to create earthquakes, but something has changed. As I got closer to him, people started getting horribly sick. Not knowing if there were any other immortals in existence, I sought him out. Naturally, I ended up here in London. A small black cat led me here, and I found this journal which explains there are more of us, but I'm not mentioned..."

"How do you know you are Hotan's son?" A chill slithered up his back; Talib was afraid to hear the answer. "Have you even met Hotan?"

Iapetos covered half his face with his hand as he recalled the painful memory. "I remember being in a dark place; I was choking, the ocean's salt was bitter on my tongue, and my lungs stung. There in that abyss, I heard him calling for my mother, Liora. She looked to me and told me she would give me life, so that my father would have the son he prayed for. Then I found myself banished, naked and afraid… alone and angry. I know that I have seen him, but I can't remember … as if it's locked away. It hurts to even attempt to look within myself for him."

So much had been stolen from us both. If Hotan had listened to reason, would this plague have even happened? Over sixty percent of the world's population was wiped out over his denial to face his son or even his own brother. Mistakes built on top of mistakes…

The plague mask dropped at his feet and tumbled down the stairs, flinging potpourri across the steps. Talib leaned against the wall; he knew the feeling of pain when trying to remember certain moments in the past.

"What has he done to us?" Looking into the bleakness of the ceiling, his emotions swelled with remorse. "Hotan, what are you doing to us? Have we met many times before and you broke us apart? Why do we both feel like we have seen one another and spoken?"

"Yes, I feel like I can trust you, as if you've done something for me…" Iapetos was at a loss for words before he gripped the book tighter. "Is it possible that I have discovered his journals in the past, and he's been cautious not to write about me this time?"

"That is something he would do." Talib rubbed the back of his neck. Suddenly, he had a realization. "Abigail, are you still here?"

"Abigail?" Iapetos stood, alarmed. "You weren't alone?"

A black cat raced up the stairs from the shadows; it giggled like a small child as it weaved through Talib's legs.

"I beg you, please talk to me." Furrowing his brow, he pleaded with her, "Was it not you who led us here?"

She paused, looking up at Iapetos with her little yellow eyes, then back to Talib. "Yes, I did."

"Who is she?" The tension in Iapetos increased, but Talib motioned for him to calm himself. "What is she?"

"Iapetos, this is Abigail, the element of Body." She sat and began licking her paw. "My dear, why have you brought us here?"

"To give you two a chance to remember." She ran up the stairs past Iapetos and stopped at the doorway. "For centuries, I have watched Hotan destroy you two in hopes of buying more time to undo his power. In the end, it has only caused more destruction; now, it is distorting everyone's power. The journal must stay in exchange for not having your memories wiped. He will return soon enough and wonder who has been here."

Talib looked to Iapetos, and they shuddered from the idea of her phrasing—destroy you. Looking to the book in his hands, Iapetos turned and marched back to the room where he came from. After a minute or two, he came out empty-handed. It frightened Talib how easily he made the decision.

The feeling of my body turning to ash is a new memory I would gladly give back … but this, this time I have forgotten?

"I'd rather give up my search for him and join you in your travels," Iapetos said as he walked down the stairs. He picked up the mask and handed it to Talib. "If we can create distance from him, my element should stop killing at this rate. I apologize for my numbness to the damage it causes."

"Understood." Peering down at his mask, Talib agreed with the decisions made on his behalf. "We will leave London and find a safe haven to exchange information. Perhaps we have answers for one another."

"Something tells me we do." He opened the door but looked to the black cat peering down the rails from the loft. "What about her?"

As he tightened the leather straps and pulled his hood over his silver hair, he looked to the lonesome girl hiding as a cat. "She stays with him, always. Someone must keep record of the damage he continues to do to himself and the world…"

So we did travel together after all. For a long time perhaps? Was Iapetos there in the Roanoke Colony before we came back with supplies? Is that where Hotan discovered we had met and erased this time from me?

The door thumped shut behind them, and Iapetos followed closely. With caution, they weaved through the ashen streets with only the eerie orange glow of the fires to light their way. After several turns and blocks, they came to Talib's door. He threw an arm out to signal Iapetos to stop. Locking eyes, he pointed to the ashen ground where fresh steps led inside, and the door was still ajar. A sickening twist in his stomach told him what he feared—*Hotan is inside waiting for me. Whether he is aware that Iapetos is with me is hard to say.*

Talib quickly changed plans. He pointed for them to go further down the block and motioned to be quiet. He looked to the windows, praying he would not find Hotan peeking down on them. Seeing the dark panes free of prying eyes, he picked up pace. They marched toward the harbor, and Iapetos followed without hesitation or rebuttal. Even if his brother had watched them walk away, he looked like a doctor searching houses for bodies. He was avoiding looking at Iapetos at all costs and he was fortunate to have put the plague mask back on. The dock echoed under them as they walked. At the end, a sleeping sailor waited with his feet propped on a crate near a flickering lantern.

"You there," Talib bellowed ominously from within the cone beak.

His only reply was a groan and snore. Talib kicked the man's heels from their perch, and the sailor stumbled to his feet, swinging wildly and angrily. Talib caught his forearm and slammed a heavy pouch of gold coins into his palm. The man broke free and opened the bag to count its contents.

"You two looking to get the hell out of London?" Placing the bag inside his coat, he whistled loudly. "We've got ourselves two more bunkmates!"

"Aye…" grumbled someone on the ship.

After a long moment of silence, a plank banged against the dock. It didn't matter whether this ship took them to Spain, Italy, Africa or even India. All that mattered was gaining distance between Hotan and Iapetos, so the Black Plague could be nullified and Talib could help him control the powers of Death.

The deck of the ship was filled with barrels marked with the ship's guild mark. Iapetos twisted his mouth, lifting an eyebrow to signal his unease. Many of the guilds did not allow backdoor-deal passengers without the guild master's approval. Not even a captain had the authority to sign off on anyone, regardless of how much they paid. It was a sacred trust between the crew and the guild master, so that funding and supplies ran smoothly and were profitable. A sailor with a lantern coughed under his bandanna, waving them into the captain's cabin.

A weathered old man popped the cork off a bottle of scotch, cursing under his breath. He glanced up groggily as he finished filling his glass. He took down the sharp liquid and banged it against the desk, sending a rolled map tumbling to the floor. Iapetos grabbed Talib's shoulder, but Talib motioned for him to be calm.

"Exactly who do you think you are that you can buy passage on a guild-owned ship?" He snorted a grotesque sound deep in the back of his throat. "Not to say I don't blame you for wanting a ship out of this hell hole."

Talib unbuckled the cone mask, and a coy smile came across his face. "What if the guild master wishes to ride his own ship?"

The old man squinted his eyes, and Talib let the hood fall onto his shoulders. "By God, it is you."

"Y-you're a guild master?" Iapetos had a perplexed look on his face. "Why on earth would you bother?"

Rasping laughter came from the captain as he rose to his feet to shake Talib's hand. "It's been a while. I cannot thank you enough for the investment and chance you took on me, sir."

"I see you have taken my advice to heart, old man," he said, chuckling. "This is … my apprentice. I wish one day for him to take my place, but until then, he will need many years of hands-on experience in all parts of the business."

"Aye, aye." He shook Iapetos' hand, looking him over with great interest. "Is he your nephew?"

Talib blinked, peering over at Iapetos before answering with caution. "Why, yes … how did you know?'

The old captain tapped at his temple with a warm smile. "These eyes aren't as good as they used to be, but the genes in your family are strong. You two are built from head to toe like toy soldiers meant to stand side by side. Even your chin and brow line match."

"We will leave you be, Captain." Talib opened the door, motioning Iapetos to follow. "Sorry to disturb you at such an hour."

"It's not every day I meet the guild master," he said as he poured himself another round. "Glad to see you in good health despite the fall of London."

Talib nodded, and a grim look came across his pale face. He walked across the deck, looking for a quiet spot near the railing on the other side of the barrels which crowded the ship. Iapetos marched close behind. They watched the crew members who took no heed in where they were going. Iapetos gripped Talib's shoulder as he made it to the edge.

"Exactly what is your plan?" He motioned to the ship. "Are we to hide on this vessel and pray Hotan does not find us?"

"Not exactly." Talib pulled his hand off and leaned on the railing. "First, we need to take you some place far from people to master your powers. The wilds of India, Africa, anywhere such as that should be fitting for the task."

"And what if he follows?" He paced behind him, his heavy steps echoing on the wooden planks beneath them. "Hunts us down?"

"He will not," Talib murmured. The morning light made the ship's shadowed silhouette on the water ominous. "I think if we stay clear of him, not meddle with whatever his tasks are, we should be safe. He will avoid us, and we will oblige."

"Then what is the plan? What else do you intend to do with me?" He paused, his black-eyed stare burning into Talib's back.

"I will teach you everything I know." Straightening himself, he turned and locked stares, his silver eyes flashing in the sunlight. "Who we were, when we became immortal, how I survived all this time without anyone, and how to use that dreadful curse attached to your soul."

Strangely, I can feel the heaviness of regret lifting from my soul as I see this. Even Iapetos' eyes feel at peace as I look upon this forgotten moment from my past. What travels did we have? This was the trade ship from India and back. The old man had convinced me he knew how to navigate the southern point of Africa and had proven himself. We would have made a good distance from Hotan in this first trip together. India… what a wonderful place to have gotten lost in to help Iapetos. How much time passed before he mastered controlling Death? Was Judgment able to overpower it so easily?

12

A FAMILIAR
TASTE OF POISON

1587 AD

Watching the time and effort put into this forgotten life is sickening. Iapetos and I were lifelong companions, both victims of Hotan's plight, both seeking the comfort of companionship after years of being alone. It took decades to wrangle the full depths of the element of Death. He could devour the soul of any living thing, and when the power did so, he could not bring them back. Not even the element of Rebirth could bring back a soul which had left the realm of the living.

We travelled from one wild frontier to the next until we had to pull ourselves back to manage neglected business affairs. With him as an aid, it is clear why I was so successful with capturing roots and connections on a larger scale. Why had I not realized all these forgotten moments with Iapetos? There were days of laughter and rejoicing, and as decades turned to centuries, we gave up on Hotan. Instead, we turned to adventures and exploration. We helped those *who were brave enough to take chances and put their mortality to the test. We were tattooed angels, guarding the first settlers to the Americas.*

The ocean was a frightening force of nature to cross and face. Back then, we were unaware of the hurricane and storm seasons, let alone the massive Mid-Atlantic trench which interacted with the world in unpredictable ways. We spent months without seeing a hint of land or even a bird in the sky. It was a daunting sign of how far into its expanse we had travelled. Our advantage was our immortality. No threats of hunger, scurvy, illness, or malnourishment would plague our bodies. As time went on, rats became fearless, willing to nip and eat at the flesh of those stuck in the ship's cramped quarters.

"Are we sure he's not already there?" Iapetos' voice broke Talib from his thoughts where he leaned on the railing of the ship. "Talib, are you even ready to face him?"

"I doubt we will ever be ready," he huffed, staring across the endless horizon of navy blue. "At least this time we can attempt to prevent another disaster like so many times before."

I remember sailing back, but this… this is not what I remember?

"With each day that we get closer to this new land, I cannot help but feel…" Iapetos paused, staring down at his hands with a worried expression, "that he's already there."

Something went horribly wrong here. Roanoke's population disappeared without a trace. Was I there? Did my powers play a part in its disappearance?

"If that is the case, we have a plan intact." Breaking away, he left Iapetos to his thoughts as he stared at the endless waves sloshing against the hull.

I was there on the first trip, but how did even Captain John White not realize it? Why are there no records? What happened to all those people… all those innocent lives?

"Ah! Mister Bithloa!" A booming voice came from near the mast, and he halted in his steps. "I wanted to thank you for helping fund this mission, good sir!"

All this time, I thought I just simply provided funds, but I did go. I went across the Atlantic to Roanoke Island with Iapetos by my side. My God, what happened?

"Ah, Captain White!" The captain tightly gripped his hand with a vigorous shake. "You must really stop showering me with gratitude. As I mentioned before, I have my own personal interests involved here. A chance to be the first to establish trade, make a profit from it all."

"You can insist all you want, Mister Bithloa, but without your funding, we would have been short on many of the supplies, including rations." He released his crushing grip, gracing Talib's throbbing hand with the smooth tap of rolled parchment. "As promised, here is a copy of the coastal map I have been working on."

Talib unrolled the map, noticing that John had taken the time to add elegant touches of watercolor that made the waterways stand out against the land. "You have a skilled hand for mapping as an art, Captain."

"So I've been told," he laughed. "Is your benefactor well?"

Looking over his shoulder, Talib saw Iapetos pale as he stared at one point on the horizon. "He will be fine once we dock. How far away do you suspect we are?"

"A day or so," he replied, scratching his beard and still watching Iapetos. "You may want to check on the young lad. That's a look of fear if I ever saw one. My men said seasick, but that's the look a man gets when he thinks he's facing the end of his existence or going to Hell."

Leaving the captain behind, Talib went to stand near Iapetos. His shoulders were tense, and he gripped the railing tight. A shudder shook him from head to foot and back again. He opened his mouth but stopped. There were no words of comfort for what was starting to happen. Hotan was indeed there on the shore of the Americas, possibly even waiting for them both on Roanoke Island. Hotan's intentions were not clear to them. Over two hundred years had passed with no signs of him, yet he waited for them on the shores of a wild, untamed land.

It was never about if I was ready; Hotan had planned so much of this in advance. Is it possible that he requested Abigail to arrange for us to meet in London? Was he heeding my advice from thousands of years prior and allowing the centuries to pass and the relationship to grow between Iapetos and I? I can see it, but why destroy what was a time of peace?

As the elements of Rebirth and Death came near one another, they drew their wielders ever closer. The abrasive feeling pulled at Iapetos' soul like magnets being drawn together. It took a great deal for him to resist the enraging sensation it brought on as Rebirth coaxed the element of Death to lash out at the world around it. The unstable power within Hotan reacted violently to Death because it was part of the element itself. Perhaps it was due to Death's stability—that is until they came too close to one another. Throughout the years, there were times when we sensed Hotan near and chose to venture far away, doing everything we could to learn more about the powers he had bestowed upon his unborn child.

"If I start to fail, use your power to send me away, Talib." A cold sweat seeped from his pores. "We are about a day out; I can feel him."

"I wish I had wings like you, so I could just fly away from it. Are you going to be able to keep it under control?"

Iapetos shuddered. No words came to him as his element tangled itself into knots. "I, I think so." A drop of sweat trickled down his cheeks, and he winced and clenched his teeth. "I must admit, I never thought it would be this painful. Then again, I can see how in the past I would have fled to the point of interference, angry and ready to fight."

"We can only assume it is something he has designed. Just as I was drawn to the areas where your elements converged." The sun faded, falling slowly and steadily toward the darkening waters below. "Let us try to remain sharp. Neither of us knows his intentions in cornering us here in the Americas. I can assure you that he is aware of the closeness of our travels. He is far more clever than either of us. Honestly, he has outwitted me plenty of times…"

It seems I was aware that things might go south there. And to think, Iapetos had such an adverse reaction when trying to maintain stability with his element. Hotan's powers have a substantial pull on all of us, including Death, but what was he planning? What was the purpose of remaining connected to them and continuing this madness of uncontrollable power?

The screeching of gulls was a warm welcome, and the sun rose high in the sky. Iapetos was still pale and sickly in complexion and movement. The crew suspected that he had come down with scurvy or even fallen victim to dehydration like so many who died on the trip across the Atlantic. He held his stomach, but Talib knew it was the sensation of his element and soul struggling with one another. It was a relief to see the land, and as they drew ever closer, landmarks made themselves known. Captain White's map proved most efficient; Talib mused if history would even recognize his skills later.

Each person had a task awaiting them when their feet hit the beaches of Roanoke Island. Captain White would venture out to the local natives to establish trade and peaceful rela-tions—essential to survive the first winter in this new place. The more experienced and stronger hands set to work clearing the trees and staging the walls of the colony to create a safe barrier between them and the carnivorous wildlife. Women and children had also come, including John's daughter. They had their own tasks of surveying supplies and mending clothes and equipment for both the men who were staying in the colony and the sailors who intended to depart again for England. Once they were settled, John and the core crew would resupply and head back across the Atlantic with no guarantee of returning.

Within a week, they had finished the walls, hoisted up and built the Governor's lodge, and started on individual cabins for the families who would call this place home. There were no signs of Hotan, yet the struggling within Iapetos' soul hinted that he was not far off. Captain White returned with excellent news from the natives, and soon they were trading and learning life skills from one another. Everything in Roanoke went smoothly except for one daunting detail: they lacked the supplies to last through a hard winter. Determined to maintain peace with the natives, the idea of raiding them for their winter reserves was out of the question.

As the leaves changed to brilliant reds and oranges, the wind carried in the colder weather. There were still no signs of Hotan, but the local hunters spoke of a winged man passing through the area. Iapetos' struggle continued; his body was in so much excruciating pain that being touched caused him to scream out on multiple occasions. The priest feared he was possessed and would bring about the colony's downfall. Superstition was just another disease in the way the world functioned then. Food was rationed out in meager proportions, and hunger rolled in their stomachs.

"Mister Bithloa." Captain White's voice was grim as they huddled in their heavy coats against the chilling winds. "The crew wants to set sail soon before the bay freezes over. I intend to go with them to ask the Queen and a dear friend in Raleigh for support. If they can survive this winter, I am sure we can return in time for the next with supplies."

"You are wagering even your new granddaughter's life on an outcome you cannot promise, dear John." Talib stared into the thick forest that surrounded them, hoping to see a glimpse of his brother among its shadows. "Have you at least left a contingency plan in place in case you are delayed? In case winter comes again before you gain the Queen's blessing?"

"Of course. I have even asked the chief to aid them in travelling to the nearest port. There is an active lumber trade not far from here where they should be able to get word home or even take the women and children back to England." Sighing, he patted Talib's shoulder. "And if that task fails, I have left strict instructions. In fact, I made two more copies of my maps with markers of the tribes and expedition landing points for England, Spain, and anyone else who would recognize my name. Are you staying behind?"

"I do not know. Though I may send my benefactor back to England until his health improves." Talib's thoughts were conflicted; *Is Iapetos too stubborn to leave after struggling this far.* "If he can make it to the ship at all…"

"Understood." Shivering, the captain's hot breath puffed out of his lips onto his numb fingers. "Please let me know in the morning what you plan to do. We will depart as the tide rolls out after sunset."

"Thank you, John." They shook hands, and each walked back to their cabins.

Opening the door, Talib was greeted by a flurry of black feathers. Iapetos was doubled over, leaning on the table; physical movement was laborious for him. He panted, markings crawled across his skin, and sweat dripped from his chin as if burning up from a fever. Closing the door, Talib swiftly drew the lock before turning to stare at the losing battle washing over Iapetos.

"He's horribly close," groaned Iapetos, continuing his internal fight. "I'm… I'm going to have to leave in the cover of night. I can't get them to go away."

His wings folded reluctantly as pain rattled their owner. Talib had seen them a few times but not this close. The feathers were as black as a crow's, but the bulk of them seemed tattered, broken, even rotting away—fitting wings for the element of Death. A flash of off white caught Talib's eyes. In the folds and flurry of black were glimpses of bare bone, a sickening aspect. *I cannot believe he can carry his own weight on such frail, decrepit appendages; to carry me as well is amazing.*

"Understood." Talib said. He paused momentarily and added, "But can you even wait for nightfall?"

"I pray so." They exchanged a cold stare. "If not, I may risk leaving in front of them in hopes of not repeating a decade's worth of deaths."

Swallowing, he agreed; seeing the Angel of Death was far safer than coming into contact with his power. Talib could feel the waves lurching out from Iapetos; his wings flared out each time one gripped him. Iapetos fought to fold them back, and a sense of shame overcame him each time he failed to hide the outward struggle. The cabin was cramped, so it didn't take much for the feathers at the tip of his wings to brush the wall next to the door where Talib stood. Reaching out a hand, he wondered, *Is there a way for Judgment to soothe the turmoil raging at Iapetos' core?*

"Do not touch me!" roared Iapetos, his eyes wide with fright. "If you use your power, I will lose what little control I have. I must manage this alone, or I will never learn to control it in Hotan's wake."

Retracting his fingers and forming a fist in frustration, he unlatched the door. "Lock this after I leave. I intend to do something about this. Do you suspect he is in the colony?"

"Y-yes." The door smacked loudly behind him, and the latch locked as Iapetos isolated himself, desperate for help.

He looked around the colony and its well-over a hundred occupants. Considering all the time he had spent on the ship with these individuals, the chance his brother could blend in was nearly impossible. Ears open, eyes sharp, he walked through the cabins and tents, looking from face to face. Eavesdropping into conversations, he searched for clues of something out of the ordinary from the routines they had created since landing. As he rounded the far end of the settlement, a woman rushed out of a nearby cabin. He flinched from the speed in which she fled toward him; he halted his search and brought his full attention to her panic.

She sprinted to him with urgency on her face as she called to him, "Talib! I need your help! Quickly!"

He stood frozen as she tugged at his coat sleeve. Staring down at her, he took in her pale face and the dark locks of curly hair which fell out from under her bonnet. Her dark brown eyes reflected his stone-faced expression. Her fingers tightened further on his coat and gave another hard tug. Puffing out her bottom lip and furrowing her brow, her cheeks reddened with frustration. Still, he stood like a marble statue, unresponsive to the frightened woman pulling at him.

"Please, we need you!" she pleaded. "Why do you look at me so uncaring!"

He furrowed his brow and smirked. "Because ... you got her eye color all wrong, Abigail."

Gasping, she laughed and shifted the eye color to the correct one. "Is that better?"

"Yes." Sighing, he was relieved to see her in human form for a change. "I suspect Hotan waits for me in the cabin?"

Nodding, she looked back to it, and her smile faded. "He has a plan to help Iapetos. He's come back around to the caring man we adore, Talib. I believe he means well this time around."

"Is that why he has allowed us to stay together all this time?" He raised an eyebrow. "Following advice I have certainly insisted upon at least once in some forgotten century?"

"Very true." She hugged him, catching him off guard.

"Should I be frightened to go in?"

"N-no." Rubbing her face hard against him, she squeezed him tighter. "It's just been so long since I've had a hug. You always gave such wonderful hugs…"

Another sigh steamed out of his nostrils as he hugged her back. "You can always start following me around instead, Abigail. You were never forced to follow him…"

"I know…" Breaking away, she wiped the tears from her face. "Don't keep him waiting. He may suspect we are plotting against him. He's still rather paranoid about things."

"Was the eye color on purpose?" Another tender smile crossed his face.

A giggle escaped her. Still wiping tears, she confessed, "Maybe…"

Taking a deep breath, he marched to the cabin. Gripping the latch, he gave one last look over his shoulder to Abigail. He didn't know the mental state his brother was in, but he had to trust her. *She has gotten me this far with clues and hints; why would she think this time is any different?* The door creaked open into the tight quarters. Hotan sat at a table with only a single candle, which wavered from the breeze the open door let in.

He gestured for Talib to take the empty chair across from him. The door slamming behind him sent chills across his body, and his muscles tensed. As usual, there was no smile or readable expression on Hotan's face as his dull green eyes watched him. Shivering in the cold darkness of the cabin, Talib marched to the chair and sat, unsure what negotiations would unfold.

"I'm sorry; I didn't think to make a fire." Hotan raised his eyebrows, looking to the hearth and back to him again. "I suppose I have forgotten the luxuries of being mortal, the sensations of heat and cold, of pain and pleasure."

"What do you wish to speak with me about, Brother?" Talib leaned back in the chair, observing the rags which clothed Hotan's body.

"Iapetos." Hotan's eyes were sharp as they connected with Talib's. "I see you've managed to help him stabilize and control his abilities?"

"Except when he is near you." Hotan broke the stare, ashamed of the news. "Do you know why?"

"It wasn't intentional…" Hotan grimaced as if in pain. "It still all comes back to my powers being too unstable, even after relieving so much of it on you and the others. Despite this, I am asking for your advice and, more importantly, your wisdom."

"I wished you had done so sooner." Talib's assertive tone made Hotan flinch like a child being scolded by a concerned parent. "I know you are very aware of the destruction your rash decisions have caused."

"And I fear more will happen as the wake of what I started begins to push further from me." Hotan rubbed the back of his neck and stared at the dancing flame atop the tallow candle which invaded his nostrils with its putrid smell. "I suspect my element is incomplete."

"Incomplete?" Talib leaned forward in his chair, motioning for him to continue with his theory. "How so?"

"Everyone else has met their element in some shape or form. All but myself. I have never been reincarnated, therefore, I have not evolved into the true meaning of what Rebirth represents. Life and death, the birth of a new existence rising from the ashes of the old." They both shifted, knowing what this meant for Hotan. "Which means I have to kill the unkillable..."

"How do you propose to do that?" Talib scratched his smooth jawline, trying to hide the anxiety this news brought over him. "I assume you have tried on your own but failed?"

There was a dull look in Hotan's pupils as they reflected the flickering flame of the candle. "More times than I should have. Often, I would back out, at least in the beginning. After a while, I hunted Iapetos, enraging him and praying his element could overcome my own. At least it would feel like justice to die at the hand of the son I have betrayed time and time again..."

Talib grunted. *This makes the situation far graver than I realized.* "So the element of Death is incapable of overpowering Rebirth?"

"Right." Blinking a few times, Hotan found the courage to meet Talib's stare again. "But it seems I would have to use my power to destroy or reincarnate itself. This might undo any spells I have set in motion ... including giving the others mortal lives. I am here to seek their guardian's opinion."

"Saphellia and the others would awaken?" Terror and excitement rattled him at the thought. "And what would happen to you?"

"Might awaken," he corrected. "As for me, rebirthing my element doesn't work like the tethering system I formed between myself, you, and the others. Instead, my power would become like a calm ball or seed. Someone will need to carry it within themselves for some time before it finds a suitable host to reincarnate into. Whether I will be this person before you or someone new is still unknown."

"And exactly how will it know there is a suitable host? How does it leave the carrier and enter the new host to begin with?" Leaning his elbows on the table, Talib filled with questions to consider before he could make a decision. "And even then, how would you transfer this seed into someone? What is the outcome? How long will it take? Decades? Hotan, there is much to resolve here before you take action."

"You are right." Covering his mouth, he hummed as he considered the questions offered and the others they created. "I need time to find answers. When I find them, I will meet with you again for advice, Brother, but it will take quite some time to begin the process of rebirthing my element. In the meantime, be aware that others may start to awaken because of it."

"Please consult me before you take action…" He furrowed his brow. "You do not have to do anything alone. It never ends well."

"I, I know." They both stood, ready to end their short meeting. "Oh, as for Iapetos…"

"Please leave him as he is," Talib barked; It was a threat, not a request. "He has done nothing wrong since the Black Plague in London."

"You're right." His eyes saddened as this fact was brought to light. "I am to blame for all his large mishaps, and even now, he struggles to keep himself contained."

"And he is failing. So much so that he intends to leave tonight to create distance to untangle himself." Talib shot an angry glare at Hotan, and again, he winced under his big brother's silver eyes. "I understand now that his powers may be beyond your control, but I cannot help but feel your meddling and abuse of your own abilities within the boy created this result."

"I cannot deny it." Again, the shame pulled his eyes away like a child who felt guilty for misbehaving. "I will keep my distance for now, but he may play a part in my final stage."

"Make sure it does not hurt him further." He opened the door, feeling his rage build toward Hotan.

"Wait!" Hotan's hand gripped his shoulder. "I need your help for one last thing."

Again, the sensation of his power snaking within me, but what for? Why here and now?

Hotan gained control of the element of Judgment within an instant. Talib's blue flames and tattoos came forward; the power peaked at an alarming speed. Failing to shove them back within himself, Talib was taken aback by the grin on his brother's face. Talib froze, frightened and unsure what it meant as it grew across Hotan's face.

"You are so close, Talib," Hotan said as he gripped tighter. Talib's flames shifted to a red hue, and his eyes widened. "This is the true color of your own power. Blue represents your connection to me, but this… this is not mine."

Puzzled, Talib stared at his hands with wonder. "R-red flames?" Closing his fist, he could still feel Hotan's grip on his powers. "Why did you show this to me? What is your plan, Brother?"

"I wanted to see for myself what I have speculated." Sighing, tears rolled down his cheeks. "I will take this chance to give you the boost I know you would never normally take. Without me around, you have used it on rare occasions, but I need you to bring Judgment into its full form, its final fruition."

"W-wait." The sensation tightened within his core. His soul squeezed in a new, startling way; it was like being on the edges of death. "Hotan, what do you intend to make me do?"

"Simply save these people. We both know the captain will not be back in time, and winter is coming too soon for them to make up their poor supplies." Looking out to where a crowd gathered in awe to see Talib on fire, yet not expressing pain or fear, he gave a reassuring nod. "You, the captain, his crew, and all who plan to return to England shall do so tonight. As for the rest of the colonists, they shall leave behind this failed attempt and will be accepted into the ranks and arms of the natives who know this land best. Iapetos, leave here now, and leave behind the memories you have of me and Talib along with this place."

Talib flinched, attempting to refuse the commanding words which echoed through the minds of those they were intended for. The overwhelming reach of his power was terrifying as it touched over a hundred colonists and sailors, stretched itself through the dense forest, and grasped the minds and hearts of the natives who lived miles away. His body ached—a sensation he hadn't felt since the infancy of learning how to use his powers. Waves of power exploded from him unlike anything he had experienced before. Tears fell from his eyes; he knew Hotan would request the same from him as he had from Iapetos. Their time of peace and companionship would be ripped away by his own element— by his own brother.

"And Talib, leave behind your memories of Iapetos, of coming to this colony, of all the times you have ever crossed paths with me and my son. You shall continue your tasks as guardian as before, but know that someone may awaken at any moment." His voice softened before he continued, "And once more, I am sorry to do this to you. I promise, in time, all three of us will gather, and I will have my solution."

Why did he find it so necessary to make me forget? Did he fear I would tell him he was wrong? That I would interrupt his plans? Maybe I would have, but I should have been made aware of his plans and given the opportunity to help him of my own volition. What happened to the trust we once carried with one another in the fields? Did I mislead you or leave you hurt at some point to create this wedge between us?

I always assumed John White had mistakenly thought I was on the ship the first time. In fact, he had not been a victim of his memories being wiped. He did what he promised, but it took three years before he was cleared to travel back. The poor man had left behind his daughter and newly born granddaughter. I wish I could assure him, tell him that they did survive by integrating with the locals thanks to my element of Judgment.

For once, Hotan's abuse of my power led to something good, and thankfully, the violent cycle of turning Iapetos and me to ash had ceased. This means what happened barely thirty years later was the start of Hotan moving forward with reincarnating himself and his element. What other unknown costs are there?

13

FORFEIT

1611 AD

I know this forest, though not much of it remains in modern times. This moment, yes, this is the first time one of us awakened. There we were, thirty years later, in the beginning of the monstrous wake of Hotan's horrible decision and refusal to let me help him. At least I now understand what happened as I see it all unfold without the forgotten bits and clouded mindset. Was it worth putting them through the torturous events? Some even made their way into the pages of history, Brother. This could not have been the life you intended for them—to awaken to harsh disasters made from man, nature, and our own, and to have memories of the vile actions from this century.

The horse under him huffed with each stride. Leaning deeper into his saddle, Talib pushed the hooved beast further, faster toward Hondarribia. He had felt the release of power from one of the Levites and travelled in pursuit for days, changing out two horses in the rush after receiving news the Inquisition was also happening in the area. Talib feared what would happen in these days of turmoil and chaos. According to the merchant he had spoken with in the last town, the area had become a target of the Spanish Inquisition.

Worse, the aftermath of the Basque Witch Trails commenced, further stirring the rebellion of people who knew many of the victims. One battle had been fought in the seaside port in 1521, but Talib assumed the presence of the witch hunters was another cover for scouting the town—an excuse to secure a valuable trade hub. As history proved time and time again, it would be a matter of time before unrest transformed to a siege like he had seen in the century before.

By 1638, barely twenty-seven years later, the Siege of Fuenterrabia unfolded and left three hundred survivors in a destroyed city. I think the horrific side of this was the number of women and children who died in their wake. The strong-minded females in this town were responsible for its success, but they made a prime target for the Inquisitors looking to justify the mishaps of the Basque Witch Trails.

Rain fell steadily harder as the ocean and city came into view. He felt surges of the element of Intelligence waving out from where he rode over the top of the hillside. The horse coughed and wheezed; if Talib dared to stop now, the horse wouldn't go any farther. Swallowing, his muscles tensed. The rain thickened, attempting to wash out the town his eyes locked onto. His clothes were pasted against him from the cold downpour, and steam rolled off his horse's overheating body. Time was of the essence. There was no mistaking; Fae had awoken and was attempting to use her element. *Why is it coming in short, harsh waves?*

The horse's hooves clattered against the cobblestone street, announcing his arrival. He focused on the pull of her power and galloped as close as his senses and the town would allow. She was in the courthouse. The Inquisitors had targeted her, and there was no telling what he would barge into. His horse skidded to a halt, foam dripping from its mouth. It struggled to catch its breath after being pushed so hard by the urgency of its rider. Two well-armored and armed Inquisitors stood guard at the court-house door. They unsheathed their swords at his approach, ready to prevent him from entering. He did not slow his march or even grant them a look of acknowledgment.

He paused as the tips of their swords pointed at his chest. An angry flash came across his silver eyes and sweat formed across both men's faces in reaction. Their hands tightened, and they readied their stances for a fight.

"You shall stand here until I am finished," he commanded, glaring at them as he pushed past without a word spoken or action taken in response. "You will cease what you are doing at this very minute!"

He marched through the doors and found himself in the back of a giant crowd. Pushing and making his way down the aisle, he reached the floor of the room. He was appalled by the scene that flooded his eyes. Fae sat shackled on the floor, panting, beaten, and hanging on the edge of consciousness. Auburn strands of hair stuck to her skin, glued there with sweat and blood. Her bottom lip was swollen, split, and still bleeding. A red line rolled down to her chin where it dripped, *tip-tap-tip-tap*. She was pale, with red, purple, and yellowish patches decorating her exposed skin. Metal cuffs dug into her wrists, and her fingers were black and blue.

Often, they broke the fingers of women under the excuse of preventing them from casting spells. It was all lies. An act of disgraceful human greed using violence and fear to achieve goals, wants, and satisfy sick pleasures for destruction.

The Chief Inquisitor was stopped mid-stride with his whip. The leather tethers adorned with iron spikes dangled and swayed.

His mirror-like, silver armor was splattered with blood from the punishment he had ripped across Fae's back. Long, red clothes flowed from under it, showcasing his rank, position, and affiliation. It disgusted Talib to see a cross worn on such vile creatures.

Iron. The hard, brittle metal soaked in the blood of so many victims. The whip's spikes, the shackles, and on the table not far from the Chief Inquisitor, an assortment of tools and devices were all stained red. They assured onlookers that iron reacted to witches and evil spirits, but he knew it was to help coax the wild screams of pain from the victims. When watchful eyes were turned away, they coated these with salt and anything else that would add to the agony of open wounds. The necklace which clanked against his chest plate had the symbol of a cross guarded by a branch and sword. Around it was written their motto, inspired from Psalm 73:

"Rise up, O Lord, and judge thy cause."

If they had grasped the lessons in Psalm 73, they would know they had become the arrogant and wicked it spoke of. It was they who were strong-bodied, wearing pride as their necklace, and clothing themselves in violence. Yes, their evil imaginations had no limits, and they scoffed and spoke with malice. Their mouths lay claim to heaven, but their tongues aimed to possess the earth and all who walked on it before them. Psalm 73 was one I had favored before all of this, and to see it used as a justification for the wretched on-goings before me twisted my stomach. In my mind, one verse from the Psalm rang true:

"Behold, these are the wicked..."

"What are you doing?" Talib started toward the Inquisitor. "Answer me! Loudly so all can hear you!"

"I-I am beating a confession from her." The man was baffled by his own reply at the command of a stranger. "Who are you? What are you?"

"It does not matter." Talib held out an expecting hand. "Give me the keys to her shackles."

"Y-yes." Fumbling at his belt loop, he found the key and gave it to him without hesitation. "What do you intend to do with her?"

"Rescue her." The iron shackles clunked to the ground, and Fae slumped forward onto him, moaning and shivering. "Was she innocent, Inquisitor?"

"What?" Several times the man had reached for his sword but was unable to finish the motion. The element of Judgment was still pulling the strings; Talib owned every fiber of the man before him. "This is witchcraft!"

"Was she innocent from the start! Answer so the court will know!" His bark made all in the room flinch. "Tell them your true purpose for being here!"

"I-I chose her because she is clever and could pose a threat." The watching court whispered at the unsettling answer. "It is our job to rid the world not only of witches, but women and men who would challenge the laws and authority which oversees them."

Sweat poured from the man as he covered his mouth, frightened at his own confession. Lugging Fae over his shoulder, Talib stared at the fearful man who was no longer the beast he had come into town as. He shook, knowing the angry eyes around him recalled all the excuses, and lives he had taken to get there. Satisfied the confession had set the rebellion in motion, Talib tightened his arm around Fae and started for the door. The crowd parted like the Red Sea; no one wanted to stop the mysterious stranger. The Inquisitor would be lucky to leave the room alive in his wake. Ignoring the growing aggression in the room, he made his way to the door where he paused and placed his palm flat against it. Looking over his shoulder, he gave them one last instruction.

"You will forget the girl and I were ever here. Instead, you were holding a trial on whether the Chief Inquisitor's purpose here for a witch hunt was justifiable. You have heard his confession of aiming to keep everyone fearful of oppositional forces with violent beatings of anyone deemed a threat."

Perhaps I was the one who seeded the cause of the Siege that lay waste to this city and its people. Sadly though, it was not I who put the Inquisition into play, destroying so many innocent lives before it reached this breaking point.

Pushing against the door, Talib left the sea of roaring and screaming mouths directed at the devil standing in the back of the room. The two guards observed the siege within the courthouse with paling faces. Talib looked to his horse, and she was still panting, her hocks shaking from the exhaustion. He dared not push the poor beast any farther. The horse had done its job by getting him there in time to save Fae. There was no telling what would have happened if she continued to push her power outward in ever larger waves. He still did not know if she was aware of who she was or what she was doing, but it could wait until he nursed her back to health.

Looking at the well across from the building, he saw the decorated horses of the Spanish Inquisition squad at his back. He smirked and thought, *A large war horse such as these could carry two people across its back. Better yet, I would hinder their ability to escape the wake of the violence they had set in motion.* Glancing to a guard, he gave him a toothy grin.

"Which horse belongs to the Chief Inquisitor?" Without hesitation, they pointed to the broad chestnut Andalusian, one of Spain's treasured horse breeds and an uncommon coat color.

"Thank you. Remember, he gave it to a family as recompense for one of his victims."

"Y-yes." The soldier nodded to the other, confessing further that they were aware of the chief's dealings. "One of many families…"

He positioned Fae gently over the saddle. It was awkward sitting on the back half of the horse, but the saddle would provide some padding for the ride. His eyes locked onto the bleeding gashes and grooves that the whip had dug into the flesh of her back. The last thing he wanted was to add to her agony. With a sigh, he was thankful he wouldn't need to use the stirrups and reigns to lead the horse—another bonus to being the element of Judgment. Fae groaned and whimpered as the horse started down the cobblestone street. His heart sunk at her broken appearance; if he had been there sooner, he could have stopped the beating before it escalated. Sweat poured over her as a fever began to take hold. The wounds swelled, and he coaxed the horse to pick up its pace. He needed to get someplace safe to clean her wounds before they became infected.

It took her a very long time to wake up. I settled for a small mountain cottage away from society to await recovery. It was a blessing that she was awakened enough not to need food or water, but she slept for over two months before coming out of her coma. It was frightening when her eyes finally opened; I did not know if she knew who I was, who she was…

Talib paced the floor as he glanced over at Fae who was still deep in her sleep. Her wounds healed in the first few weeks, but that was months ago. A creak from the bed brought his steps to a stop. Peering over, his heart skipped a beat with hope. She cringed, and a moan of discomfort came from her for the first time since he had taken her from her torturer. He held his breath, unsure if he should rush to her or wait further.

She fumbled her hand to her forehead and rasped, "Water, water, please…"

"Of course." He rushed to the ladle and scooped water out of the bucket by the table. "Here…"

She sat up, shaken and feeble, eager to quench the dryness of her lips and mouth. After gulping it down, she sighed in relief and took in deep breaths. Looking up, her dark blue eyes froze as they met his silver irises. Her shoulders tensed, and she paled. Her forehead creased as her awareness increased. She connected the memories at an alarming rate. If anyone could grasp the severity of their situation, it was Fae. After several minutes of silence and watching her eyes dance side to side, she sighed.

"Talib," she whispered, breaking the tension and bringing him instant relief. "I see the spell broke after all."

"Only yours." His voice was soft as he informed her of the news. "I take it you remember who you are?"

"Indeed, and all the mortal lives in between." She frowned but forced a smile back onto her face. "I am glad to see our trust in you as guardian proved a good choice. Thinking back, you checked on me at least a few times. And then, just in Hondarribia, when I fell victim to the Inquisition, you saved me."

"Yes." Talib's face reddened. "I may have abused my own power in a moment of rage. I may have added fuel to a fire that may claim more innocent lives."

"It was rightfully placed, and you did no one harm." She twisted, placing her feet on the floor. "Good lord, how long have I been lying here?"

They looked to the skin and bone of her legs. She may not have needed food or water while in her coma, but the state of her body before awakening had taken its toll. She had been denied several luxuries, and her power let loose in a desperate attempt to survive. This had added to suspicions that she was indeed a witch or possessed by the Devil himself. She had gone without food and water before Talib arrived, and now, she needed to build herself up to a healthy plateau.

"Two months at the very least." She grimaced at his response. "Fae, I fear I…"

"As I recall, there is always a fire burning." She huffed as she struggled to stand but failed. "My body feels so horribly cold and weak…"

"I am sorry; perhaps I should have somehow fed you…" Pulling her arm over his shoulders, he helped her to the chair by the hearth. "I suppose I could have done a better job."

"No, you are fine." She shivered, enjoying the heat from the fire. "It's not like I am hungry. I'm sure you would have fed me if I had showed signs of needing food. All this damage is from being imprisoned, beaten, and the failed attempts to use my power."

He handed her the blanket from the bed and started for the door. "I will retrieve supplies from the nearby village. Rest."

"We will have much to discuss when you return." The gleam in her eyes when she spoke sent a chill across his spine.

We spent the whole winter there, trying to figure out why she woke and what complications it would bring. Looking back to what little I remember of Hama involving Geliah, if it was done in a moment of panic, he would have awoken. I am troubled by the nagging sensation that if my memories at Roanoke Colony had not been taken from me, then I would know why she awoke at this time versus all the other lives. Hotan had begun the process, and I could only assume he had found the answers to those horrifying questions I asked.

14

SHADOW ON THE SUN

1772 AD

My dear friend Lucius was next to awaken. To this day, he has not forgiven himself for the suffering his power caused in India in the late 1770's. We all discovered the terrifying side to the element of Light in that horrible decade. I had joined a regime of British missionaries and troops who were travelling to Doab and Rohileund. Our mission was to record what we saw there and give support when able. Supplies were limited, especially in means involving food and water, due to the condition of the region.

This was not the aftermath of a war, but the active fight to survive a drought unlike any in known history before or after it. To this day, no other drought conditions have even come close to the scale of starvation the Doab region felt. What frightened me was the constant pulse of power I felt emanating from the core of the region. Rivers and lakes were barren, and people and wildlife were dead or dying in the wake of the deteriorating vegetation around them. Like a thirsty beast, the sun licked up every drop of moisture from the land and the living. Bengal endured only by a thin *thread of relief supplies, but how long could they fight this force of nature? It had gone on for four years by the time I realized the element of Light was at its center...*

"Tim!" A hand shook Talib's shoulder, snapping him from his thoughts. "Are you going to be able to stomach this?"

"Sadly, I have seen worse, Henry." They left on foot because horses were now a food supply. "I heard many cannot make it to the rural regions..."

I regret saying I had seen worse. This was the most horrific moment in mankind's history. Sadly, it is also the least known in modern times. Looking back, why would anyone want to share stories of what was seen there from those desperate to survive at any cost? Of course this moment would be sealed away, praying never to be recalled...

"It's true; the poor lads living here haven't seen rain in four years now." Henry's expression was grim. "When they go back, I try to send children with them. To see men and women suffer is nothing compared to seeing these young ones. Most are abandoned, parents dead or no longer able to feed them. You'll see, if you can stomach it, Tim."

"Are we headed for the Doab region?" The pulse of power pulled at him. Being so near it, he could no longer doubt that it was the cause of the drought. "Or is it a lost cause?"

"Unfortunately, we'll be headed there." Henry penciled something in his journal. "I haven't been there myself just yet... not that deep into the mess."

"I see you have been recording what you see?" Furrowing his brow, he patted the man on the back. "I pray your written words do not haunt you as much as the nightmares this place will give you."

"You're a frightening man to talk to at times, Tim." Grunting, he put away the journal, and they marched on.

It took weeks before they came across a village with living, breathing people within its streets. Those who remained barely survived in the decaying landscape that the drought left in its wake. They passed trenches of dead bodies and watched a dying man march himself into one—dead before hitting the pile. Sickening twists knotted themselves in Talib's stomach as he watched the man slide down the side of the trench. When he caught up to the rolling body, the man's pulse was gone, but his face was at peace to finally be free. The lions in the desert had been far more forgiving than the sun in this place.

They found themselves in a small town, once vibrant with activity from the now abandoned wagons and merchant stalls. Packs of starving dogs as thin as the people watched and took account of the living. The frail skin-and-bone appearance of the natives was sickening. Their grotesque physical conditions, starved and malnourished, made them appear inhuman. A dog approached a man leaning against a wall, sniffing at him as drool dribbled from its lips. Tensing, Talib watched, unsure of what he was about to witness. An excited yelp made the rest of the pack pause. A slight wag of the yelper called them back to where he stood. Like vultures, they circled patiently around the dying man. They waited for him to pass on before relieving him of the little flesh he retained. The dogs were too weak to take down a victim who might fight back.

"They pick them clean in two days, if that," Henry's voice cracked, tears fighting to be set loose at the edge of his eyelids. "But that's not the worst of it, Tim."

"It seems the dogs have some respect for those still alive, even if they seem dead to us already." Swallowing, he pulled the scarf further over his nose. The decaying dead around him reminded him of the smell of bodies from the Black Plague in London so long ago. "So many dead and lying on the road, the fields ... wherever they fall."

"Y-yes. Bed rest cannot heal or relieve the hunger that eats them alive." His shoulders tensed, and he nodded at the shambling remains of a young woman who worked her way toward them. "She's got a little one, I bet..."

The woman made it to where they stood and gripped at Talib's uniform with her skeletal fingers. "Please! Sir! I will sell my child for a rupee! For food! Water!"

Grimacing, he looked into her sunken, bloodshot eyes. "I am so sorry... I do not have any of those things to give."

It was the one time I damned myself for not carrying food or water. I may not need those things, but the people in the world around me needed them for sustenance. There in the Doab, I realized how much of a blessing my immortality was for not needing the simple exchange of food and water to thrive. I was spared— but cursed—as I walked among these men, women, and children who needed the things I did not.

Henry pried her away. Her tears could not fall; there wasn't enough blood to spare for tears in her starving body. Many of the dead left very little splatter behind. Even if they had water or food, it would make little difference to the poor souls who waited for Death's reprieve. With no way to offer assistance, they marched away to the next village.

"It is hard," whispered Talib to Henry, "witnessing all of this."

"Tim, if you want to head back..." Henry paused, his deep brown eyes dulled from the emotional turmoil which smashed through him.

"The drought or the mother having to eat her own child?" Henry's eyes met his, astonished by the firm tone of Talib's question. *I want to hear what he thinks is the worst part of the whole ordeal. Could I condemn someone for wanting to live even if it means eating their dead child?*

"The drought, Tim." Color came back to his face, and he nodded. "The travesty is this blasphemous drought…"

Another week passed before they arrived at the destination which they had failed to reach in prior missions. The missionary station in the far village had gone months, maybe over a year, without contact, and it was unknown whether those stationed there were still alive. The sun beat down on them with intense light, much brighter here than anywhere else they had travelled. They felt blinded by the sheer amount of sunlight which fell upon them; looking in any direction was as if staring directly into the sun. Lucius' power originated from this spot, and Talib's heart thumped in his ears. He could no longer deny that Lucius was to blame; he was the source of this natural disaster.

Most of the regiment had turned back. Considering the gruesome conditions of the living in the villages, most of the sights were too much for them to bear going any deeper. The farther from Bengal they went, the more horrific and desolate the villages became. Here, in this village, nothing but the bones remained. Dust stirred on a mild breeze in the heat, but the wind did nothing to relieve them or the world around it. Henry and the last three men were setting up camp; their faces were drawn and phantom-like from discovering that no one remained alive there. Talib took the chance to venture away to find the core of the power of Light, knowing it resonated somewhere within the buildings. Swirling waves of heat rose off the ground and buildings. Some of the wagons and rooftops had turned into charcoal, crackling and still warm with fire.

Walking ever deeper, he came to a small building bearing a crucifix above the door. His body tensed and his muscles twitched. *Lucius has always been drawn to religion, to the idea of an inner light. This has to be the missionary's station and the starting point of the horrible drought raging around us.* The door was cracked, and he pushed it open. Pausing, he saw a priest on his knees, rocking to and fro. Mumbled words in several languages flowed from his lips; his hands were clasped in prayer and bound by rosaries.

His black clothes were faded across the shoulders, and holes showed the deterioration of the cloth itself. Dust and ash coated his head and arms, and the rocking did nothing to shake it free. From the appearance of the wooden floor, he had not left the spot in days—possibly weeks. The priest fell silent, his body stopping all motion. Peering over his shoulder, the pain-stricken face was familiar. Lucius sat on the floor in front of the altar. He looked up at Talib with tears soaking his face and lips trembling.

"I can't make it stop…" he pleaded, "The sun… I can't make it stop shining its light."

His body shook from anxiety and crushing guilt. His blue eyes revealed how scared he was of what was happening within him. The blonde hair on his head was ruffled from being tugged at it in frustration. Candles and an overturned table lay not far from him; at one point he had lashed out angrily. Pews were jumbled and tossed, and dried blood was smeared across part of the church. Lucius had attempted stop himself by any means, including suicide. There was no question that his immortality had awakened. The signs of his strength and undying condition painted the church in an emotional display of panic and self-hatred.

"Lucius…" Talib felt guilty for not having the ability to get there faster. "Do you remember who I am?"

Looking up, he said softly, "Talib."

Nodding, he closed the door behind him. "You have been here for four years, have you not? Trying to stop yourself the entire time?"

"Y-yes…" Choking sobs and mangled confessions flooded from him. "I didn't even notice the first year. Though it was odd not having any rain the second year, it seemed like a fluke. As the third year peaked, those around me started to starve and wither away, and I became so afraid. The fear I felt only made it worse; the light from the sun became stronger and more intense. Then I realized I was alone. There had been no food or water for months, yet I was still here. I was angry at first, then I started to remember… I've never used my powers much, and now, I cannot pull it back. I cannot control it…"

Talib sat next to Lucius and rubbed his back. "It is alright. You never meant to harm these people…"

"What will happen to me now?" He peered up to the ceiling, waiting to hear God's judgment. "Is there punishment for this abuse of power?"

"No, no abuse of power has happened." Pausing, Talib gathered his words with care. "Your only punishment will be the memories that will haunt you for all of eternity. I can take you some place safe, some place where we can bring your powers under control."

"My God, how far has this light reached?" More tears rolled from his eyes. "What suffering have I caused to innocent lives? How many have I killed?"

"Bengal even feels it." Swallowing, he answered honestly and truthfully. "Many lay dead in the wake of your power, but it is the starvation that kills them."

Gritting his teeth, Lucius' face fell into his hands, and he begged, "Talib, if your powers can make it stop, please do so!"

Wincing, Talib confessed, "I can. If you want me to, I can."

"Do it!" The determination in Lucius' tearful eyes took Talib's breath away.

Gripping Lucius tightly and digging his fingers into his shoulder, Talib swallowed his unease. His power seeped into his friend's body, turning the outward lines of the element of Light back to its core and pulling the pieces back to their foundation. Lucius' power responded easily; unlike Geliah or Hotan, he was a willing patient, not an opposing enemy. They both breathed slowly and steadily. Each deep inhale allowed him to push Lucius' power back to his soul where he could better control it. After several minutes, the deed had been done. Goosebumps rippled across Talib; he was unnerved at his own abilities and their power over another immortal.

Lucius gasped, and Talib removed his hand from his shoulder. "Oh, dear God, I remember that sensation well. To think you have the ability to put my powers back in place… if Geliah had been here, he would have surely ended my life somehow."

Looking away, Talib balled his hands into fists. "Very true."

"Tim!" Henry rushed through, knocking the door off its hinges. Water dripped from his beard and clothes. "By God, it's raining! A miracle!"

Mustering a smile, Talib looked to Lucius. "Perhaps your prayers have been answered?"

"It still won't wash away what happened here." Lucius shook and tears streaked down his face. "This should have never happened."

The second the element of Light was stabilized, it started to rain. Within a year, Doab and the nearby regions were fruitful in their crops for the first time in four years. One would have never known a dry spell lasted four years with the speed in which nature returned to normal. Lucius didn't give up his missionary work. Instead, he embraced it in hopes of repenting for the lives damaged in the wake of the drought. The guilt in his eyes as he took in the scattered bodies on that walk out of India was heart wrenching. Images of the dogs eating and fighting over the starved figure of the woman who had been alive weeks before still haunt me. I do not think Lucius will ever use his power again, even if his life depended on it.

I recall aggressively using my powers. Geliah had forced my hand, and Hotan had used his refusal to make me stronger. As for Lucius, he needed me to seep into him, to aid him in pulling his power back into himself where it belonged. For the first time, even with these lost memories restored, I had made the decision to use my powers to control another immortal. It was frightening. How could I control them with such ease, with such force? Although, looking back, I would have had trouble saving Lucius otherwise. He found himself in such a terrible and out-of-control state, and if my sense of duty hadn't driven me, perhaps I would have abandoned him in fear of facing all these tragedies.

As for why Lucius awakened with the outburst of ever-flowing power remains a mystery. With all my memories and all I know, Hotan's unstable power puts us all at risk of becoming erratic. Perhaps at that very moment, Hotan was pushing forward in the next stage of whatever he had planned. I imagine a rebirthing of the caliber he prepped himself for would have drastic consequences. Lucius is a prime example of such aftermath.

15

DESTROY MYSELF

1863 AD

We went almost an entire century before another incident occurred. As the years passed, there were instances of power leaking out into the world. Elements influenced people and nature around the reincarnations, but it was minor—nothing alarming like with Lucius. At this point, Fae and Lucius travelled with me, and we worked in tandem to track and observe the others.

I did not force them to do this; it was of their own volition and desire to prevent a repeat of what happened to them. In fact, I often encouraged them to explore the world and do something they wanted rather than the stressful tasks that were essentially my duty. Granted, I enjoyed the companionship. For once, I could reminisce and talk to someone who understood the difficulties of immortality. Though I now realize I had gotten that first from Iapetos. Deep down, I wanted them to live their lives without feeling the chains I still bore across my shoulders and around my neck.

When Fae was not tracking anyone specific, she spent her spare time in institutions and libraries. It was her way of keeping *a sufficient stream of knowledge. Often, I found her in the Al Qarawiyyin Library in Morocco or the Biblioteca Marciana in Venice. She requested identification documents or enrollment paperwork to join colleges, so she could expand her knowledge and quench her thirst to know more. Her active hand in society was a blessing which allowed us to pass information and even investigate anything we suspected could be an awakening.*

As the times changed, it became more difficult to forge documents to get through the invisible walls the governments created. We used my power to blend in with the masses and make our lives as immortals easier. By the 1800s, most of the languages I knew and spoke were extinct or had evolved into something different. The art of making books shifted in miraculous ways. Machines worked in the place of hundreds of men; books were no longer written in the great rooms of scribes but printed in a matter of minutes.

Mankind bettered itself without our aid, but as we had seen in the past, it turned on itself with ease. Wars and crusades had ravaged and scarred the land in unspeakable ways. Politics, religion, and vendettas destroyed the lives of innocent people. Regardless, humanity pushed forward to something better, where their plates could be filled with more than gruel or potatoes. America had broken away from British rule and formed its own country. As we travelled across the jungles of South America with its mix of native dialects and Portuguese, the United States experienced the Civil War. Rights, beliefs, commerce, and political strongholds were to blame for that unruly war which raged between families. I must admit, looking back, I am shocked no other civil wars broke out. The stain and taste of that single, bloody barrage was something no one wanted to happen again.

It was a rare treat to have a reincarnation happen while in South America. As the population grew, it became more common and confusing. It wasn't that there hadn't been any people there, but perhaps Hotan's spell relied on some connection to their former bloodlines, and it had taken time for that ancestry to spread. It required a genetic connection and bond to DNA in some unseen manner. Considering the Levites were sent out to other nations before our downfall, most of us had some genealogical connection to those in this modern time. It is a comforting thought that part of who we once were survived and was carried through the generations by mortal means.

"Who do you suspect is here?" Fae came along to see Chile, a new region she had only read about. "I can't help but wonder if you always know who you are looking for. I've never even thought to ask; can you feel who we are?"

"I do. This time it is the element of Fire." They were riding in on the main train into Santiago. "Remember, he is not awakened yet, so be cautious if you encounter him before me."

"Is it safe to assume you can feel all the elements?" She folded her newspaper in her lap, watching him stare out the window. "Unlike the rest of us, you've always seemed to know when we are using our abilities or where we were when reincarnated."

His jaw tensed as her dark blue eyes burned into him. "Hotan gave that ability to me since I was chosen guardian…"

It was a half lie.

I had the ability from the start of our immortality, but she had no evidence to prove otherwise. In the beginning, we all could feel the wave of power in one another, but after awakening, that connection seemed lost to Fae, Lucius, and the others. All I could do was continue watching over those still caught in the spell while providing support to those who were rediscovering their abilities. For some reason, their powers were different when they came back. In fact, I must confess the powers were stronger and more dangerous. It took far more physical effort to keep themselves from collapsing or falling into deep comas. Is this the cost of stabilizing the element of Rebirth?

"Hmmm, Hotan…" She balled her hands and pressed the paper tight against her thighs as she prodded further. "And why do you never check on Hotan's reincarnation?"

"Because I can never find it," Talib confessed; his silver eyes flashed his frustration. "Neither Hotan nor Abigail. They are beyond my ability to detect. Even though I can sense them, I might as well be looking at a spinning compass when it comes to narrowing down their locations."

"Did he do that on purpose?" Her brow folded and her face softened as her eyes showed empathy for him. "Is he even reincarnating?"

"I do not know," Talib sighed. The train slowed, screeching as the brakes gripped the tracks. "Regardless, my promise was made to all of you to be a watcher, a guardian, and that is where my focus remains."

"Understandable…" She looked to a picture of a cathedral on the folded newspaper in her lap. "If you don't mind, I would like to see this in person."

"Of course…" He returned his gaze to the window, wishing it was Saphellia by his side.

She would have loved to see these places in all the stages of time…

"Are you alright?" Fae blinked, leaning forward to get a better look at his face which had a tear sliding down his cheek. "I… I didn't mean to upset you…"

"No, it is not you…" His voice was hardly a whisper. "Sometimes my heart can be cruel."

"If it means anything at all, I miss Saphellia too." She mustered a smile. "She always knows how to brighten a room."

Closing his eyes, he let another tear fall. "Only she knows how hopeless I can be at times…"

Fae's lips parted, but her voice fluttered away. There was nothing she could say to comfort him. Every passing decade took its toll, and he felt lost without her. Talib cried as he replayed the memories of his wife and the time they spent together. As the conductor's booming voice shouted for those unloading, he rubbed the tears away on his coat sleeve. *It is time to focus on the element of Fire which tugs at me from someplace here in Santiago.*

Kyle was still a dormant reincarnation. Talib kept himself occupied by chasing each recreation down, aiming to see them at least once for himself. As they walked the streets of the thriving Latin American city, Fae walked beside him with her arm interlocked with his. Most assumed they were a couple on their honeymoon as they headed for the cathedral. Many of the merchants offered flowers or pretty, shiny objects like gems and jewelry. Much to his relief, his connection with the element of Fire was growing stronger. As they broke free from the crowded vendor street, the cathedral Fae was interested in appeared before them.

"Guess we get to kill two birds with one stone." He patted her hand which still grasped his arm.

"So he's some place inside?" She lifted an eyebrow; the heat of the sun painted her forehead with sweat under her hat.

"Definitely inside." Grunting, they increased their pace. "And it seems abnormal."

"Abnormal?" She tightened her grip. "Is he trying to awaken?"

"I do not know…" Eyes forward, Talib rushed to find him and confront Kyle's reincarnation to know for sure. "Something is not right here…" He thought, *Considering the culture in the area, he should be inside praying like many do daily.*

They paused outside the crowded, magnificent building. The archways were reminiscent of Roman architecture during the fourteenth century. Unlike most cathedrals, this one lacked the spires commonly seen on Gothic style churches and was rectangular in its overall bulk, save a single bell tower. Its walls were adorned with large flowing sweeps of engravings which looked as if rolls of wind and water filled it. Every alcove showed the etched face of a prophet or saint; candles and flowers gathered at their feet from the patrons who believed in them. This was where people kept their hopes alive.

"It'll be impossible to get inside," Fae scoffed as a patron bumped into her shoulder. "I can't believe how many people are stuffing themselves into its doors."

"Kyle is here." They gave each other an exasperated look. "We just have to confirm, not shake his hand."

"Right." Nodding, they pushed through the throng of people toward the church doors. "Does he still have his outrageously red hair when he reincarnates?"

"Indeed…" Talib spoke loudly to be heard over the hum and chatter around them. "He should be easy to spot from afar. Then again, it depends how much thicker it is inside…"

"*Bon.*" Separating would increase their chances of spotting him, so Fae initiated a better means of communication. She projected her voice within Talib's mind, *We'll just have to use this instead. There's no way we'll find or hear one another in this mess of people, mon cher.*

Agreed, Talib responded. *Good luck to us both*. Fae vanished so quickly into the crowd that it startled him.

The mass of people rubbing against each other created waves of smells which were both delightful and dreadful. Perfumes, spices, and incenses all mixed with the dirty, foul, sour, odorous scents from sweating bodies within the boiling sea of people inside the cathedral's walls. Halfway through the building, Talib caught a glimpse of red hair. It took several more shoves inward to get a better look. Kyle's reincarnation kneeled before a statue of the Virgin Mary, rocking as he prayed at its base where a great number of candles and wax flooded the floor. Colorful wall coverings and oil lamps created a spiritual ambience around the statue. It was easy to see why so many came here to pray and be in touch with their faith. As for Kyle's reincarnation, he looked pale; perhaps some tragedy had struck him in this new life.

No, it was not that. Later, I discovered it was the result of something far more dangerous… far more tragic. That was a man fighting inner demons, or in this case, power.

Did you find him, Talib? Fae's flustered voice entered his head.

Yes, we should leave, he responded, heading back for the doors. *I am done when you are.*

Oh, I've had my fill of this place, she retorted. *Meet you at the train platform?*

Yes. He smiled, knowing her fantasy of Chile had been tarnished by the crowded smells, awkward touches, and overall humid heat of the cathedral she desired to see in person.

Looking back, there were so many people… Men, women, and children scrambled between my legs. It was hard to see with so many there. If I had pressed forward further, I still would not have been able to tell something was wrong…

It was much easier to pass through the crowd on their way out, exiting through the massive, wooden doors of the building. Talib paused and peered up at the open doors. *I am astonished they chose to build them to the ceiling.* Thick dark brown timbers were bound tightly with iron straps and hinges. It was a wonder they had managed to hang the doors at all.

Those doors proved worthy of their strength…

Fae had arrived at the platform before him. She smiled playfully and winked, teasing that she had beaten him on their escape. Laughing, Talib got into the line to purchase tickets for their speedy retreat. There were no other immortals in South America. They would travel north or back across the sea to

Europe, Africa, the Middle East, or even parts of Asia. There were plenty of options to choose from depending on Fae's interests. After all, they had all the time in the world. The time it took to travel and even the dangers associated with it were nothing to an immortal.

"Where are you going from here?" Curiosity danced in Fae's eyes. "England? Some place in Europe?"

"Actually, I am heading to New York first. I plan to contract a cathedral of my own there." They took a few steps forward, and the line shrunk in front of them. "I figured with some of us awake, it would make a fine center to meet and do business together. At least in the future."

"It's a great idea." Sighing, she furrowed her brow. "But are you not afraid of the civil war? I'm sure no train passes over the battle lines at this time."

Blinking, he looked to her. "I suppose I had not considered how I would travel, with everything pitted against itself."

"You're a mess indeed." Giggling, she added, "How in the world Saphellia ever kept you in line, *mon cher*, I will never know."

He felt his cheeks redden as he approached the teller. Speaking Portuguese, he requested tickets for their return to the closest port town. The smooth tone of his tongue caught the teller off guard, making him pause; it was rare to encounter non-natives who spoke the dialect so well. Refocusing, he took Talib's money and provided them with boarding passes. Once more, he offered his arm to Fae, and on command, she interlocked her own in it. They had several hours before the train would even arrive, let alone be ready for departure.

And then I felt it.

Talib gasped, and sweat poured over him. A wave of power made him pause mid-step. His smile vanished as he looked in the direction of the cathedral. The element of Fire had released a startling amount of power without warning. Muscles across his body tensed, and Fae was unable to pull her arm from his as she panicked at his sudden shift in behavior.

"Talib! What's the matter?" she pleaded, still trying to free her arm.

"The… the cathedral…" He released her and pointed to a rising pillar of smoke in the distance. "K-kyle … he awakened… I think."

Talib ran toward it, and Fae could barely keep up as she shouted after him, "What do you mean, 'you think?'"

"It does not feel like the time with you…" His heart beat fast and hard against his chest, and his nerves pushed him to hurry as he answered, *It feels more like the time with Lucius.*

No! The smoke! Panting, she struggled to keep pace with Talib despite her long skirt and heels.

He left her behind, and she slowed, knowing she could never keep up. As he came over the hill, he felt the heat of the fire on his face. The flames were massive; waterfalls of red, orange, and blue reached high above the building. Screams from inside and outside the church rattled his eardrums. No amount of water could quell the monstrous fire devouring the cathedral. Covering his nose and mouth with his coat sleeve did nothing to prevent the stench of searing flesh. A piece of Hell was brought up to the living to claim lives.

He skidded to a stop, fixating on the closed wooden doors. His eyes watered from the stinging heat. In the rush to escape the fire, the people within had shoved the massive doors shut. The doors had been hung in the wrong direction and swung inside the church, instead of pushing outward. There was no ability for those outside to open them against the weight of so many people inside who piled in behind them. Furthermore, the swelling heat prevented anyone from coming closer.

Tears and wails washed out the roar and whoosh of that massive fire. I stood among the onlookers. We could not see their faces, but their cries of pain and pleas for help reached us loud and clear.

Falling to his knees at the sight, Talib was speechless as he held his head. Unlike the rest of the crowd, he could feel Kyle's power surging and then failing. *The element of Fire is fading away; is he destroying himself with his own flames?* Flashes of the sickly face of the red-headed reincarnation rocking in prayer made themselves known. *Had he felt it coming?*

Yes, even though he was not aware of who he was, he was aware of the unbalanced power surging within his soul…

Fae's footsteps fumbled and stopped behind him as she joined him on the ground. Tears fell down her cheeks, and helplessly, they watched with the rest of Santiago as loved ones burnt to ash. After the flames died away, they speculated that well over two thousand died within those holy walls. They confirmed the starting point of the fire: the statue of the Virgin Mary. Unlike the masses, he knew it wasn't the oil lamps and wall coverings that had caught fire. Kyle had burst into flames, or perhaps surged the nearby candles and lamps.

He died there. His power went dormant again. It was not until I discovered Hotan's reincarnation that I understood why I never found Kyle's reincarnations again until modern times. Again, Hotan's meddling with his own power of Rebirth caused such chaos with the other immortals. Power surges, instability, awakenings, and a scary amount of whiplashes resulted from his intentions.

16

FADE AWAY

1902 AD

Exactly what were his intentions? He had spoken of a seed, someone to carry it, reincarnating himself. At this point in my memories, that was nearly five hundred years ago! Did he ever finish, or are we still in the center of unfinished business and mistakes? He is gone, dead, and we are left with a tangled web of questions with no answers! Did you ever achieve your solution, Brother? By the hand of Iapetos, I lay dead on a rooftop with your reincarnation! What good has wiping our memories done! If Iapetos could just remember the years in which we travelled with one another, I could have salvaged this! Your meddling has only hurt us further!

Talib landed at the docks of St. Pierre on the island of Martinique. Having felt a strange mix of powers emanating from the island, he requested Fae, Lucius, Peter, and the others stay behind in case something terrible happened. They fussed about it, but something in his gut told him Hotan would be there waiting for him.

Another hidden memory from April 1902. Was Mt. Pelée your doing, Hotan? All those lives… but then again, had you lost control over your own powers at this point?

He made his way to the local shop to purchase climbing gear. As Talib peered over the city, there was no mistake that the surges of power came from the smoking mountain looming over the horizon. Shuddering off memories of Herculaneum and Mt. Vesuvius, he prayed he would not have to endure a repeat of such an event.

That is why you chose the island. I may not have found you in Herculaneum, but I know you and Iapetos fought on the mountain the day it erupted. What exactly were you planning to do here? I doubt a fight, but I had no idea what I was walking into since all my memories were taken from me.

"Sir, I do not recommend you go." The local Carib man stared at the items and cash on his counter. "Mt. Pelée has been acting very angry for the last four days. It is not safe to climb to the top."

"What sort of activities?" Furrowing his brow, echoes of the chain of events from Italy clawed at Talib's soul. "Please, I am a geologist here to do a survey of these activities…"

"Well, they say the mountain smells like Hell, sulfur coming from it, and just yesterday, it rained ash." Shakenly, he took his money and continued, "Some climbers said it rained rocks and ash at the top two days ago while visiting Etang Sec."

"Etang Sec?" He motioned with a hand for the man to keep the change—a small thanks for the information. "Is that the dry lake at the top?"

"*Oui, monsieur.*" Sighing, he put the extra money in his register. "Back on the twenty-third, they felt some underground shocks, and cinders rained down in the south and west of Mt. Pelée … but the authorities don't seem to be concerned."

"Have the horses been uneasy and difficult?" he asked, giving a concerned look at the man. "Does your heart speed up at random or your legs feel the need to run away at any moment?"

The man looked astonished; his eyes grew wide as he nodded, not sure how else to answer the questions.

"Leave this place," he commanded. "You and your family must leave here; I have seen this before. She will blow soon, if not at any minute now."

Swallowing, the shop owner grabbed Talib's wrist as he reached for his items. "Sir, even knowing this, you still intend to climb to the top?"

A faint smile crossed his lips. "It is my job. I have to go see for myself and confirm it so your authorities will take this threat more seriously."

Releasing his grip on Talib, he sighed. "I see. You are the person who can help them decide to evacuate the city."

"Sadly, yes." Frowning, he nodded goodbye and headed out the door.

Looking over his shoulder, the shopkeeper flipped his sign to "closed." He would take his family some place safe, and hopefully the extra cash he left behind was enough to aid him. Throwing the rope over his shoulder, Talib headed for the mountain. Again, ash fell, and he pulled out a handkerchief to cover his mouth. Fear built up inside him, and it took all he had to fight it. He recalled the way it had burned the last time he experienced a volcanic eruption in person—an experience no mortal would survive to tell the tale.

It was painful. Worse, it took a very long time to break from the pile of hardened ashes that weighed me and the dead down. The fear of being buried alive again with no hope of being found for months pulled at me. But this memory is new to me, and I do not remember what I felt as I made the hike to the Etang Sec caldera. I know Hotan was waiting there based on the power washing over me…

Climbing over the last ascension, Talib came to the mountaintop; steam plumes filled the area with heat and the aroma of sulfur. It felt like Hell was crawling out from under the earth here on top of Mt. Pelée. As he marched for Etang Sec, his eyes widened. What had been a dry lake crater for hundreds of years was now filled with water. On the far edge, a heap of earth was pushed up, and boiling water steamed from it. The lake was unnatural as it boiled and bubbled. Even the steam was odorous of volcanic sulfur. He squatted at its edge and observed the weathered, dead grass. Heat licked at his cheeks when he pulled his bandana down. Looking to the center of activity, he knew it would not be long before the lava flow would surface and destroy the city at its base. Talib felt helpless. *Will I even be able to command all the people to leave? Even then, how will I begin to cover the tracks of using my powers in these times?*

Knowing what I do now, I wish I would have remembered it was my powers that had moved Roanoke Colony to safety! I could have saved St. Pierre, both its citizens and the refugees who gathered there…

"Talib." Hotan's voice caused the hairs on the back of his neck to stand on end. "I'm glad you made it."

"Hotan?" Talib stood and spun around to see the solemn face of his brother.

His body, painted black from his tattoos, was alarming to witness. He was no longer the nostalgic, striped beast he remembered from those days training on the beach. Instead, he was an ebony-colored figure; what few slithers of skin remained were being choked out by the power tarnishing his flesh. Talib's stomach knotted as his mind raced. *Something is wrong, even deathly, about the aura eminating from Hotan. This is not right. Something dark and dreadful has overtaken my brother's body.*

Talib found the courage and asked, "What is happening?"

"I will be reincarnating myself as soon as the vessel appears." Furrowing his brow, Hotan looked to the boiling fissure which steamed at the far end of the lake. "Sorry I couldn't make it to an island that wasn't inhabited, but my powers are far too unstable now for me to keep them hidden."

"Vessel?" Talib asked confusedly.

A low rumble shook the ground under his feet.

Chills ran up his spine, and he pushed for more answers. "What do you intend to do?"

"I've created the seed which will carry my reincarnation, but I still need a host." He held out his hand and summoned forth a tiny blue ball of flame. "This holds it all, and once it leaves my possession, my body will fade to ashes. It's taken all my strength to co-exist with it."

Talib's heart fluttered at the thought. "What will happen to you? Will you return?"

A sad smile graced Hotan's face, and he closed his eyes. "In a way; I will return in essence. When it will happen depends on *him*."

"Him…?" Nerves tightened around every joint.

Hotan opened his eyes, turning to face the pathway on which Talib had travelled.

"Who in the world…"

A man stood there, panting in pain. He reached the summit and paused to glare at them. His black hair and eyes adorned a face identical to Hotan's. Catching his breath in his throat, Talib realized a power similar to Hotan's spiraled out from the man. The stranger grimaced again, and the ground rumbled under them and dissipated. The powers pulsating from them were causing Mt. Pelée to become volatile at an alarming rate.

Looking back to Hotan, Talib gave him a heated glare. *Hotan has kept too many secrets and put innocent lives at risk for this one selfish moment. How can he disregard the lives of people? Their lifespans are only a breath of his own in comparison, and he didn't care about snuffing them out so easily for his own greed.*

"What is happening, Hotan!" Talib demanded, his stomach tensing and aching. "Who is this, and what do you intend to do with him?"

The stranger stumbled a few more steps, then hit his knees. Groaning, the man fought against the pain of his powers colliding within him. The markings which crawled across his skin made it known he was an immortal. Talib grinded his teeth as his anger built to a level far deeper than he had ever allowed it to reach. *All of this is unacceptable. Hotan has dragged someone else into this curse of never dying, never able to live a life, never able to bear children, or feel human ever again.*

"Your name … is Hotan?" the suffering man before them rasped. "You've plagued my dreams for hundreds of years. Who are you?"

Hotan sighed and answered the questions yet again, "I am your father, Iapetos. Today, I intend to make things right by you and give you the life and opportunities I squandered and denied you."

Talib locked his eyes onto the seed. This thing—this unknown ball of chaos—would be given to Iapetos, whether he was willing or not.

"What will it do to him?" Talib's voice called out to Hotan like a warning to answer correctly—or else. "What will *you* do to him?"

Looking down at his hand, Hotan gave a faint smile again. "It will give him a single opportunity to create life. As the element of Death, he has only known a life of rejection, surrounded by the destruction I have wrongfully forced on him. It was your efforts that aided him in his renewed ability to control his powers, but unfortunately, I do not know what will happen."

Even though the memories had been wiped, the training to control his element had stuck with Iapetos. But that statement was drowned in my thoughts. My focus was the glowing orb in my brother's hand and what it meant to us all...

"It's the same concept; someone from our lineage has to be involved for a reincarnation to be successful." Talib's nerves heightened and sweat trickled down his temple. "Why does Iapetos have to carry your seed in particular?"

"I think you already know..." Hotan closed his eyes, and his face tensed, willingly giving answers. "It can only be carried by two people: my brother or my son. I thought and hoped that Saphellia would awaken. I was afraid to force it myself. I realized that between you and him, I have wronged Iapetos the most. My son never experienced childhood, a mother's touch, a father's guidance, falling in love. To repent for my sins, I will give him something we have been denied."

"No, you cannot possibly..." Talib's heart pounded at his eardrums. "Is he even strong enough to contain it?"

"I... I don't know."

They looked to Iapetos.

The dull, unfocused state of his eyes meant he was in too much pain to be aware of what was about to happen.

Hotan continued, "The more I reflected, it made sense for Death to give birth to the reincarnation of Rebirth. From the ashes, we will be born again; it is mentioned in multiple folklores and religions. The true meaning of life is what comes after death; this is why I chose Iapetos. Fate guided me this time, not my selfish desires like in the past."

"Why am I here?" Talib's muscles ached from his defensive stance as his brother's skin gave way to the black and began to crackle like coals in a fire. "It seems my advice is not needed."

"You're wrong." A blue glow engulfed Hotan's eyes, steaming out like smoke from a flare. "It was your advice that led me this far."

"And how much and for how long did you ignore my advice before heeding it?" Talib balled his hands into fists, fueled by anger. "Why do I not remember giving you this advice?"

"I took those memories away." The smoldering ebony statue tilted his featureless face toward the orb floating in his palm. "I apologize for my abuse of power. In the end, I still want to hear what decision you would make. Who would you choose? Which immortal should take this once-in-a-lifetime gift to bear a child?"

How could he even ask me this! He knows this subject has forever stung in my mind and heart!

Talib winced at the cruel question placed on him. He had no desire to answer it. "Do you realize your powers have made the other elements unstable? How many lives have been claimed because of it?"

Did Hotan not care for the risks and troubles it caused the others?

"I never had control of my powers to begin with, Talib." The glowing eyes turned to Iapetos who fell to the ground, wheezing from the growing pain in the presence of Hotan's unstable powers. "He is stable until I am near. Perhaps he holds a key, but again, your abilities have grown beyond what I gave you."

Gritting his teeth, Talib looked at Iapetos as he wailed from the agony consuming him. The fissure bubbled and steamed more aggressively. Hotan waited with great patience for him to answer. *Before me is the rejected son and his broken father, the maker of immortals. How can I have the answers to the unknown?*

His chest tensed, making it hard to breathe. The sulfuric odor stung his nostrils and lungs as he huffed. The longer he took to answer, the more Iapetos' pain and instability grew, making Mt. Pelée more dangerous. Again, Talib gritted his teeth hard as he fought back tears. Time was precious and short here in this moment of chaos.

"Who should be chosen: the childless brother I hurt or the child I rejected and abandoned?" There was an eerie lack of emotion in Hotan's voice as he pressed further. "I am confident both of you can handle it. As for how it will become stable, I cannot promise anything."

Damn you, Hotan! What was the purpose in further mind games! If I had known about all the other times, we both know I would not have been so calm or empathetic for you!

Closing his eyes, he gave him the answer he sought, "As grandfather begets father, father begets son, son begets the new generation. If you wish to pass down your legacy, this is your only chance to honor the memory of the mortal life you longed for while giving him a piece of humanity he would have never been able to experience…"

Hot tears fell down Talib's face, and he squeezed his eyes shut, angry to have given away his one chance. Hotan's cold hand was like a steel blade in the snow as it gripped his shoulder. His eye flew open, and fear rattled through him as his powers were tugged by Hotan.

This is different; instead of the tangled wrenching of two souls, this is like a power pushing mine outward…

Red flames crawled across his skin, and his markings came forth. The pain gripped him and took his breath away. He watched a small part of his fire join the ball in Hotan's obsidian hand. He looked, bewildered, at Hotan's glowing eyes. *Why is this part of me being taken and placed within the ball?*

"I want this reincarnation to have some part of you in it." There was a warm smile on those blackened lips. Hotan pulled Talib toward Iapetos who lay on his back, wheezing and eyes rolling back. "Perhaps the next version of me will have a better sense of self and not repeat the mistakes I made. As for my son, I pray he finds someone to love and knows the excitement and fear that fatherhood imprints on one's soul."

Talib still struggled with the agony and sensation that part of his soul had been ripped off. Grimacing, he rubbed his chest and asked, "How are you not in pain?"

Hotan sighed. "I am, in many ways. Physical, emotional, mental, and even in my soul as it lies here in my hand, embracing a small part of you."

"How does this work?" Talib asked as sweat poured, and he began to feel ill. "The seed… exactly how do you give it to someone else."

"With the help of your element, of course." It wasn't the answer he wanted to hear. "He will take it from me and swallow it."

"S-Swallow it?" The simplistic answer was terrifying. Asking someone to swallow someone else's soul was demonic in nature. "What will happen then?"

"I simply do not know." Talib felt the strings of Rebirth pulling out his power—asking it to do its bidding. "Iapetos' element allows him to swallow souls, Talib. Frightening, isn't it? Regardless, I pray this will be the last one he ever devours."

Nodding, he let Hotan take control of Judgment.

"Iapetos, I give you the soul of your father and the seed to make a new life of your own." Hotan's green eyes lost their light, and the ball in his hand brightened. He gripped Talib's shoulder tightly. "Please accept this as reparation for all the sins I have committed against you and others in my life."

As if a spell had been broken, Iapetos rose to his feet. Talib's stomach knotted further at the unnatural reaction. He appeared possessed; his eyes were rolled back into his head, and he was no longer awake or aware of his actions. A commanding hand reached out, and the seed of Hotan's reincarnation willingly flowed into Iapetos' palm without hesitation. Talib watched in horror as Iapetos jaw fell open, and he raised the blue ball and inhaled swiftly. The seed rushed inward. Hotan's fingers dug deeper into him, and he began to buckle and moan. It was the first signs of pain he had seen from him in thousands of years.

Iapetos fell to his knees, screaming. Black-and-blue-feathered wings exploded from his back—a reaction to absorbing Hotan's soul. Mt. Pelée rumbled and smoldered more heavily from its fumaroles. Stumbling away, Talib watched helplessly as blue light poured from Iapetos' eyes and mouth. The tortured man leaned forward, grasping at the ground. The wings were magnificent and frightening as they spread wide, casting a shadow over them amongst the brewing chaos from the volcano underfoot.

"Talib…" rasped Hotan, leaning heavier onto him. "He's struggling to stabilize it…"

"What can we do?" Talib tried to go to him, but Hotan pulled him back. "We must help him!"

"I will do this." Half his other arm was turning white and flaking off into the wind. Panic filled Talib to witness the rapid deterioration. "Listen closely…"

There was a strong grip around his element within himself that he couldn't break away, "Please do not do this, Hotan!"

"You leave this place," Hotan demanded with the aid of the element of Judgment. "Do not remember this place or the whereabouts of myself or Iapetos. You will have a full plate since this will break the reincarnation spell further. Because of Iapetos' weakened condition when he arrived, I doubt he will even recall you being here. I will do everything I can to stabilize him. Now go!"

Talib gripped the hand at his shoulder. "No … I cannot!"

He was too weak to force it…

"You must," Hotan pleaded desperately. "He is my son, and as you said, he is my responsibility. I will stabilize him before I allow my soul to be swallowed completely. Please leave, for I fear the task may cause an irreversible explosion like that of—"

"Mt. Vesuvius," Talib answered. They looked to one another knowingly as he figured out the forgotten gaps. "How do you propose I leave?"

"Lend me your element." Hotan leaned his forehead onto Talib's shoulder. "And I will prove you that have your own wings…"

Could it be?

Closing his eyes, he let Hotan take control. "Fine, do what you will with this last moment of Judgment."

"Forget this place, and fly back home on your own two wings, my dear brother." He released his grip, and with one great *whoosh*, Talib lifted off the ground.

Wait!

Why is everything falling to black!

Where is the rest of this memory!

Has he taken this from me completely?

HOTAN, WHY!

Have you not learned anything at all?

Hotan's voice reached him in the darkness of his mind, *I was afraid to let you remember me turning to ash under your wings. I see my reincarnation did not make the same mistakes after all.*

Hotan? Trembling, he spun every which way in the dark abyss in search of the voice. *How are you able to speak to me? I felt you fade away from the boy that very night when he grasped the power of Rebirth.*

One part of me, yes. The last of me has been dormant, waiting inside Iapetos in case a day like this happens. The voice was sad as he continued, *At this moment, you are recollecting memories as your life flashes before you. You are neither dead nor alive in this state, and I am doing my best to slow it.*

Slow it? Talib spun around, thinking he saw movement in the corner of his eye. He shuddered, and his skin crawled from this momentary pause of his memories. *Have you been listening in on my thoughts this whole time?*

Talib knew that Hotan's silence was an admission of guilt. Indeed, he had watched and heard every thought in and out of the memories. *I pray the boy senses you here and brings you back,* he finally answered.

I lie here now because I was not strong enough! Talib protested, angry at Hotan's silence this far into his flashbacks. *What good can I do?*

I... There was a nervous pause before the voice stammered, *I will give you back what I stole from you.*

Stole! A small, red flame appeared before him; it was held in the hands of his brother's form which appeared from the shadows of his mind. *But I thought...*

It is more than that. Hotan looked at him woefully with tears dripping from his chin. *I embedded part of you into the seed, but I also locked away your true self. Here, in my hand, is the key that I regret ever taking from you on that faithful day on Mt. Pelée. With this, you can overpower Iapetos and unlock his abilities just like he has unknowingly done for you.*

Rage swelled and he swung at Hotan, but the form faded away. The small flame remained, floating in place where hands had once held it. Talib reached out; the warm flame tingled in his hand as it pressed against his palm.

Sighing, he humored, *Do I need to eat this?*

No, snorted Hotan from the darkness. *It will simply go back to where it belongs… absorb back into your soul.*

What happens to you now? He sat and rolled the tiny flame from one palm to the other, watching it shrink with each pass. *Will you shatter away as you did within the boy?*

If I chose to let go, I suppose so. There was a lonesome sigh somewhere in the darkness.

You may stay here longer if you like. The flame disappeared, and he fell back, entertaining the peaceful prison shared with his brother. *What memories shall we travel through next, alef chet?*

From here, they are all ones you are aware of… Again, he materialized from the shadows and stood looking down at Talib.

Which memories would you like to see next?

He thought long and hard, a grave expression on his face as he glared up at Hotan's green eyes. *Allow me to show you the more painful ones, the ones caused by your neglect and insistence on hiding memories, Brother.*

Do you think watching everything this far was not painful for me? Through your eyes, I realize the magnitude of the mistakes I have made. Hotan sat next to him, looking upward as if wishing he hadn't fallen into Talib's mind. *I suppose I should learn what happened after I lost myself to my reincarnation…*

17

PANIC PRONE

1965 AD

T his memory is barely fifty years old. It scared me when I sensed Geliah's awakening. Out of everyone, he was the last I wanted to see come to light. Strangely, he was weaker than his former self, but still more powerful than those who remained as reincarnations.

I watered down his ability when we forced him into the spell, Hotan replied, holding his chin in thought. *It was punishment for abusing his abilities, but I'm sure it only added to his rage when he woke…*

You have no idea, little brother. I was in New York at the time, looking into multiple sources of power I had felt within the city: the elements of Fear, Lust, and lastly, Wind. My goal was to verify if Geliah had indeed awakened and make sure he did not seek out the others in the meantime. Unfortunately, by the time I arrived, he had already started using his powers.

Unlike the others who woke physically weaker than their former selves, Geliah had been a bodybuilder and wrestler. His body had far more endurance than Fae or Peter or Metsy, who had awakened centuries before. I did not go alone; I brought Metsy, hoping that the element of Spirit would be able to undo any damage he had done. She was the strongest next to Fae, who was attending Harvard University again.

Exactly what happened when Geliah awakened? The muscles in Hotan's face tensed.

You will see for yourself, little brother. If I had known my abilities were stronger and you had not locked them away, this moment in my life may have played out far differently...

The taxi headed for the Empire State Building where he felt the surge of fear rang out. In this era, 1965, Talib was a well-traveled journalist; it allowed him access to many regions and made sliding in and out of places more acceptable to the public eye. In this moment, there were reports of a group experiencing mass hysteria from the Empire State Building's observation deck. Talib wasn't surprised to feel the waves of the element of Fear pushing out from that location, and he assumed that Geliah was the cause of the chaos. Innocent lives were at stake; fear can overrun reason, leading to desperate decisions like ending one's life.

"You two be careful," grunted the taxi driver as he took his fare from Talib. "There's some crazy stuff happening lately around the city."

"Thank you, sir." He nodded and tipped his hat to him as he and Metsy slid out. "We have to hurry; Geliah's power is the source of the hysteria, and it is getting stronger."

"Geliah?" Metsy jogged after him as they rushed down the crowded sidewalk. "What should I do?"

"When we get up there, you will need to use your power to break Fear's hold on them and get them out of the building." Peering over his shoulder, she smiled and nodded with confidence. "I know you are capable in your own unique way, but try not to push yourself too hard."

"Understood." As they reached the front of the building near the main entrance, she slowed, and her eyes widened. "How are we going to get past the police?"

"Go to the back and find a maintenance door." She nodded and disappeared into the crowd.

Unlike Talib, Metsy didn't have reporter pull or passes to gain admittance. Armed with a pad and pen, he elbowed his way through the mob of concerned citizens gathered at the police line. As he reached the rope at the doors, his heart fluttered. The cop on the other side of the barricade was Jacob's reincarnation. Talib had neglected to notice any other element besides Fear. The pulse rung out again from the building overhead, renewing his urgency. The purple eyes locked with his silver ones, and they both froze. Inklings of Jacob recognizing him started to surface, and he held his breath. There was no time to explain. He wouldn't be able to gently break the news of what was happening to him—around him—with the crisis unfolding.

Last he knew, the element of Lust had not awakened, but as they stood there, speechless in the swirling chaos of shouts, there was no mistake that seeing Talib face-to-face affected Jacob, unlike the centuries before. Talib recoiled and turned to leave, but a hand grabbed his upper arm and pulled him back against the rope. The fingers dug deeper, and he couldn't pull his arm free. He stumbled backward under the lifted bridge of yellow cautionary rope. Catching the anger on Jacob's face did nothing to deter Talib's turning stomach as butterflies danced inside and made him nauseous.

"Sir, we could use your help on the observation deck," Jacob said with a scowl.

"Yes … yes." The rope dropped behind Jacob, and Talib stumbled closer to him and followed him into the building.

No words came to mind as Jacob tugged him through the lobby toward the elevator. Jacob nodded at fellow officers as they reached the doors, and the questioning faces faded away in an instant. The elevator doors opened, and Jacob shoved the elevator attendant out and dragged Talib in; it was an odd gesture for a police officer. Talib's heart pushed at his chest, and he wanted to flee as the doors closed. With a hum and creak, the elevator started its ascension. He was trapped with no idea why he had let himself be tugged along this far. His best friend's reincarnation glared at him. Jacob finally released his arm, leaving it throbbing. He looked down at his feet, unable to stomach the unhappy, confused look across Jacob's face.

"Talib." Hearing his name flow so easily from Jacob's lips was frightening. "Am I right to think Geliah is at the top of this building? Answer me!"

"Y-yes," Talib stammered. *I cannot bear to look up at his face, but I must ask…* "How long have you been awake, Jacob?"

"Since I arrived at the doors of this building," he answered, rubbing the side of his face. "I figure the fear and panic compounded with Geliah's powers caused my awakening. It all flooded back to me in an instant. So many lives, so many deaths… I'm not sure if I care for this aftermath on an emotional level."

Talib sighed in relief. "Perhaps it was fate that you awoke. If not, I may not have gotten through the front doors, let alone dragged onto an elevator to the source."

"I doubt you would have; sorry, I didn't mean to scare you, buddy." He gave him a few hearty pats on the back. "What should I know about being back? Any side effects I should be aware of before I try to do anything rash?"

"Use your powers lightly. They are stronger, but your body is very weak." Finding the courage to face Jacob, Talib was relieved to see the familiar smile of his best friend. "Metsy is here as well. You two can evacuate the civilians while I deal with Geliah. She may provide further details which I cannot accurately describe since I have remained untouched by all of this. Let me take on Geliah's wrath."

Jacob's smile fell away. "It won't hurt my feelings if you throw the asshole off the building."

"I cannot do that, Jacob," Talib scoffed.

"Real shame then," he snorted.

The chime of the elevator announced their arrival at the observation deck. As the doors slid open, they were relieved to see that Metsy had already amassed people to go down. Talib gave her a befuddled look, and she pointed to the maintenance staircase not far from there. Several people showed signs of paranoia and fear. Some sat and rocked themselves, mumbling or praying, while others tugged at their clothes or hair while hugging the inner walls. The waves of fear made even Talib sweat as he fought back the sensation that Geliah urged into existence.

"Jacob!" Metsy blinked. "I didn't think…"

"Yeah, it's me, Metsy," He blushed, rubbing his shoulder, a phantom motion from his original, injured body from long ago. "I'm here to help snap these folks out of this mess. How the hell did you beat us up here?"

"The maintenance staircase. The staff elevator is a few levels lower, and apparently, it moves faster than the main elevator." She touched a woman on the shoulder, snapping Geliah's spell and pointed her in the direction of the staircase. "It holds a lot more people, so for now, I can get most of them out of here before he notices me."

"I will leave you to it." Taking in a deep breath, Talib scanned the faces of the crowd. "I do not see Geliah, do you?"

"No, not yet," she answered, "but there were screams on the other end … and that laugh he makes when he's … enjoying himself."

"That dickhead…" Gnashing his teeth, Jacob turned his focus to those he could help. "You get him good, Talib."

Nodding, he left them behind. He walked slowly, directing people where to find help. The element of Fear weighed him down. The wind gusted around him, and Fear tried to make it a scarier sensation than what it truly was. A shift in the wind made him pause. The urgency with which it pushed and pulled him made his muscles tense. His heart sped up, and he swallowed to drive the cloud of fear away. He closed his eyes to shake the thoughts in his head from going further. *This air—this wind around me—is from the element of Wind.*

"Oh, come on!" Geliah shouted; his boastful laugh could be heard from around the corner. Talib was still not in view as he eased closer to the corner of the building. "You can't honestly still be pretending that you don't know who I am, Saphellia! Wake up, darling! I've let loose enough energy to topple Hotan's pathetic spell for anyone within a five-mile radius! Hahahaha!"

There was a yelp, and her voice trembled as she pleaded, "Please, sir, I-I don't know anything! Let me go..."

Talib gathered his nerves for the scene that awaited him. She had awakened; he could feel it in the fingers of the wind. Saphellia was smart, and she hoped that playing innocent would persuade Geliah to give up and not show further interest in her. Talib inhaled, ready to engage in the trap Geliah created for him. Peering around the corner, tears streamed down her face as Geliah held her by her hair. She teetered over the edge as he threatened to throw her off. She did her best to grip the slippery metal railing that kept her from falling. The wind pulled at him with more vigor, but Talib was afraid that if he rushed in, Geliah would push her out of spite.

The wind blew past him; it was drawn to her, and her eyes looked to where he stood. Her sudden calm broke her fears momentarily, and Geliah grinned. Now, he knew Talib was there, and worse, he knew she was awake. His wild amber eyes rolled in his direction, and Talib stepped out from behind the corner; the time to think and plan how to rescue Saphellia was over. The weight of the situation pressed down on his shoulders, making them ache. Laughter rolled from Geliah's chest at the sight of Talib, and he scowled in response. To Geliah, this was all a game of pissing off Hotan—a way to get back at him for defeating him so easily that day in the desert.

"Just as I thought, look who came to the rescue." Whistling, he yanked Saphellia to a standing pose and gripped her jaw in his other hand. "Ain't she a sight for sore eyes, huh, Talib?"

He locked eyes with Geliah and did his best to ignore Saphellia's desperate expression. "Release the girl. I am here now. Is that not what you wanted?"

"Not exactly..." His smile fell away, and he attempted to push more fear into him but failed. "Stronger than ever, I see."

"Thousands of years hardens a person." Talib took a step forward but paused as Geliah tightened his hold on Saphellia. "I see our last fight is still fresh on your mind, Geliah. You were so confident you could beat me, without knowing I was a proficient fighter myself. If you wanted a rematch, you could have asked me directly."

"Yeah, real fresh," sneered Geliah. "In fact, I already know to keep my distance, so you lost that advantage. I'd have to make this match work in my favor. You and your foul brother tricked me last time."

"You think so?" A gust of wind took Talib's hat, flicking it over the railing like a feather in the wind. His eyes dropped to Saphellia's frightened, hazel irises, fueling his anger. "What part of you thought making me angry would give you an advantage?"

"Oh, so I did poke the bear!" A devilish smile snaked across his face, and he jerked her back halfway over the railing. "What about this? How's that tickle your fancy?"

Gritting his teeth, Talib no longer cared that his tattoos were crawling out across his skin. "I demand that you let her go, Geliah, before I force—"

Before he could finish his threat, Geliah kicked her legs up and over; her fingers failed to hold the wet, smooth, metallic railing. He dashed forward but was too late. In horror, he saw her face during the last, agonizing seconds. Eyes wide, her strength pulling forward in the slowing of time, a smile came across, and she fell away from the ledge. Those tender lips, which still left their touch on his after thousands of years, had one message for him in this last, unknown moment.

I love you.

He smacked hard against the railing, peering over the edge in disbelief. A huge gust of wind threw him back. His heart thudded faster; she had managed to call a gust of wind, and he prayed that she lay on a ledge far from Geliah's reach. As the wind dissipated, he dared another look at where she fell. There were no signs of her at all. Broken shards of glass reflected in the sunlight, and hope swelled within him. *What is the cost of using her power so soon after awakening? If Fae lost over two months before waking, then how long before Saphellia will open her eyes?*

Geliah's heel slammed into the center of his back, and Talib screamed from the shocking pain of it. Again, another strike landed in its place. He crashed into the metal railing and cracked a rib. He coughed and wheezed, and the taste of blood came to his tongue on his breath. Geliah's heel rubbed deeper, pinning him against the railing.

"Go on!" Geliah roared in a fit of laughter. "Join her already! Let me help!"

As Geliah pulled back his foot, Talib twisted in time to catch his leg. He dug his fingers into the calf muscle and pulled Geliah to him. Rage burned through him as he wrapped his other hand around Geliah's throat. His amber eyes were wide with fear, but he was unable to produce even a yelp. The speed in which the motion had unfolded left him only able to wheeze. Talib was tired of the game with the railing and edge of the building, so he shoved him back the other direction. Slamming and pinning him on the wall, he dug his fingers deeper into his throat. Geliah's body was no longer able to obey itself.

"I may not be able to kill you, but I can make you regret every waking moment." Talib's voice was dark as he demanded, "You better not repeat this meddling ever again. If you dare force anyone else to awaken, you will suffer greatly."

Why did you let him go? Holan interjected, confused by his older brother's actions. *If you had passed Judgment on him here, the confrontation between him and I which happened later through the boy in the cathedral would have never happened.*

Ah, this was the point when I realized, even with so much anger, my powers did not work against awakened immortals at the same level. There was a considerable difference between this moment and the time we forced his hand to cast the Rebirth spell. I may have still felt my connection to them, but I no longer could persuade them. When the boy came along, I found that I had the ability to persuade him, but the question is, Was it because you were there inside him? Was being in touch with your element in its new form giving me back what you took from me on Mt. Pelée?

I see. Another result of me not considering the future conse-quences of my actions… Hotan sighed and started to pace in the darkness. *My desire to protect everyone did exactly the opposite.*

Exactly. The abuse of your power, my power, and life itself brought on some of the worst moments in my life as well as the others. No one ever needed you to figure out the unknown alone, Hotan. You decided that was how it needed to be done. Now, the loved ones, friends, and family pay the price for your selfishness, struggling to resolve a matter that involved more than your own life. It was for us to decide, not your right to choose for us. No one should ever deal with tragedy and hardship alone. We came from several walks of life, and there was a chance that one of us had a less harmful, more beneficial solution. You simply needed to ask.

I am so sorry… he whispered. *Once again, you're right. I went about all this so wrong…*

"DO YOU HEAR ME!" Talib slammed Geliah against the wall again, knocking his head against the brick and sending his ears ringing. "You will not touch another Levite or innocent with your powers ever again! When everyone has left here safely, you leave and walk, walk this Earth without yield."

"Y-yes…" Geliah responded, and Talib's hand fell away from his throat.

Geliah shook as a sickening sensation took hold of him at the command echoing in his head.

Jacob caught sight of Talib coming around the corner and stopped the elevator doors from closing. "What happened? Talib! What's wrong"

There was no hiding the situation from Jacob, and Talib grimaced. "Quick! We need to go down ten floors!" He stared hopelessly at the confusing array of elevator buttons. "Christ, which one!"

"Here!" Jacob felt Talib's alarm and quickly slammed the correct button.

"God, please let her be okay!" His soul was drowning in dread; thoughts ran wild as he paced in a tight circle in the elevator. "She managed to awaken, but…"

"Did he…" Jacob caught the frantic look in Talib's eyes and knew the answer. "Shit! Did you at least slit his throat?"

Looking down to his hands, he confided, "My powers… I could not get them to do anything. Even if I tried, I could not have stopped him from throwing her over, but I do not think he realized. In the end, all I could do was punish him to walk forever…"

The doors opened, and they rushed out. A startled woman came out of a far door, but seeing Jacob in his police uniform made her shoulder drop in relief.

"Mr. Officer! A woman! She came through the window!" She motioned for them to follow. "Hurry! I think she's still alive!"

They ran through the crowded office toward the windows at the far side. The floors were on lockdown to make evacuating the observation deck easier. People clustered together, scared and baffled from all the chaos. Wind whistled and moaned through the broken panes before them. Talib pushed past the circle of office workers to find Saphellia in a bed of sparkling glass shards. He dropped to her side and was comforted by the soothing pitter-patter of her heartbeat as he placed his ear to her chest. He nodded to the watching crowd, and they all sighed in relief and whispered amongst themselves.

Tiny cuts painted her bare skin, and one shoulder seemed dislocated. Clenching his teeth, he didn't know whether it was Geliah or the impact with the window that had done it. He gently lifted her in his arms. The limp and heavy sensation of her body made his heart swell in agony. Jacob assured the bystanders that she would be immediately taken to the hospital, but Talib knew it was pointless. She was cold, clammy, and pouring sweat. This was identical to the time with Fae, and he was helpless to pull her out of it. *I could not use my power to its former extent on Geliah. How can I hope to wake her when my power failed at its prime?*

Instead of taking the elevator to the bottom floor, Jacob stopped on another. As the doors of the elevator slid open, they were greeted by images of graffiti. The place was under renovation for a new company, and the damage was being removed or painted over. With Jacob's help, no one would look for them there or know they were missing. Tipping his police cap to Talib, they exchanged knowing stares. He would return when the crisis had settled. Jacob disappeared behind the elevator doors, and Talib crumbled to the floor in despair and exhaustion. A dusty couch adorned the haphazard soon-to-be lobby; it caught her limp body when his knees buckled. A plume of drywall dust made her look like sleeping beauty. Kneeling on the floor by her side, he pulled her hair from her face as tears started to fall down his cheeks. He gently kissed the lips he had missed so much, and their coldness tore his soul apart.

"I'm so sorry, my dove." His brow folded, and his lips trembled. "I was too late. I feel so horribly helpless..."

Laying his head on her chest, he sobbed; he gripped her cold hand in his, hoping for some sign that she heard him. Beneath him, the steady *ba-bump, ba-bump* of her heart joined the rise and fall of every breath she took. Questions filled his broken mind. *Does she feel my warmth, my weight, the hand trembling in her own as my tears soak her blouse?* Every part of him shook in misery and anger—*I failed.*

"I have you now. I will care for you as long as it takes for you to wake..."

Her fingers flinched, and a hint of warmth came and went; even a flutter in her heart filled him with hope. She gave him the miracle of knowing she was there, inside her body, unable to answer. Finally, his tears stopped, and he fell asleep.

What happened after this? Again, Hotan stepped out of the shadows, curious about his older brother's life. *She woke on her own, yes?*

No, she did not wake on her own. Jacob returned with a car, and I took her home. After a while, I bought a house and set up a room with a hospital bed. Her wounds healed, but as for her waking, it took nearly eighty years. It was a horribly long time to stare at the motionless love of my life. I was helpless to undo what happened; I lacked any ability or power to wake her or reverse what Geliah's sinful actions had done.

18

ANGELS FALL

2002 AD

I will never forget the first time I saw him.

The boy? asked Hotan.

Yes, your reincarnation. Talib's voice came to an abrupt stop, and he glared over at Hotan who didn't flinch against its sharpness. *Granted, he really is your grandson, is he not?*

Hotan's eyes fell away. With a sigh, Talib continued to share his thoughts and memories. *I was sitting on a park bench in one of the neighborhood areas of the city. Looking back, I barely remember why I chose that location, but perhaps it was meant to happen that way. I was growing impatient as I waited on Jacob, so I started walking along the sidewalk, pacing with the weight of my thoughts riding my shoulders. Considering his line of work, Jacob was always late, and I could not blame him.*

Kids screamed and shrieked with glee at the nearby playground. Talib watched the pack of children as they swung on the swings and slid down the slide. Boys and girls chased one another around every obstacle and squealed as they played hide-and-seek. He smiled and began walking again, enjoying watching them tuck in and out from behind trees and decorations. One tripped, stumbling to keep balance, and it brought him to a halt again. Looking down, the boy realized his shoelaces were unraveled. Flustered, he fumbled with them—something he was still learning from the way he paused periodically during the task. His lips were repeating something to remember what to do next.

Talib closed his eyes, remembering the days from his past when he chased Hotan through the fields and throughout the village. Thinking about it brought a bigger smile to his face. He remembered how they would run so hard through the tall stalks of wheat that his chest burned from the lack of air. He would fall to his back and gasp with his stinging lungs. He had nearly forgotten about being a child; after millenniums of immortality, it seemed like a dream. Closing his eyes, his heart soured at it all.

There was a numbness within his soul from surviving world disasters and watching the rise and fall of entire nations, governments, and cultures. It was easy to forget that he too had lived a simple life as a child, chasing his little brother around their version of a playground. Opening his eyes, he squinted at the bright skies above. It was a clear, sunny day, and a slight chill on the breeze felt amazing as he reminisced under the shade of an old oak. Autumn was starting to whisper its start, and soon, the deep green leaves overhead would fade to yellows, oranges, and reds. It was as if the trees set fire to themselves to stay warm as the early waves of cold rolled in from the north.

Thoughts spiraled over memories from before his body had become riddled with his curse. Tears welled up as images of Saphellia on their wedding day came to mind. He smiled, and a tear slid down his cheek. He relished in the image of her in her wedding attire with the ceremonial fire giving her fiery wings. *Maybe that is why I enjoy it when the leaves shift to a more vibrant display…*

In his peripheral, he saw a mother tugging a small child behind her as she fussed, "You have your entire life ahead of you, so you should try to make some friends now."

"Mom…" The voice of the young boy struck a nerve within Talib. He froze, afraid to look more closely. The boy continued, "You always know what to say. I hope one day I can be like you…"

"Oh, Hotan." The mother's voice rattled him, and the boy's name echoed in his ears. "All you need to do is be yourself. I thought you were friends with Kyle?"

Dropping his eyes, he stared wide-eyed at the silver-haired boy. He had found Hotan's reincarnation. The boy turned to him, feeling his stare. His gentle, silver eyes lacked his brother's vibrant, green shade. Instead, the boy carried the same silver irises as Talib, but there was no mistaking that it was him—Hotan's reincarnation. He was identical to Hotan at that age, and his voice was exactly like he remembered from so long ago. Deep within his core, barely noticeable, the element of Rebirth lay dormant and quiet. Somehow, it had been locked away deeper than any other element.

He shuffled behind his mother's legs, glaring at Talib. "Mommy, that man is staring at me."

"Oh!" Talib looked to his mother. Her eyes were tired, but her smile was soft. He apologized, "I am sorry, I did not intend to startle either of you. He just reminds me of someone."

"Normally, people comment on his silver hair." Sighing, she furrowed her brow and patted Hotan on the head. "Go on, go play on the playground, honey."

Hotan dashed away, and Talib addressed his mother, trying his best to hide the rising urgency that he felt. "May I ask where on earth you came up with his name? It is quite unique."

"Well…" Her face reddened, pausing a moment before finding the courage to answer. "His father named him."

His heart skipped a beat. "May I ask who his father is? I think he may be an old colleague of mine."

"Gone." She frowned, looking away as if ashamed.

"Where is his father now?" Talib swallowed, thirsty to hear her answer.

She turned away, hiding her face from sadness. "Excuse me, I must keep an eye on my son. He's all I have…"

She rushed away, and his heart sank for her. *How could the name come from his father?* Questions flooded him. He watched the sorrowful woman sit on the bench; her gaze was unfocused—someplace else. *She is heartbroken, so I can only assume Hotan's physical father had left her suddenly.* The idea that it was possibly Hotan himself didn't seem right. In fact, something in his gut screamed *no* to the idea. *I feel like I should know the answer to this puzzling matter. Hotan's dread over Liora locked away any desire to love another, otherwise, something would have grown between Abigail and him during all those decades on the island. Something far more frightening is unfolding.*

The phone in his coat pocket rang and vibrated. "Jacob, are you here?"

"Yeah, but where are you?" Jacob whined. "I'm on my lunch break, and don't tell me you got lost because that's impossible. I refuse to believe the oldest man on Earth gets turned around in a city with signs."

"No, you were late, so I took a short walk." Talib marched back to the bench, relieved someone else could verify what he saw. "I will be there in a second; you will not believe what just happened."

Hanging up, he shoved the phone back into his pocket and came around a large oak tree near the bench. Jacob spun around, catching sight of him, and he grinned. Jacob held a half-eaten hot dog; he had wasted no time and devoured his lunch in the short time he waited for Talib to return. Jacob showed concern and tensed at the stunned look on Talib's face; it was abnormal to see Talib walk with such alarm and speed. He slowed in his chewing before forcing the food down with a hard swallow.

"Look at the playground and tell me what you see," Talib instructed.

Jacob lifted an eyebrow, and with a grunt, he stared in the direction of the playing children. "You're making this awkward. A grown man, coming to stare at kids on a playground..."

"I need a second pair of eyes to ensure my imagination is not playing tricks on me," Talib fussed as he sat beside him with a look of panic across his face.

Jacob took in the last bites of his lunch before catching something of interest. He stood, took a few steps forward, and rested a shoulder on an oak tree. As he watched the kids dive in and out of the playground obstacles, he wiped his face and hands free of what little remained of the hot dog. Talib watched his back, anticipating the reaction when he noticed the small boy. Suddenly, he jerked his body away from the tree to stand upright. His shoulders visibly tightened under his business jacket as he shielded his eyes from the sun. Jacob looked over his shoulder at Talib in amazement before peering back to the playground.

"So you see him too?" Closing his eyes, Talib waited for Jacob's answer.

"It's him." Pulling a pack of cigarettes from inside his coat, he tapped it in his palm as he glared at the playing children. "Poor thing is built like him, silver hair and all."

"Only one detail is off..." Talib sighed. He opened his eyes, and Jacob turned to face him. "His eyes are silver, not green like my brother's had been."

Jacob lit his cigarette and took a puff of it; he blew out a stream of smoke before he said, "No offense, but that's a reincarnation of Hotan, matching eye color or not."

"Agreed." Talib crossed his legs and continued staring at the little boy who kept himself apart from the other children. "It seems clear that he does not know who I am, but his name is unusual. His mother claims that his father named him…"

"What's so unusual about it?" His cigarette hung loosely from his lips, and he searched for something in his pockets. "It must have rung a bell with you if you're bringing it up to me. I mean, I don't think any of us ever got noteworthy names. Occasionally, we'd get the same name, but mine's been a popular one in the last several decades, heh."

"She said his father named him Hotan." Jacob's cigarette fell to the ground as his eyes locked with Talib's. "As far as who the man was, I will need your help and resources to see if anything can be uncovered."

"Absolutely!" Stomping out the cigarette, he pulled a small pad from his back pocket and began scribbling in it. "I'll see what I can pull out of the records. There must be some hints as to who it may have been. I haven't heard that name since before we became immortal."

"The answer frightens me, to be honest." Sitting down again, Talib leaned forward, rested his elbows on his knees, and stared vacantly at his feet. "Part of me does not want to know. I feel as though I know the answer somehow but have no name to give him…"

I felt as if I was missing a piece of myself. Now, I know that feeling was not misplaced. Deep in my soul, I did indeed know who your reincarnation was and who had fathered him—Iapetos. It had taken almost a hundred years, but that woman with the tired eyes had somehow captured the heart of Death itself. There was very little we could find out about him. He did well to cover his tracks, even in modern times.

What kind of woman was she? Hotan asked softly as his face reddened. *Did you ever cross paths with her again?*

Of course I did. She worked at a diner not far from where Jacob worked. It was easy enough to become her regulars since she worked the skeleton crew at a twenty-four-hour dive. There were not very many options at two or three in the morning, so after a while, Jacob and I started meeting there, requesting her, and often tipping her more than our tab by threefold. I do not think she ever missed a shift and often was the one who filled in when they were short staffed.

No, I mean describe her to me... Hotan mumbled sadly. *Surely, being in the diner that much, you saw beyond the obvious with your keen eyes, Brother.*

He sighed and looked over at his brother's silhouette. His cheeks were stern, his forehead creased, and mouth tight-lipped. Talib thought to himself, *It is a fatherly desire to wonder what sort of woman blessed him with his grandchild. The weight of what he missed—even continued to devour with his powers and misplaced selfish acts—must haunt him. If he had not pushed everything through on his own and had asked for help, perhaps he could have met her himself.* Regardless, Talib gave a heavy sigh, and as her image stood before him, he told Hotan what little he knew of her.

She was tall and rather average looking. Her eyes were a wonderful brown, almost orange in tone. Sadly, they always seemed to long for something from her past; I assume it was fond memories of her times with Iapetos. Her hands were dainty and elegant, and her gracefulness and balance were stunning to watch. I never saw her drop a tray or plate or even tip a cup. She wore depression like a veil, even when she spoke proudly of her son for his schooling and such. I wonder about the circumstances in which

Iapetos abandoned her because it left her broken in a way that was painful to watch as the years went by. The faint empty smile she gave us seemed to take effort to hold as she worked.

What happened to her... It wasn't a question as Hotan's frown grew heavier.

Are you sure you want to know?

Hotan's eyes gripped him, shaking the answer from him.

Perhaps you should see it as I did...

"How long are you going to let this poor thing rot away?" Lucius rubbed the side of his jaw while he stood with Talib in front of the decaying building. "It was so beautiful..."

The remains of the cathedral Talib had commissioned so long ago after the incident in Chile stood before them. It was dark out, and Talib came to inspect its current condition after a recent report of a break in. The boards had been pulled away, but as he looked at it, he realized the passage was far too small for an adult. Motioning for Lucius to help, they broke the board completely free and opened the creaking door. Inside, the cathedral had deteriorated under dust and cobwebs. He elbowed Lucius and pointed at their feet. Small footsteps disturbed the dust as they trailed to the front of the church. A smile crawled across their faces at the thought of a child sneaking into such a scary place at night.

"You think he did it on a dare?" No longer needing to explore further, Lucius chuckled at the idea and followed him out. "As a kid, I know I would have dared someone to go into this haunted church."

"I do not know." Talib closed the door and paused, looking down at his feet where he had left the board. "I think I will leave it open and see if he returns."

"I doubt he'll come back." They were headed for his car when Talib's cell phone rang. "Who's that? It's well past midnight?"

"Jacob," Talib replied. Furrowing his brow, he answered it. "Hello, are you headed to the diner early?"

"No." Jacob's voice lacked its usual, playful tone. "There was an accident. Hotan's mother… she… she's dead."

His eyes widened, and his face paled. "How did it happen?"

"A car wreck on her way to the diner. The paramedics are pretty sure she died instantly from the looks of the wreckage." Jacob paused, and Talib heard him swallow as if finding courage for the next question. "What should we do about the kid?"

Motioning for Lucius to get into the car, Talib refocused his thoughts. "First, let us see what her will says, if she even has one. If you do not mind, I would prefer that you and Lucius deliver the news."

"Sure," he stammered. "Meet me at my apartment. I'm heading there now."

Jacob arranged standard issue uniforms for them to wear. They all looked troubled as their minds swirled around the concern of what would happen to Hotan's reincarnation. *Will his powers awaken? Is there a will at all? Who will take over raising him?* Their silence remained during the drive. Talib rode in the back of Jacob's car toward the apartment building; he watched the streetlights bloom into life and fade ever quicker, mimicking the panicked thoughts in his mind. The car rolled to a stop, and he stared up at the shadow of the building with its scattering of lit windows. Moths fluttered around the flickering yellow glow of the streetlamp, adding to the daunting atmosphere of the task before them. He dared not approach Hotan, fearing he would trigger a reaction or be recognized.

"Here." He flinched as Jacob shoved an earpiece in his hand. "This way you can hear everything for yourself without having to hide in the shadows."

"I was not intending to go in…" Lifting an eyebrow, he placed the piece in his ear.

Rolling his eyes, Jacob scoffed, "Don't even pretend you wouldn't sneak in there. You're hopeless … and a horrible liar for an old guy."

They left the car and disappeared through the apartment building's front entrance. It was pushing past one in the morning when he heard knocking over the earpiece. Closing his eyes, his heart *ba-bumped* in his ears. He waited for the heartbreak to start. The sounds of a lock sliding, another flipping, and the door opening marked the beginning of the wave of emotions that would be stirred. He imagined the confusion those silvery eyes would hold at the site of the officers.

"Hello?" A female voice threw him off guard. "Can I help you, officer? Is something the matter?"

Jacob asked flatly, "Are you the property manager, Annie Kerbowski?"

Talib was baffled; his thoughts raced, *Why would he go to another apartment first?*

"Y-yes." Her voice shook from their somber presence. "What happened?"

"We understand Miss Olivia Samuels had a son?" Jacob took on a strong, authoritative tone. "If you are able, can you accompany us to her apartment? Miss Samuels lost her life tonight in a car accident."

A squeal was quickly muffled as she began to sob.

"I'm… I'm so sorry," Jacob stammered. "If it brings any comfort, she died instantly and did not suffer."

Annie's crying went on for several minutes before she caught her breath. "I will show you to her apartment. Poor Hotan…"

He listened intently as a door clicked, and their footsteps echoed in an unseen hallway. Soon, there were the sounds of a stairwell, and he shifted tensely in the back of the car.

"Did Miss Samuels have a will?" Jacob asked as they followed her. "Any family who could take guardianship?"

I see… Talib was relieved that Jacob was coolheaded enough to think things through. *The boy is too young to know anything. A landlord might at least have some hints, clues, or even be close enough to them to take the boy into her care long enough for us to figure out a plan. Thank God for Jacob…*

The steps came to a halt, and Annie answered, "There is no other family."

"Uh, what about the boy's father?" Lucius prodded.

"No one knows who he is," she responded, sniffling from crying. "Is there some way I can become his guardian? I'd hate to see him lost in the system. Is there a way I can become his foster parent? His mother had no friends … besides me, I suppose. They just seem to never escape tragedy…"

There was a pause, and Talib scrambled for the radio between the front seats. Gripping it tightly, he held the button down and spoke firmly, praying Jacob could hear him, "Tell her yes! Let her take on the role of his guardian!"

"Yes, you can hold temporary guardianship in this case," Jacob said. "I will send someone here tomorrow to discuss how to go about becoming his permanent guardian if you wish. As long as a will wasn't left to state otherwise"

"Please do," she said, sighing. Their steps continued on for a moment before stopping again. "This is it."

Talib looked to his wrist; it was 1:13 a.m. when heard the loud knock through the earpiece. *This is a cold Wednesday night the poor boy will not forget. His mom left for her night job and would never come back home again.* Annie wiped tears from her face as she greeted him with the two police officers. The door creaked open, closed again, and locks slid open.

"Hotan Samuels?" There was a pause, and he assumed Hotan only nodded. Then Jacob swallowed and pushed the words from his mouth, "I'm sorry. We are here to inform you about your mother. She… she passed on after a car accident."

Another round of painful silence made Talib shiver. Waiting to hear some response, he wished he had snuck in, so he could gauge young Hotan's body language and the look in those silver eyes. *How much pain is striking the boy? Will his despair fall further than my brother's? Will he fall prey to the painful path as before?* Talib's chest tightened with every fearful question, and the silence of the microphone was deafening.

Hotan barely whispered, "How?"

Clearing his throat, Jacob held nothing back. "A drunk driver crossed into her side of the road from the opposite side of traffic. Considering the speeds involved, no one had a chance to survive. According to the paramedics who first showed on the scene, she died instantly."

There was a sound of something hitting the floor.

"I'm so sorry," wailed Annie.

"We leave him in your care, dear." Lucius ended it, and their steps tapped at Talib's ear as Annie's crying faded further.

He pulled out the earpiece and threw it against the dash. A boiling mixture of anger and despair tightened around his core. He held his face and leaned back in the seat. Memories of his brother's broken face after their father passed surfaced; it had been an omen, leading to the start of a dark path which destroyed millions of lives. *Did the boy have the same look on his face as he fell to his knees? No, this path was far darker than the one his brother had known. This child has no brother and has no friends.* Tears swelled up and rolled down his temples as he squeezed his eyelids tighter. He tried to keep them from flooding forward, but there was no stopping the tidal wave he found himself drowning in. *No pain hurts as long or as sharply as the ones that strike the soul. I would trade a million volcanoes, tsunamis, and earthquakes over what I feel at this moment.*

"Dammit, please do not let him make the same mistakes..." His chest ached as he spoke his fears out loud. "I pray he knows his choices. His decisions in life not only affect him but everyone around him. What can I do differently, being this far away from him? I am nothing more than a stranger who looks so eerily alike..."

The car door opened, startling him. He opened his eyes to see Jacob holding the back, driver-side door open. Jacob's purple eyes were bright and fierce without the usual smile to soften his face. Talib couldn't breathe under the crushing weight of his own emotions, and Jacob could see it, even feel it.

"Come on, you and I are going for a walk," Jacob insisted as he held open the car door. "Move it."

Shuffling out of the car, he dared not voice any rebuttal. Jacob closed the door and nodded to Lucius who stayed behind. Jacob marched him down the sidewalk. They drifted in and out of the yellow overhead lamps in a trance. A tear dripped from his chin, and he wiped his face with his jacket sleeve. No words would come from his lips, but Jacob's glare prodded him to keep walking. There was no destination in mind, just the silent rise and fall of steps in the night air.

"You're just as bad as a child, you know?" huffed Jacob as he flicked a lighter for the cigarette which fumbled between his lips. "Wiping your face with your sleeve, sheesh. Go on, might as well finish the deal and blow your nose in it too."

They paused under a light, and he motioned toward the cigarettes. "Give me one."

"Wait, what?" Bewildered, he shoved them in his pocket and snarled. "You've gone millennia without; I think you can go this time without lighting one up, old man."

Snorting, he continued walking. "How do you know I have not smoked?"

Jacob burst into laughter. "Did you forget that I am the element of Love? It's not in your heart to do something like this. It's a lazy man's habit, anyhow."

"You can be so obnoxious." Sighing, Talib quickened his pace, leaving him behind. "I am in no mood to talk."

"Ah, but I know you need to talk." Jacob jogged after him, smoke puffing out from his lips like a steam engine. "You can't tell me you're not freaking out about how much that boy's path seems to follow your brother's."

He stopped. Talib's heart raced from the truthful words hitting him.

"I thought so." Rubbing his shoulder, Jacob continued, "It may have been a very long time ago, but even I remember the regression. Hotan was a happy kid, then your father died, and the laughter stopped. Liora managed to get his smile back, but that soon rotted away when the village came under attack. I may have been nothing more than a shepherd, but I saw it too."

"Was I so blind that I did not notice?" Turning around, his face folded in pain. "How did I never see his pain in those days after my father died…"

Taking a long pull of his cigarette, Jacob let it out slowly before he replied, "Because he worked so hard to hide it from you, Talib. I think one of us should have said something. Maybe things could have ended differently if someone, anyone, had spoken to you about the awkward effort he put into hiding his despair from you above anything else. He never wanted you to know, to see, and like you, he just wanted to see you live a happy life."

"Well, his efforts proved effective in fooling me." Turning away, Talib started marching down the sidewalk again.

"Where are you going?" Once more, Jacob raced to keep up with him.

"Does it matter?" Talib growled angrily, and Jacob stared at him wide-eyed. "It is not like he ever allowed me do my part, the job our father bestowed upon me. I tried tirelessly to help him, but instead, I was handed this immortality on the simple note that I was sterile. His sense of family and brotherhood was distorted, so why bother to hide it from me at all?"

"I… I don't think I've ever seen you this mad." Blinking, Jacob dropped his cigarette on the ground and stomped it out. "Did you ever think that the moment he discovered he would not have a normal life, he immediately wanted yours to be?"

Talib's voice caught in his throat, and Jacob took the chance to continue.

"You want to know what I think?" He smiled, and his purple eyes glimmered even in the dark under the edge of the circle of light. "Despite everything he foresaw, he immediately thought of you. He knew it would become hard … on you, on him, hell, all of us. Through hiding his remorse, he kept you focused on your life and the village for as long as his predictions would allow. He knew you would be there for him when he called on you, but for the meantime, there was no reason to destroy your happiness any sooner."

Talib's fists tightened at his sides. He could not bear to look at Jacob any longer and stared off into the darkness. Despite how hard he fought and shook, his tears fell, tip-tapping on the sidewalk at his feet. His vision blurred; the moths faded from focus. Jacob noticed the stripes of Talib's tattoo across his angry fists. Talib closed his eyes as another wave of rage swept over him; deep inside his soul, his emotions were eating him alive. Without warning, Jacob's arms wrapped around him, and the rush of heat startled him. He was stiff, but choking sobs pushed forward and broke him apart as he leaned hard into his friend. He clung onto Jacob, unable to stand under the weight of his fears and the dread they brought.

"You've been long overdue for this…" Jacob cooed, patting his back. "Saphellia's situation has been eating you alive, and seeing this young boy repeat the hardships from your own childhood must have stung. You nearly blew out my ear drum yelling into the radio."

Through his crying, Talib laughed and pulled away. "I panicked…"

"I could tell," Jacob said, laughing. "You must feel better; your tiger stripes went away."

Looking down at his hands, Talib's face reddened. "I feel like I have been caught with my pants down; how long were they visible?"

"It's the reason why I pulled you out of the car." He rubbed his shoulder a moment and waited for him to wipe the last of his tears away. "Let's get you home; you could use some rest. The kid is in good hands, lots of love in that girl, and I think he'll pull through this. He's a lot different from your brother…"

I didn't realize my actions were seen so easily after Father passed. Hotan's voice broke Talib from his memory, and he rubbed his aching chest. *I also didn't realize the amount of anxiety I would bring you this far along your path…*

I suppose I failed to teach you that your actions continue to wreak havoc even after you are gone. It was wrong to assume that you learned this when Salah came back to burn the village after our father exiled him. He sought revenge against us even though we played no part in it. Consider the plague that left large numbers in our generation sterile; we were not alive during that time, but it still echoed into our lives. When you drop a stone in a lake, it takes a long time for those ripples to calm.

Hotan grabbed Talib's shoulders, turned him around, and hugged him. He stood in this dark place somewhere within Talib's mind. Blinking in confusion, Talib was unsure why he showed signs of affection now after so many years. Hotan had been nothing more than a drone—a soulless shell of a human being—for so long that it felt awkward and baffling.

What on earth are you doing? No answer came, but a growing puddle of tears gathered on his shoulder where Hotan pressed his face against it.

Sighing, he patted his back, reluctant to let his guard down. Tears fell, and he was torn between shoving him away or comforting him. Talib thought to himself, *After all the pain I have endured, should I not be the one needing this embrace? Am I not the one who needs a shoulder to cry on?* Despite it all, his responsibility of being the big brother helped him to hold everything inside, and he enjoyed the small inkling of humanity that Hotan demonstrated.

Hotan mumbled within Talib's mind, *I would tell you I'm sorry, but what good would it do? Looking back through you, I see my mistakes. When I have seen these memories from my own soul, they were blurred. I allowed my emotions, my denials, to blind me so deeply that I destroyed those who are special to me in my life. How can I begin to ask for forgiveness after the scars I have left on your heart? Your soul! Where was I when you needed me most? If I could go back…*

Talib considered his reply to Hotan carefully. *Often, we all feel regret. What counts is what we do after our failed moments in life when we aim to make amends. Nature and God did not give us awareness that our actions can indirectly harm others. Humans make mistakes, and we must grow from them. This single element is what gives us our humanity. It is how we each become our own person. We are not defined by the words we say or even what others say about us. We are defined by our actions and the rippling wake of life that follows.*

His grip tightened, and he cried more deeply. It was as if Hotan had become himself again after watching Talib's life play out. He thought to himself, *This is the little brother I missed—the one who was sensitive and worried about how his actions affected those around him, like the day he was married.*

Talib directed his thoughts at Hotan, sharing what was on his mind. *Where have you been, alef chet? I am sorry for not realizing how far you strayed after Father passed. I was so wrapped up in my own life and duties that I never stopped to ask how you felt. Instead, I shoved you into your role as chief's son in hopes of redirecting you. In my reasoning, I failed to remember that, just like the boy who carried Rebirth after you, you were still a child.*

19

SHATTERED

2018 AD

Well, if your plan was to slow down my death, I suppose it is working. He laughed, pulling Hotan away from him. *Is that not why you came here in the first place?*

Yes, but I didn't realize I would see my own follies play out. Rubbing his forehead, he sighed. *What a mess I have made, but I assure you, I will do everything I can to make this right.*

No, no you will not. He snorted, gripping Hotan's shoulders tight and shaking him once. *We will all work together for a better outcome. You should have never taken on such a difficult task alone.*

Right. Nodding, they turned to look into the abyss of black where the memories came to life. *May I ask how the other girl died?*

Talib's stomach tangled into knots at the question.

The one that looked so much like Liora. Seeing how pale Talib became, Hotan realized this was another painful instance in his life. *I see. If this is not something you want to revisit…*

No, it is just something I regret. If I had been stronger, or perhaps not swallowed up by my concerns, I might have been able to save her. It will haunt me for a long time … and like you, the boy took her death hard.

I see… He looked away, ashamed to have brought it up. *Were there any happy times for you?*

Talib smiled. *Why, yes. The night you first showed yourself within that child … though I was so angry and frustrated on the drive back. Here, let me show you why…*

Talib fought the urge to speed his Audi down the highway as anger rolled within him. Cursing himself, he couldn't decide. Was he aiming to get rid of Geliah for revenge or was it the excitement for Hotan to return? Rebirth had released its power, forcing him to make that horrendous deal. He remembered what he said, *Give me one year to prep the young boy.*

He didn't know how far Hotan had pushed himself, but he decided to leave him on the floor of the cathedral. If his friends had not found him by morning, he would send Lucius to care for him. His hands trembled, and he tightened his hold on the steering wheel to steady them. It was dark and pulling through his front gate was a relief. Following his driveway through the thick, old oaks and maple trees, he slammed on the brakes. Up ahead, lights were on in rooms of the house that he hadn't used in months. His heart pushed against his chest. *Has Geliah planned an ambush?*

Another thought rushed forward, *Saphellia!*

He flipped off the headlights and rolled to the edge of the circle driveway. He pulled the emergency brake and slammed the car in park, leaving the car in a position to block anyone who attempted to leave. He crossed the gap to the house in silence as his heart thudded through his body. Images of Saphellia in her hospital bed, alone and unable to protect herself, added to the tension in his muscles. He was ready to fight whoever was in the house. As he reached the front, he tried turning the knob to the kitchen door, but it was still locked. He quietly searched for his keys.

He felt a breeze growing stronger and tugging at him. He gripped his keys firmly to keep them from clanking against one another. He turned to the door but froze. The scent carried on the wind gave him chills, and he shuddered as he recognized Saphellia's rosy perfume. The thudding of his heart quickened, and he fumbled to find the correct key for the door. *Is she in danger and trying to let me know?* He dropped the keys before the thought finished. As he reached for them, the door opened, and he winced, afraid to see who would be standing there.

"Talib!" she gasped. Her hospital gown fluttered in the wind, and she pulled him into the house. "TALIB!"

He quickly abandoned his keys and lifted her in his arms, laughing with relief. She felt so warm in his arms after lying cold and clammy for decades. Her lips met his, and he could no longer hold back the tears of joy. The warmth of her hands on his face was heaven incarnate. They held their kiss, thrilled to be in each other's arms. He had so longed for her after seeing her in Hama during that horrendous earthquake. Countless times, he thought about going back and enjoying life with her for at least a short while. He could have easily faked his death in those days or simply faded away. Then again, he did not want to risk waking her from the spell, thus failing to keep his promise as guardian.

She pulled away, and her hazel eyes glittered from tears. "I remember! I remember all the times I saw you … and then … and then in Hama."

He buried his face in her chest at the shared memory. "I cannot believe you were able to find me there and care for me, as always!"

"You have been my tattooed angel through the decades..." He started to kiss her neck, and she shuddered with excitement. "Oh, how I have missed you, my husband!"

"And I have missed you..." Once more, he pressed his lips against hers, his tongue diving and teasing as they stumbled away from the open door. "God, how I have longed for you..."

She shoved him away. The sudden flash was cold and harsh compared to her usual warmth. Being ripped away broke his heart and shocked his system. He stared at her red-cheeked face with a befuddled look.

"I... I need at least a shower," she confessed. "From the looks of it, I've been in that bed a very, very long time. I'd like to feel like a person again before I indulge any further..."

He felt the heat of his own cheeks. "Of course. It has been... Well, it is not as if I have not..." he stammered awkwardly.

She placed her fingers on his lips, stopping him from speaking further. "I would expect you to do what was necessary, but a proper bath is in order."

Smiling, he pulled her fingers down. "Down the hall, a little past your room on the right, my dove."

She started down the hall but paused.

"Is everything alright?" he asked, his smile faltering in fear.

Looking over her shoulder, she gave him a coy smile. "Well, husband, are you not joining me in the bath?"

A sheepish grin came across his face, and he chased her down the hall. It was exhilarating to have her awake and well. He relished hearing her voice and being able to run his fingers across her warm skin. Those hazel eyes had always mesmerized him, but now they were enchanting. He felt drunk with passion—something he had been starved of for thousands of years.

She was still sickly in appearance, but it did not take long for her to regain the lost weight and restore her complexion. Nights of holding onto one another in our bed was soul-repairing. I would kiss her shoulder as we talked, and she fussed over my thoughts. For once, life gave me something pleasant.

How did she awaken? Hotan asked. The memory had ended with her running through the bathroom door before going black. *Was she showing signs of pulling out on her own?*

No, she showed none of the signs I had seen from the rest. I can only assume that the release of power that night triggered a shift in many of us, including Kyle.

Kyle? The element of Fire? Hotan brought his hand to his chin as he thought for a moment. *He was the one who died in Santiago, right?*

Yes. Something unusual happened with him, and I was not made aware of it until the very next day...

It was hard leaving Saphellia at the house alone, but he had to make sure Hotan was sent to the hospital. He wondered if he would be in a coma after the exertion from facing Geliah. He called Lucius and discovered that he had travelled to New York to check on a situation possibly involving one of the elements. Talib had felt a disconnected presence there, but he was unsure who it was. He had been relying on the others more since Saphellia fell. In fact, most had taken on roles to aid his efforts in finding out more about Hotan's reincarnation. Metsy posed as a fellow student. Peter was appointed as the principal of his high school. Jacob spent years to gain the position of police chief. Tina, though unreliable at times, worked well as a book shop owner near his mother's old diner. He considered appointing more but needed others to go investigate incidents involving the remaining immortals who were still being reincarnated.

As he arrived at the rejuvenated cathedral, it looked elegant in the pink and orange hues of the sunset. Taking in a deep breath, he prayed someone had found Hotan before now. He pushed open the doors to see the glistening marble floors and new pews inside the massive structure. Much to his surprise, he saw a red-haired boy looking up at a small statuette of the Virgin Mary. She looked down on those being blessed at the holy water fountain. *Perhaps he thinks the church is open again to the public.* As he approached the boy, he realized it was Kyle's reincarnation. The element of Fire was still dormant and locked away within him. He was staring so hard at this reflection in the fountain that he hadn't noticed Talib at all. Guilt filled Talib, knowing how he was unable to track him since that horrible day in Chile.

"Can I help you?"

Kyle flinched at the sound of his voice. "I… I'm sorry, I—" Turning around, he paled. "T-talib?"

Talib flinched, not expecting to hear his name. Kyle was still being reborn and living mortal lives, even now. Something twisted in his stomach, adding to the daunting reality of the disconnection that happened so long ago.

"Talib! Where have you been!" He gripped the front of his suit. "Is there some way to break the spell?"

"You know who you are?" he asked as his heart pounded in his ears. "No, I cannot break the spell, but it seems to have become … unstable."

"Shit." He let go and turned to lean on the fountain. "This is Hell…"

"How long have you been aware?" The answer he knew was coming made his nerves rattle. "Was it that time … in Santiago?"

Tears started to land in the fountain's bowl. "Yes…"

Furrowing his brow, he continued, "I was afraid that would happen. After Chile, I could not find you again. It was as if that outburst of power imploded and was sealed away so deeply that it disconnected me from you."

Kyle sighed, and his shoulders sunk further. "I figured as much. In all my memories before Chile, I always saw a glimpse of you at some point."

"Wait, so you are still reincarnating but with awareness?" His heart leapt to his throat, and he tried to swallow it back down.

"Yes." He pulled away from the fountain, turned to Talib, and took a deep breath. "I am born knowing and acknowledging what is happening, and I grow old knowing the moment this body gives its last breath, I will have to face it all over again. Perhaps I brought this on to myself as punishment for all those lives lost in that church…"

"You did not understand what was happening then." Furrowing his brow, he prodded further, "When did you discover Hotan's reincarnation?"

"Somehow, were placed in the same Kindergarten class, and I clung to him. I kept looking into those silver eyes, praying some spark of him would recognize me. As time passed, I realized that his reincarnation is not the same man I feared for millennia."

Nodding, he confessed, "I thought the same. His eyes are different, both in color and soul."

"If I remember right, he had the same color green as mine. Regardless, he seems to have stirred his powers in such a way that I can feel him stabilizing my own power whenever I am near him." Rubbing the back of his neck, Kyle continued, "I assume being his best friend and aware of who he is might come in handy, considering the way things are unfolding."

"In fact, yes, it will." Pushing the glasses up on his nose, Talib sighed. "If he becomes suspicious, confess that you became aware of yourself the night he released his power. It may take a while for him to piece it all together, but then again, we are confused ourselves. The instability in his power over the last four hundred years or so is responsible for breaking the spell."

"Understood. Do you have any other means for me to contact you?"

"Of course." He pulled a business card from his pocket and handed it to him. "If you need anything at all, Kyle, please do not hesitate to call me. I may not show, but Jacob or someone else will definitely offer assistance to you or Hotan."

"I'll do my best to keep you up to date." Tucking the card into his wallet, he started to walk away but paused. "Do you plan on introducing yourself to him?"

He blinked at the question. "No, I did not intend to…"

Rubbing the back of his neck, Kyle's tone saddened. "No offense, Talib, but that kid could use some family, especially a long-lost big brother. If there's a way, I would give him a chance to know you, even if you keep him at arm's length."

"I see." He tapped at his lips as he took in the idea. "If I decide to do so, you will know."

Kyle smiled. "Thank you."

A sincere smile echoed back. "And Kyle, thank you for giving him a best friend. My brother never had any friends, so seeing this boy with someone caring and trustworthy is comforting."

"I'm not the only one. He's got plenty of friends in his life." Kyle waved and headed out the door. He shouted one last hope, "I pray that he asks us for help this time around."

The door shut, echoing throughout the building. Talib was left with only his thoughts. *Despite his horrendous situation with a dysfunctional reincarnating cycle, Kyle has remained optimistic. Back in the days of the village, or even on the island, I never realized Kyle was such a strong-willed person.* Huffing, he smiled to himself. *All these years and I still do not know the other immortals as well as I thought. Every time one wakes from their spell, I discover a side of them that I was unaware existed. Is it because I did my job as a guardian so effectively? Does that allow them to open* up and speak freely to me, remembering how I checked on them and kept them safe? Often, they confess their terror of my brother, but did that fear damage my earlier relationship with them?

Hotan interrupted, *They feared me so much that it hindered your ability to get to know them...* He looked over apologetically. *I don't think I can blame them. Seeing all of this, I was a monster.*

Yes, yes you were. Time and time again, people fear what cannot be seen but is simply felt at their core. It creates some terrifying situations, including wars. Geliah never should have held the element of Fear. In fact, he should not have been an immortal at all. Of all of us, he was the weakest-minded. He had no respect for humanity, let alone his fellow Levites. Being immortal, controlling fear, he saw himself as a god.

And I was a close second. Hotan smiled half-heartedly. *At least I meant well...*

Sometimes, I doubted your intentions since they seemed to depend on your state of mind, Hotan...

The knot between Hotan's brow wavered. *Honestly, you are right. I certainly did not aim to be friendly in Hama...*

No, not at all. You were selfish and thought only of your own needs. Hotan winced at the statement, not able to deny it. *Regardless, it was a relief that Kyle was there to befriend the boy. It was pure luck that they crossed paths. Kyle's awareness aided him in breaking down the natural barriers within Hotan's personality. Much like you, he has a hard time letting people in and rarely shows his true self. It frightens him to feel exposed, as I am sure you can relate.*

Yes... He tugged at his hood, shielding his face. *I went from not letting people in to pushing those who were close to me out.*

You asked me about the girl, Shelly.

Yes, he said solemnly as his green eyes finally met Talib's again. *What happened to her?*

She died, Talib answered. *But you knew that much.*

Hotan's eye widened. *How? I wanted to know how she died.*

Geliah. He grew impatient and decided to take advantage of all of us. It was … horrific, and to know that you left me power-less is a bitterness that will last for eternity. If I had full use of my power, I could have even saved Saphellia. You gave me something, and I then found its true meaning within my own soul. Instead of leaving it for me to decide how to best use it, you ripped it out of me on Mt. Pelée.

Hotan frowned. *But my intention was to give you a way to have a child…*

A seed of your making could never replace the ability to make a child, or even adopt one by my own means. I never needed that, but I needed my brother to trust me. Your misplaced intentions caused pain and destruction because you never stopped to con-sider our thoughts and feelings on any level. You have been nothing but a selfish brat squandering what is within his reach.

For once, Hotan did not look away as Talib reminded him of the implications of his actions—his choices.

Let me show you yet another example of how your actions destroyed lives…

The cathedral was eerie in the silence. Talib looked up at the Crucifix and sighed. Within his soul, he was at peace for the first time in a long time. He scanned the elegant feathers on the wings of granite behind the figure of Christ; each one was unique in its chiseled strokes. *I may not have my little brother, but I have a second chance with this boy who carries the same name. Saphellia is awake, ending my torment and longing. The only worrisome thing that persists is Geliah's intent to fight the boy; less than six months remain, as promised. Thankfully, he has unlocked the ele-ment of Rebirth, so progress in learning to use the powers could start.* An orange light trickled in from the front doors opening behind him, and he turned to face who entered. Since Lucius had been sent home, it was unexpected. Jacob waved, closed the doors behind him, and joined Talib in admiring the church's center piece.

"You plan on going to see Hotan's band tonight?" Jacob asked, giving him a side glance.

"No, I figured I would let the boy enjoy his last farewell to his mortality." Sighing, he pushed his glasses up on his nose. "Besides, I cannot help but feel like the haunting phantom for the life he is about to face."

Jacob burst into laughter. "You've been a phantom in all our lives!"

He smirked. "I suppose that is true. All those times in your past lives when I crept near and faded away…"

"But you did what you promised to do, Talib." Patting him on the back, he exhaled in relief. "You were indeed our guardian."

"Are you planning to go?" Looking at his wristwatch, he blinked. "If they advanced to the second round, you might be able to catch them before it ends."

"Ah, geez…" Rubbing the back of his neck, he looked at his own watch. "I didn't even pay attention to what time it was when I left headquarters…"

Patting Jacob's shoulder, he laughed. "Come, I will go with you. If they ask why you were late, just blame it on me."

"Like I wasn't going to do that." He took a few steps but stopped, looking off to the alcove where the holy fountain sat. "Did that thing break down already?"

"Did what break?" His smile fell away as he followed Jacob's gaze. "It runs on a natural spring."

They looked to one another quizzically. The water had stopped running. *What could stop water from flowing and even take it away?* They turned back to take a closer look, both standing straighter as tension grew.

"The bowl is … dry," Talib marveled, stepping back a few steps to look for water on the marble floors. "What on earth…"

"Did Lucius forget to tell you?" Jacob squinted one eye and attempted to look down the hole. "Maybe something fell in and clogged it?"

"No…" he said quietly as he paled. The familiar wave of power from the element of Water grew closer.

"Please, forgive me," a frightened male voice whispered from behind.

Water erupted from the fountain, slamming Jacob in the face. He stumbled back, and the weight of the gushing water fell on top of Talib as well. Callan, the element of Water, had managed to keep his power and distance far enough away until he was ready to attack. As Talib's back slammed against the marble floor, he saw Jacob holding his own throat. His eyes bulged and he gurgled. Callan was drowning him. Talib's only chance was to grab Callan and attempt to use his power. Jacob would recover, but he had no way to stop the water from filling his lungs.

Scrambling to his feet, he caught sight of Callan crouched behind the podium. He ran toward him as another stream of water exploded from the fountain. In a moment of sheer grace, he slipped off his coat and blocked the stream. Water splashed in all directions, but he had closed the gap between them. Reaching out for Callan, he saw the weight of fear that Geliah had forced on him. It was enough for him to falter. Callan threw water into his face from the glass he held tightly with shaking hands. Water crawled like wet snakes between his lips and teeth. There was no defense to keep it from invading his lungs.

Gagging, he fell at Callan's feet as he watched with a tear-soaked face. *This is not his doing but one last, harsh push from*

Geliah. Talib didn't fight what was happening. *The sooner it takes me out, the quicker Callan will remove the water. Once the water retreats, I can start healing. I just hope I wake in time to help Hotan in the war Geliah is about to wage.* It was dark inside his mind as he waited for his body to wake again. Screaming reached his ears, but despite how hard he tried, his eyes would not open. Scrambled words echoed around him. At least he could breathe, but it did not help the panic.

Talib recognized Geliah's maniacal laughter. They were still in the church, and he was relieved to be on familiar ground in case he was weakened further than expected. A wave of power washed over him—warm and chilling. It made him flinch, jolting his body awake. Clinging onto the wave, he knew Hotan had released a surge of power. He had to trust that the boy knew how to use what was given to him by his little brother. Silence fell, and his heart began to race. He urged his ears to please listen.

Saphellia! PLEASE COME! he pleaded, hoping his words reached her.

Warm fingers cut the ropes at his wrists. Callan whispered, "I'm so sorry. I was too weak to fight the fear I was under. Please hurry and wake, Talib. Hotan needs you now more than ever."

Saphellia's panicked whisper hit his mind, *I'm on my way!*

He pushed harder to wake up, but his lungs still stung as he took in deeper breaths. The blood in his veins warmed, and much to his relief, his eyelids started to part. Blinking the blurriness from them, he saw Callan rocking and holding his own face. He wobbled to his feet, confused. Jacob had his back turned and Cassie sobbed. Jacob turned and held onto a pew to steady himself. His purple eyes were filled with tears, and he gave him a grim expression. Then his eyes hit the red-covered floor, and his heart shattered. Hotan knelt in a pool of blood, silently staring down at Shellie's lifeless body as shock took hold. Talib gritted his teeth and pushed back his tears. There was no time to waste.

"Jacob." He flinched at his name. "We need to get him out of here, now."

"Right." They both rushed over to him. "Hotan…"

As they closed the gap to Hotan, they stumbled to a stop and gasped. They had not seen the wound in his abdomen until then. The lake of blood he sat in was not from Shellie alone but his own which still flowed out of him. If they didn't act swiftly, he could die. No one knew if he had completely become immortal or if he would reincarnate like the others. It wasn't a risk they wanted to take. Jacob was gentle with him. He squatted on the other side of Shellie's body, desperate to snap him out of it.

"She's gone. We need to get you out of here. I wish I were able to stop it. I tried, and I let you down. I'm so sorry," Jacob pleaded, hesitant to touch him just yet.

"I let you down…" Talib's balance failed, and he leaned onto a nearby pew, frustrated to feel so weak. "I let my guard down. I did not want it to end this way. It should have never gone this way. Hotan… Hotan, you need to leave."

Hotan's tears fell heavy on her body as he sat, listening to their words but unmoving.

"What should we do?" Jacob couldn't hold back another wave of tears as he watched Hotan fall deeper into despair. "He's in shock. I hate to move him, but the police are bound to be on their way. I can only do so much explaining."

"Saphellia is on her way." He felt so useless and sat down on the pew, covering his face. "She will take him to my place. I will stay and use my power to help smooth this over."

"I can bring her back." Hotan's words struck him like an offer made by the Devil himself. "I could bring her back. I know how."

"What?" Fear gripped Talib's soul. Hotan sounded like his brother for the first time. "What do you mean, bring her back?"

"I have the power to bring her back." Breaking his stare from her body, his silver eyes locked with Talib's. "But it wouldn't be her, anymore. It wouldn't be her at all."

"What do you mean?" Jacob shuddered as he glared at the wound dripping from Hotan's stomach. "We need to get you to the hospital, Hotan."

"It wouldn't be her anymore," he muttered repeatedly as if trying to keep himself from doing something rash.

"You can resurrect the dead?" Despite feeling weakened, Talib gripped Hotan's shoulder, ready to use his power if necessary to prevent such a travesty. "You can bring her back?" *I needed to know, I needed to hear what I had feared for so long that my brother had attempted.*

"No, not her," Hotan murmured. He leaned heavily onto his shoulder against Talib's grip; he was tired, cold, and weakening by the second. "It would be another person, a look-alike, a fake. Shellie would still be gone. She's gone. It only works if they are still here, and she left so fast… so fast…"

"Hotan," Jacob said, unable to stop his tears from falling.

He helped Talib lift Hotan to his feet. He had lost too much blood for medical attention to aid him. Blood still dripped from the wound as Hotan fought against his healing abilities, deeply wanting to let go of life. Hotan was numb. *He couldn't see the fear and horror of losing him on the faces surrounding him. He was unable to see beyond this painful moment which replayed itself in his head. He could not see the pain his death would cause those who were not there like Anne, Hisota, and even the peers in his school who he never bothered to spend time with. Death was not the answer. He had people to lean on, but it was up to him to pull himself out of despair. Shellie would have wanted him to live…*

"I am so sorry. Dear God, I hate this. I'm sorry I was too dumb to figure this out in time." Jacob shuddered, overwhelmed by the realizations pouring forward.

Being the element of Rebirth is a curse... Talib shot a glance at Jacob when his words hit him. *No wonder your brother distanced himself. How could he fight the urges... Never mind, I don't want to think about that now...*

My brother was left broken, and I will not allow that to happen again. The tension in his face struck Jacob. *He is stronger than my brother, and I will be here to help him through this.*

"It would be Shellie without her soul, another soul," Hotan mumbled again as they ushered him out the door to the car that waited for him. "Shellie is gone. I've lost her. I failed her. Alone, I am all alone."

Saphellia! Help us get him in the car! Talib's words reached her, and she quickly exited the vehicle.

"Jesus." Saphellia's face drained of color as she watched them drag Hotan's blood-soaked body. "Is he going to make it?"

"I... I don't know." Jacob's expression made her shudder. "He was wounded before I even came to, and that was quite a while ago."

"Let's get him in the car quickly." She jerked the backseat door open and rushed to pick up his feet to speed the process along. "Please don't die on me, kid. We've only just met!"

Placing him across the backseat, Talib realized Hotan was letting himself slip away.

"Dammit!" He ripped open Hotan's shirt; the wound was gruesome, and his body was paling. "He cannot do this to me!"

"He'll never make it to the hospital, Tal." Pacing outside the car, Jacob called for aid. "The paramedics are too far out..."

"What can we do?" Saphellia started to cry. "Is there some way to heal him?"

"If Abigail was here, but…" His heart raced, and he dove into the back of the car.

"Talib!" Jacob dropped his phone on the sidewalk and followed close behind. "What are you doing?!"

"Hotan!" Screaming, he gripped Hotan's jaw and forced him to look at him. "Heal yourself! I know you can do it. Damnit, heal yourself!"

"Why?" whispered Hotan before closing his eyes again. "I don't want to. I'm dead."

"I said to heal yourself." Talib had to try; he had no other choice. Pushing his element into Hotan, he prayed that his powers would not falter. "I will make you, if I must. You hear me, Hotan? I will make you live!"

Sweat trickled down his temple as his power gripped the element of Rebirth. If this failed, Hotan could die before becoming fully immortal. There was no resistance as Judgment tangled itself with Rebirth. Tattooed lines crawled across Hotan's body. The pounding of his heart added to his tension. Talib held onto what was left of Hotan's soul, not allowing it to slip any further.

"I said to heal yourself," he commanded.

Hotan's eyes opened, but all they saw were the whites of his eyes. He took his hand and covered his wound. A blue flash glowed under his palm; Talib's last-ditch attempt had worked. As Hotan pulled his hand away, the wound closed and disappeared without a scar or mark. Color returned to him—a sign the blood loss had been reversed. *Rebirth truly is a very powerful element.* Satisfied that his soul was climbing back from its abyss, Talib retracted his powers. Relief flooded him, and he collapsed on top of Hotan. He had struggled with his powers lately, and if this had failed, it would have destroyed him. Tears crawled down his face as sirens wailed in the distance.

"Talib, stay with him." Jacob closed the car door, satisfied that Hotan would be fine. "Saph, take them home. I can handle this. After all, I didn't get my position by using powers."

"Of course." Saphellia nodded and scrambled to the driver's side. As they pulled away, she asked Talib, "Are you going to be all right?"

He mumbled, "I'm fine, but that was too close…"

"No, that's not what I asked." Her voice stung at his heart, and the hairs on the back of his neck prickled. "Are you going to be able to do *this* again."

"I, I do not know." Lifting his head, he watched the streetlights pass over them and fade in the distance. "But I plan on handling *this* far differently. Mistakes were made, but this boy is not my brother. Sometimes I feel as if my brother tried to bring her back, and when it went horribly wrong, he hid us away in this spell to cover the shame and guilt. We may never uncover what he actually did. It does not matter whether my speculation is true or not. It matters how we carry on from here, what we do now and the future we build for ourselves. We can help one another become stronger and understand who and what we are."

She reached back and grabbed his shoulder. "You have always known who and what we are. Like you said so long ago to me … we are tattooed angels, both physically and emotionally."

"Indeed, we are." Talib lowered his head onto Hotan's chest, relieved to hear his heart still beating.

Warmth was fading back into existence within the boy. As the last of his worries melted away, he drifted off to sleep.

Within his mind, Hotan spoke to him again. *I see. If you had your full powers, you wouldn't have needed to touch them directly…* He sighed and turned to Talib. *But I brought that piece back to you. At least that is a step toward undoing what I have done…*

I am dying, Brother. How does that power help me as I come closer to the end of my memories? There is not much of my life left to watch before I take my final breath and my heart becomes still forever. Even then, what good can I do against Iapetos?

Hotan smiled, and his green eyes glimmered. *Now that touch is not needed, you can call to the boy.*

Talib was in disbelief.

Once awake, you will need to touch Iapetos for my next plan. His smile faltered. *You must force his power to kill him like it attempted to do to you. Through your touch, I can unlock the memories from there.*

Hotan is able to revive me because my soul has not left... Talib was already astonished, then it hit him. *Have you planned everything, even this moment?*

Yes, Hotan replied sternly. *Since the day we spoke in Roanoke, though I did not realize the destruction it would cause for everyone else. If I had known or stopped to consider... regardless. The boy proved to be a stronger person than myself, and now, I must stop this cycle of father and son wanting to destroy one another.*

Talib paled as he realized something else. *If they are this close to one another, does that mean another disaster is about to strike?*

No. His smile returned, providing Talib with a sense of relief. *Rebirth is finally stable. Partially because of the reincarnation, but it helped that he chose replacements for Earth and Fear. As long as Hotan keeps his powers balanced, no large-scale dangers should occur from close proximity to Death.*

After I call out to Hotan, what exactly will happen? His brow knotted, unsure of the plan pushed onto him by his brother. *Attack Iapetos head on with my full powers? When he wakes, what do you think will happen?*

I don't know. He shrugged sheepishly. *My intentions are to undo what I did wrong. Restore your memories, do the same for*

Iapetos, stabilize Rebirth, and leave the decision making to you and the others. I have already proven to be far more incompetent than I even realized.

I pray your plan works. Otherwise, we are all dead if Iapetos can eat souls.

Talib took a deep breath and called out to Hotan. *Hotan! I am still here, but my time is fading fast! Revive me! I know how to stop Iapetos!*

They waited in the bleakness of his mind for a response from the boy as the last remnants of Talib's life flashed by like an hourglass running out of sand.

20

SNUFF

Present Day

The heated stare between Hotan and Iapetos on the rooftop could stop time itself. Talib lay dead or dying in Saphellia's arms behind Hotan. For the first time, Hotan faced the man who haunted his dreams—his own father. Cold black eyes glowered at him. Clenching his jaw, Hotan took one more deep breath before launching full stride at Iapetos. As they ran for one another, black and blue flames collided forcefully in an explosion of bright light. Hotan failed to realize that his father was far stronger than him and stumbled backward. His feet tripped over one another, and his shoulder slammed into the pea gravel. Iapetos was quick to leap toward him but was met with an explosion of flames.

Kyle stood behind Hotan. Another ball of fire left his hands and pushed Iapetos further back. The seared flesh left behind was grotesque, but the gap between him and Hotan kept the nightmare at bay. As Hotan scrambled to his feet, he watched Iapetos' flesh quickly rejuvenate, a sickening, crawling of flesh snaked back into place. Again, he ran at Iapetos with renewed confidence. This time, he dodged his father's blow and attempted to knock him off his feet with a low, swift kick. He misjudged Iapetos' speed, and a hand caught his leg, jerking him close. A ball of black flames came racing down on him from Iapetos' hand. Instinctually, Hotan met it with his own ball of blue. Another blinding spark loosened Iapetos' grip, and Hotan back-stepped to Kyle's side. They panted in exhaustion from their failed attempts to harm him.

Gunshots rang out as Jacob unloaded his Desert Eagle into Iapetos' head and chest. Laughter rolled out of him. It did nothing to slow him down, and he began to charge again. Kyle pushed out one last fireball before his legs gave out, but it successfully stopped his approach.

Concentrating, Hotan gripped a handful of pea gravel. A burst of blue flames erupted, leaving behind an elegant sword as they faded. With all his friends at his back, Hotan mustered his courage and pushed forward yet again. Enraged from frustration, he screamed and swung with all his might. Iapetos reached up to catch the blade, but it sliced through his fingers and lodged itself halfway through his skull. Hotan stared at the eye he had cleaved in half. He tugged at the blade but couldn't dislodge it from his father's skull.

In horror, he watched Iapetos grip the blade with his other hand, and it turned to ashes and fell away in an instant. He stumbled backward, and his heel locked on something; Hotan landed next to Talib's lifeless body. His chest sunk as his nightmare began to play out in real life. Even with this power, he was falling back in line with the dream that foretold his death. Black flames restored the missing fingers and scurried outward from Iapetos' palm, fading to reveal a katana. Each step closer broke his mind further. *This is it; this is the part where I die.* Every crunch of gravel gripped Hotan's soul tighter, suffocating all hope.

Hotan! I am still here... Talib's voice pulled him from his anxious thoughts.

"No!" Annie slammed her hands against the rooftop, and a massive wall of earth rose in their defense.

Hotan seized the opportunity to crawl over to Talib's body. Tears streaked his face as he summoned a ball of flames in his hand. With all the weight of his desperation, he slammed it into Talib's chest. His mind raced: *There is no way of knowing if I'm doing the right thing... if anything I'm doing is right or wrong. Talib is here, I heard him, and I need him more than ever.*

"Please, let this work. I need you!"

Talib's body arched from the surge of power thrust through him, and he gasped.

It was cold as he stood in the darkness. Talib could no longer hear what happened outside the place where his death had taken him. His life flashed before his eyes. He thought, *My time is ending.* Long forgotten thoughts and emotions from centuries ago felt as if they had just happened, but none of that mattered if he couldn't be revived. He looked over at his brother; they both felt his life coming to an end.

He muttered the question he had asked himself at the start of this fight, *How does one defeat Death?*

You give him life, answered his brother.

Hotan! Hurry! Gritting his teeth, he balled his fists as he felt himself teetering at the edge.

Suddenly, a warmth exploded from his chest. He looked down as the tentacles of power from the element of Rebirth wrapped themselves around him. He smiled at his brother, and a single tear fell. He waved in return, and a harsh tug sent him soaring backward. Talib gasped in the blinding sunlight, and Hotan looked down at him in awe. Blood painted the side of his face where he had fallen. Elation took hold, and Talib scrambled back to his feet. Much to his surprise, a wall of earth had risen, shielding them from Iapetos. He looked to Jacob's tear-filled, purple eyes as he held a ghostly Annie in his arms. She had only been in control of the powers for a few hours but already showed more control than Cassie ever had. Kyle was unable to stand and had exerted too much power as well.

The wall began to crumble, and Talib gritted his teeth. He thought, *I was told what to do, but can I bring it out?* He looked over his shoulder and saw everyone he cared about watching the earth collapse with mind-numbing fear. Anger poured out of him at a radical speed. Soon, they broke their attention away from the failing wall to the red glow that surrounded Talib.

"W-wings..." gasped Saphellia.

As he heard the word, he felt them flare wide as if confirming their existence. Red and orange feathers covered the massive appendages like fire. They were much more massive than Iapetos' wings or even the cerulean blue ones his brother brandished. A smile crawled across his face; the gap between the Angel of Death and himself had closed. The wall had fallen, and Iapetos glared at him from the other side. His cold stare was nothing like the past versions he recalled. The centuries had destroyed him, but Talib knew this was not the man Iapetos wanted to be deep in his soul. Memories of the kind-hearted, tortured immortal who had been abandoned stung at him.

"You…" snarled Iapetos. "You're the one I remember flying away, leaving me for dead on Mt. Pelée all those years ago."

"That is not exactly how it happened. I was forced to leave, and I would have taken you with me if given a choice in the matter."

"I was crippled on the ground!" he roared. "What sort of threat was I!"

Closing his eyes, Talib responded, "We were not alone. Your father is to blame for how it all happened. He is also responsible for our forgotten memories of one another."

Iapetos flinched at the idea, but Talib's words struck something deep within him that made his rage falter. Seizing the chance, Talib took to his wings and launched himself at Iapetos. Iapetos leapt back, and Talib's hand missed his throat but caught his wrist.

"You missed," scoffed Iapetos, failing to jerk his wrist free.

"No … I did not." His eyes glowed red, emanating the fiery steam of his power. "Let me remind you of everything my brother has wrongfully taken from you…"

Iapetos fell to his knees, screaming. He grabbed the side of his head with his free hand, his eyes rolled back into his head, and he fell to the ground. Talib released him but stood over him, waiting to see if any immediate whiplash would surface. The palm of his hand tingled where he had gripped Iapetos. Looking down, he saw the tiny blue flame absorb back into his hand. His brother had done his part as well; now, they had to wait.

"Talib!" Hotan ran up behind him, his eyes still fixated on the elegant, long-feathered, red wings. "What happened? Did… did I do something to you?"

Laughter erupted from Talib, and he patted Hotan on the head. "All you did was save me from death."

"Do we all get wings?" Jacob cut in; Annie was fast asleep in his arms. "How come you never told me you had wings, old man?"

"I was not aware..." He looked to his palm where the blue flame had been. "It happens when we resonate with our element. I guess Judgment was a perfect fit for me..."

"Is he dead?" Hotan stared down at the lifeless face of the father who had haunted his dreams. "What did you do to him?"

Talib felt at ease. His nerves calmed, and his wings burst into a swirl of power and faded away. "Ah, technically, he died. However, since he is the element of Death, he will eventually wake up. When that happens, he will remember the things my brother took from him."

"Is it true that my dad is Hotan's son?" he whispered as if he wanted to keep it between them. "And somehow, he was able to conceive a child because of something the old Hotan did."

"Yes..." He gripped Hotan's shoulder, catching his attention. "Do not judge him so swiftly. The mistakes he made were based on confusion from missing memories."

"Missing memories?" Saphellia knelt next to Iapetos, looking him over with great interest. "Good lord, there's no mistaking his relation to you both."

"As my life flashed before me, I discovered that I really did not know what was happening." Swallowing, he willed himself to reveal more. "Over thousands of years, Hotan used my power to erase my own memories and Iapetos' as well. Disasters in Antioch, Hama, London during the plague, and many more resulted from his clashes with of the element of Death and the turmoil created from an unbalanced Rebirth. On Mt. Pelée, my brother, Iapetos, and I met, and it was there that Hotan essentially destroyed himself to create a seed for reincarnation, which he left within Iapetos."

"You can't be talking about the 1902 volcano eruption..." Hisota found his voice, breaking himself from his stunned state.

"If those two drawing close together caused natural disasters, then that means in 1902…"

He locked eyes with Hisota, and everyone shuddered.

"It took Iapetos nearly a hundred years…" Hotan's brow folded as the information settled. "But in the end, he really did fall in love with my mother, didn't he?"

"Knowing who he was before rage and sorrow destroyed him, I can easily believe that." Iapetos started to show signs of shallow breathing. "Get him back to my place. I would like to be there when he wakes up to gauge whether he intends to continue his aggression or wants to start his life over."

Hotan started to walk away. "I… I don't know how I feel about any of this."

Abigail stood by the stairway door. "Hotan…"

He ignored her, brushing past and leaving out of sight.

She began to follow, but Talib stopped her. "Abigail?"

She flinched and looked to him with tears streaming down her face. "Y-yes."

"You and I need to have a very long talk." He locked eyes with her. "Out of everyone here, you are the only one who has never been wiped of her memories. You remained by my brother's side without fail through it all."

The heated glares stung at her.

Shaking her head, she pleaded, "You don't understand! After Roanoke, when he wiped your memories without needing to do it, I left!"

As she ran down the stairs, he paused to reach back through his memories. The last time he recalled her at his side was indeed in 1587. At that point, his destructive actions had gone too far for even her to watch.

"Your brother was a monster," Jacob said quietly.

"Agreed…" Talib huffed.

Hotan's voice whispered inside his head, *Indeed I was…*

"Is she going to be okay?" Saphellia broke the morbid conversation, bringing everyone's focus back to what needed to be addressed first. "Annie gave Hotan just enough time to save Talib, but it may have been too soon."

"She's fine." Sighing, Jacob kissed the top of her head. "It wore her out, but she'll pull out of this. I think she's a much better fit for the element of Earth. Never thought I would see someone so new to this have that much control and power at a time like this."

Smiling, Talib sighed. "I am relieved to see that he is far wiser in his choices than my brother ever was."

"No kidding…" Jacob looked down to Iapetos. "But still … this whole situation is so twisted, I'm not sure he'll be able to keep it together."

"I am hoping the Iapetos I recall from my past returns when he wakes." Squatting down, he checked his pulse. Iapetos was cold and clammy, and his heartbeat was horribly low. "It seems he will be down far longer than I was."

"Maybe it'll give us time to sort ourselves out…" Saphellia stood up. "Where did you leave the car?"

Talib's face reddened. "In the middle of traffic."

Jacob groaned. "You've got to be kidding me."

"Kyle…" Talib's voice broke him from his shock where he sat on the rooftop, exhausted. "Are you well enough to move?"

"I think so…" He wobbled to his feet. "I'm fine. I'll see about following Hotan; you guys have a bigger problem to solve."

Talib grabbed Iapetos arm, slung it over his shoulder, and lifted him from the rooftop. Hisota took his other arm. An exhausted silence resonated among everyone as they brought him down the stairs. Jacob carried Annie close behind them, and Saphellia rushed ahead to find the car. They made it to Annie's apartment and laid Iapetos' limp body on the couch.

After putting Annie in her bed, Jacob walked out and closed the door behind him.

"What should I be doing?" Hisota rubbed the back of his neck, still fighting the shock of events. "This is all so much so fast; I feel useless."

Jacob gave him a few hearty pats on the back. "Be yourself."

Hisota's face turned red, and he glared at him. "You sound like my school counselor."

Laughing, he gave him a more accurate answer, "Right now, you simply need to be Hotan's friend, no different from before. Don't feel useless because you didn't use those newfound powers."

Hisota's brow knotted, and he looked at his hands. "It was frightening … feeling everyone's fear while I was up there. It was overwhelming when it hit me."

Talib interjected, "I am glad to see you take in that sensation with caution. Your predecessor would be intoxicated from a wave like that." Hisota grabbed his stomach; the idea of it made him ill. "My thoughts exactly. Regardless, there will come a time when your power will be needed. I do not think altering anyone's sense of fear any more or less today would have done any good."

"Agreed," snorted Jacob. He nodded at Iapetos. "I can't help wonder if he even felt any fear."

"He did." Hisota's eyes fell to the sleeping body on the couch. "In fact, he's horribly afraid right now. Realizing Hotan was his son was the highest sensation of fear during the fight. But now… now he's even more afraid of that."

"That is because my brother is undoing the chains he wrongfully put into place." Rubbing the side of his jaw, he looked down on Iapetos with pity. "Out of all of us, his suffering has been the worst from the mistakes put in motion…"

"Wait, your brother is undoing the chains?" Jacob rubbed his shoulder out of habit. "I, I thought Hotan died, Tal?"

"Not in traditional manner that we understand," he replied. "Right now, the last piece of him is trying to make things right. I pray he makes amends with Iapetos in this limited time he has left to do so…"

A car horn blared its arrival outside the door. Nodding to one another, Talib and Jacob grabbed Iapetos and dragged him to the car where Saphellia waited. Closing the back passenger door, he and Jacob gave one another a hug and hard pat on the back. They knew the tasks ahead of them: Talib would oversee Iapetos, and Jacob had Annie to care for in the meantime. As for Hotan, they left it to Abigail, Kyle, and Hisota to console him.

Exactly what are you doing inside his head, Brother. Staring out the window of the car, he looked at his reflection, knowing his brother could hear him. *How are you going about this?*

First, I will give back what I have stolen… His voice was clear in Talib's mind, making him shudder. *Then, it's his decision whether I will allow him to wake from this…*

His stomach twisted. *Now, it is Death's turn to decide what he truly wants his life to be about… whether to die, live, or allow his legacy to continue.*

The story concludes in *Death…*

BOOK CLUB
DISCUSSION QUESTIONS

1. Do you feel Talib sees Hotan as a second chance with his old brother or a fresh start with a new brother?

2. Do you think Hotan was more afraid of what he had done or that Talib would find out?

3. Who do you feel was the primary reason for the disaster that happened? Death or Rebirth?

4. What mistakes do you think Talib made in the past that impacted the present?

5. How has Talib changed over time? What events do you think aided in him changing or staying the same?

6. A few events in this book are historically inspired. Which one do you feel captures that history best? Did you discover something new?

7. Do you think the old Hotan is cleaning up his mess and truly making amends by the end of the book? Who do you feel he owes the most?

8. Why do you think the author chose to represent a strange cycle of old Hotan begets Iapetos who begets new Hotan? Do you think this compliments the idea of Rebirth as Life begets Death which begets Life renewed?

9. How impactful is it to see and experience the past through Talib and his tribulations? Would seeing this through a different character have made a significant difference in how the past was experienced?

10. When Talib discovers Lucius, do you feel he was lonely or at a turning point in his life? How do you feel Lucius impacts this moment with his tragic event?

AUTHOR BIO

Valerie Willis is the COO at 4 Horsemen Publications, Inc., an expert digital typesetter, co-host to Drinking with Authors Podcast, and an award-winning Fantasy Paranormal Romance author. Her works include a workbook series, *Writer's Bane*, starting with *Research* and *Formatting 101*, and novels inspired by mythology, superstitions, legends, folklore, fairy tales, and history such as in *The Cedric Series*. Many have experienced her hosting workshops or being a guest speaker at events where she shares her expertise in publishing, novel writing, research for fiction, worldbuilding, character development, book design, reader immersion, foreshadowing, and more.

www.WillisAuthor.com
https://linktr.ee/WillisAuthor
OR
Instagram: @WillisAuthor
Facebook: facebook.com/ValerieWillisAuthor
Twitter: @Valerie_Willis
TikTok: @willisauthor
Email: Willis.author@gmail.com

MORE BOOKS FROM
4 HORSEMEN PUBLICATIONS

PARANORMAL & URBAN FANTASY

AMANDA FASCIANO
Waking Up Dead
Dead Vessel

BEAU LAKE
The Beast Beside Me
The Beast Within Me
Taming the Beast: Novella
The Beast After Me
Charming the Beast: Novella
The Beast Like Me
An Eye for Emeralds
Swimming in Sapphires
Pining for Pearls

CHELSEA BURTON DUNN
By Moonlight

J.M. PAQUETTE
Call Me Forth
Invite Me In
Keep Me Close

JESSICA SALINA
Not My Time

KAIT DISNEY-LEUGERS
Antique Magic

LYRA R. SAENZ
Prelude
Falsetto in the Woods: Novella
Ragtime Swing
Sonata
Song of the Sea
The Devil's Trill
Bercuese
To Heal a Songbird
Ghost March
Nocturne

MEGAN MACKIE
The Saint Liars
The Devil's Day
The Finder of the Lucky Devil

PAIGE LAVOIE
I'm in Love with Mothman

ROBERT J. LEWIS
Shadow Guardian and the
Three Bears